Who's Watching the Tower?

Dr. Gregory Vilner

Who's Watching the Tower?

Dr. Gregory Vilner

HAWK
PUBLISHING
G R O U P

TULSA
HawkPub.com

LIBRARY OF CONGRESS CATALOG IN PUBLICATION DATA

Who's Watching the Tower? / Gregory Vilner

[1. Vilner, Gregory - Fiction-United States.]

Copyright © 2006 by Gregory Vilner

Cover Design and Interior Design by
Müllerhaus Publishing Arts, Inc. | mhpubarts.com

Cover Photography: ©Marino Colmano Photography
For more San Quentin images see: http://marinocolmano.com/quentin.html

ISBN 1-930709-59-5
Library of Congress Control Number: 2006921076

Published in the United States by HAWK Publishing Group.

HAWK Publishing Group
7107 South Yale Avenue #345
Tulsa, OK 74136
918-492-3677
HawkPub.com
HeartlandAuthors.com

HAWK and colophon are trademarks belonging to the HAWK
Publishing Group. Printed in the United States of America.
9 8 7 6 5 4 3 2 1

DEDICATION

FAMILY

My wife, *Kelly Hughes Vilner,* for her deep affection, love and appreciation.

My mother, *Louise A. Vilner,* who taught me unconditional love.

I WISH TO EXPRESS MY DEEP AFFECTION AND APPRECIATION TO

My son, *Gregory Israel Vilner*

My daughter, *Jessica Lee Vilner*

My sister and brother-in-law, *Vince and Vanessa Lee Triscell*

My sister and brother-in-law, *Mike and Anjela Quecke*

My aunt, *Clara Tartala*

My aunt, *Verner Bee Chaffin*

My cousins, *Jack and Elaine Reusser*

My cousins, *Cosmo and Mike Violante*

AND IN MEMORY

My father, *Israel Izzy Vilner*

My grandpa and grandma, *Isaac I. and Easter Vilner*

My grandpa and grandma, *Phillip M. and Angelina Vella*

My grandpa, *Frank Baccaro*

My grandpa, *Attilio Sollini*

My uncle, *Braxton Chaffin*

My aunt, *Mary Violante*

My aunt and uncle, *Art and Amelia Azevedo*

My mother-in-law, *Anne Louis Hughes*

My sensei, *Sosai Mas Oyama*

My sensei, *Donald Irving Buck*

My sensei, *Henry Augusto*

My good friend, *Tom Lazio*

My good friend, *Sergeant England*

My good friend, *Raymond (Duke) Moore*

My good friend, *Geary Gilden*

PROLOGUE

At 12:01 p.m. the gates to the lower yard's football field were opened. Small and large groups of people streamed in from every direction. On stage, band members plugged thick wires into amps. The inevitable squelches and hums followed. Fans smoked cigarettes and drank homemade or store-bought booze. Black leather and rubber-soled shoes scuffed loudly against the blacktop then fell nearly silent on the dead brown grass as people hurried to the staging area.

Kenny Boyd with the "Band of Gypsies" belted out one of the songs that made them famous. The sounds of "We Gotta Live Together" with Jimi Hendrix on guitar, Buddy Miles on drums and Billy Cox on bass made the ground shake, rattle and roll. Men gathered around the grassy stage area, smiles on their faces, dancing, clapping, and cheering.

The San Quentin State Prison's lower yard had never been so danger-ously filled with inmates. Guards in the towers and on the gun walks with their stainless steel mini-fourteens and thirty round clips watched a sea of men rising and elbowing each other while the music roared. Inmates in blue jumpsuits swallowed the outnumbered correctional officers. As the hot sun bore down, groups of inmates gathered around the bikers and engaged in intimate conversation, not unlike a reunion of old friends.

"Code Red, Code Red, lower yard!" someone yelled frantically over the facility's portable radios. The crack of two nearly simultaneous gunshots brought the revelry to a halt. One bullet hit the singer in the head during the middle of the first song. He took a single step forward, opened his mouth as if to sing the words "We gottaaa…" before bright red blood began gushing from his mouth. It flowed down his chin onto his white shirt as he leaned backward then crashed to the stage floor.

Another bullet hit the leader of the Hell's Angels as he was enjoying the music with his fellow bikers. His fresh pink brains and shiny red blood sprayed across the highly polished black and chrome motorcycles and onto the stage. His enormous four hundred and eighty pound barbarian body dropped to the ground like a lead weight in water. There was a second of complete silence before bullets flew everywhere. Correctional officers, bikers, and inmates scattered for safety. When the gunfire ended thirteen seconds later, five men were dead and scores more wounded. Silence hung over the lower prison yard like fog hangs over the San Francisco Bay on a cold November night.

Kenny Boyd was horizontally silent on the stage. One guard, two inmates, and one biker also lay motionless on the prison grounds. Men walked around like zombies, blood gushing from their bodies. Alarms and emergency horns blasted every two seconds until over fifty officers and a handful of doctors responded to the incident. The National Guard arrived to help maintain control of the facility.

Gunfire had grazed the well-known drummer and star, Buddy Miles. However, it was the death of the popular singer Kenny Boyd, which focused the media spotlight on San Quentin. Boyd had been using his new-found wealth and influence in local communities and prisons as a catalyst for reform. Unfortunately, his efforts at San Quentin had ended in deadly silence.

1

I didn't answer the phone when it rang on Monday morning. Didn't care. I sure as hell didn't need any telemarketer touting the latest bargain on long distance rates. Certainly not before I finished my first pot of java. What I needed was a job. A stack of bills leaned toward my plate of cold, scrambled eggs. The last freelance job was a couple of weeks ago and Dad's oncologist and chemo costs kept growing. Damn. I needed some serious money to keep both my parents and myself afloat.

Finally, the phone stopped ringing.

Sebastian, my thirty-five pound orange tabby cat, jumped onto the kitchen table and sniffed my empty coffee cup, then checked for any leftover breakfast. I should have cleaned it earlier. Then again, I should have done lots of things earlier. These past few days, visiting Dad and dealing with his illness, had dragged me downhill. Sleeping on my folks' couch hadn't helped my chronic back pain either. Every movement rippled with agony this morning. I'd like to blame the ache on some glorious college football record, but the truth was I suffered the same fate as all writers who spend long hours at the keyboard.

When the phone rang again, Sebastian gave me one of his slow blinks. How cats caused guilt and shame in just one look always amazed me. Oh, what the hell, I reached for the phone, hoping it might be an editor. Whether I felt like working or not, I needed the money.

"Yeah, who is it?" I grumbled into the receiver. Sebastian wandered to the edge of the table and flicked his tail, as if declaring victory and dismissing me all in one action.

"Matt! How the hell are you?"

DR. GREGORY VILNER

1

The guy sounded familiar, sort of like my old roommate from college...

"Sal? Sal Tarantino?"

"Of course it's me! Hey, it's only been a couple of years—forgotten your old buddy already?"

Talk about a voice from the past. We'd been friends since the good old days at the University of San Francisco. Sal Tarantino...man, I hated how he kidded me about my dorky black glasses and the way he always called me Columbo. I'm sure my nosey nature, however, is why I became an investigative reporter in the first place.

"No, no, I haven't forgotten you. I've just had a lot on my mind. Dad's been dealing with cancer."

"Shit, Matt, I'm sorry, man. How's your dad feeling...does he have insurance?"

"Actually, he *feels* like crap and no, things are pretty tight money-wise."

"Anything a D.A. can do for you?"

That's right...Sal had been in the District Attorney's Office for the past year or so. Saw it in the paper, but never called him. Truth was I couldn't stomach congratulating the guy. Sal was always more handsome, more moneyed, and more charismatic than I was in college. His personality eventually irritated me so much I quit hanging out with him after graduation.

"Thanks for the offer, Sal, but no—I think I've outgrown bumming cash off of you till payday."

He laughed so loud Sebastian heard him and hopped off the table. He headed for his saucer of milk on the floor.

"I wasn't thinking about loaning you any money, but I was hoping to hire you if you're not busy on another story."

A job? What's the catch? I'm glad I didn't say that aloud, but I did have my doubts. Sal had a slick quality about him, even when professing he'd been a decent friend. When the girls dropped me after meeting him, he always waited a couple of days before asking them out. And he expected me to be happy with that concession.

So much for old times. I needed a paycheck.

WHO'S WATCHING THE TOWER?

"What kind of job and what kind of cash?"

Laughter again. "You haven't changed a bit, have you, Columbo? You'll like this, really. It's investigative work and it pays a thousand bucks a day—plus expenses."

I nearly dropped the phone. A thousand bucks a day? And expenses? That would help Mom and Dad a hell of a lot. Before I drooled too much I needed more facts.

"Investigating what?" My voice was cool, steady. Sweat, however, slipped under my arms and stuck to my robe.

"You've heard about the rock concert and shooting at San Quentin?"

I moved the plate of eggs off the morning paper. A grisly photograph of the scene appeared above the caption: Murder at San Quentin. "Yeah, I've seen it in the news." What I didn't tell Sal was that I'd heard rumors of internal problems in the prison weeks earlier from my buddy, Don. He'd been a guard there and told me he'd been beaten up and almost killed because he didn't bow to the "system." My reporter mind kicked in gear at the time, but I'd just learned about Dad's cancer and couldn't talk to Don for more details. I made a mental note to phone him. "What can I possibly do for you as a reporter?"

"Good question, Columbo. Look, Matt, this investigation is highly political. All my staff members are too close, if you get my drift. I need someone outside of our department—someone I can trust. That's you."

"But Sal, I know squat about investigating a murder. All I can do is interview people and get their stories."

"Yes!" He laughed again. "That's why you'd be perfect! And I need someone neutral—who doesn't have anything to gain or protect when asking the tough questions."

That revelation didn't set well on my just-downed bacon and eggs. What the hell was I thinking? I had no business poking my nose around that prison. On the other hand, maybe I owed it to Don to find out what I could, and that thousand bucks a day sure would be nice.

"Matt, you still there?" Sal's voice had dropped in volume, turned serious.

"Yeah, I was just thinking it through...trying to figure out where to start."

"For Chrissake, you're a reporter! Just ask the questions and get the answers—simple answers to simple questions. And, Matt, I need them fast."

Something didn't feel right about that last plea. "Aren't things like this usually handled by a state task force?"

He sighed into the receiver. "Yes, yes, but the Governor wants to know who's to blame for the whole damn thing. And he wants to know now. Hell, Matt, if I put a task force together, it'll take months to get any answers." He paused to clear his throat. "We've only got three or four weeks before the legislature gets all carried away with this issue and the last thing the Governor needs is this bullshit in his lap. So he appointed me and now I need your help." His voice gained a bit of strength. "And just think what this kind of a job could do for your career!"

Sure, it would be a scoop. Of course, if I asked the wrong person the wrong question I could end up dead. That wouldn't help my career much at all. Still, the bottom line was I needed the money.

"Okay, Sal, I'll take it. Tell me what to do first."

"Great! Thanks, Matt, I'll get it set up. You can talk to the people who were directly involved. Use your trusty tape recorder if they'll let you. Make sure they understand that no one except the Governor's legal staff can examine the tapes or your notes without a court subpoena." He inhaled, then slowly exhaled. "Sort it out for me, please, Matt. I need you on top of this one."

It wasn't like Sal to sound so desperate. He was always on top, always in charge. I wondered if he'd been backed into a political corner of some sort and really did need his old buddy for something other than making him look better to women. If so, that was his problem. I only wanted the paycheck.

"I'll do what I can, as long as you keep the funds coming."

"No problem. Just collect as much info as possible. Oh, and my forensic investigator will work with you on the technical aspects of the case."

"I remember him, we met while I was doing another story. Isn't he a little strange?"

Sal laughed again. "Hey, in this business, everybody's strange. And, of course, my staff will be available to help if you need it."

"Thanks. Again, what's first?"

"I made an appointment for you to meet Warden Cooper at the prison tomorrow. He'll see you at ten-thirty, sharp. Good luck."

He hung up before I could blast him for committing me to meet the warden. Now that did sound like the real Sal—so convinced I'd do anything for him that he'd already made the plans.

I looked at my empty cup of coffee and felt a throbbing push at my temples. Some things never change. I hadn't endured a "Sal" migraine in years, but this one I hoped to cut off before it started. Best way to do that was to try to get ahead of the game, which meant doing research on my own. I glanced at the paper, picking apart each sentence in the article about the San Quentin riot.

> *Shortly after 12:01 p.m. yesterday, all gates to the lower prison yard's football field opened. The specially invited "BAND OF GYPSIES," as well as local bikers, mingled with the crowds. Loud music blasted over the audience with Kenny Boyd singing, Buddy Miles on the drums, Billy Cox on bass and Jimi Hendrix on guitar. Within seconds, shots were fired and Boyd lay dead. A riot broke out leaving many inmates and guards dead or wounded. At this time it is uncertain who fired the first shot and why.*

Ha! What a joke. A hard-up reporter in need of cash was investigating those questions. Before checking the prison, though, I needed to call Don Barrett. Maybe he'd still be willing to help with this job. I sure as hell hoped so.

After a search through the pile of scrap papers on my desk, I found Don's number and dialed. Damn. His machine picked up and I left a quick message. Something cold troubled my spine. If Don was in over his head at San Quentin, there was a real possibility he might not be able to call back.

Sebastian pounced around my leg, startling me so much that I nearly kicked him. I had to quit being so jumpy if I hoped to present a calm front at the prison. Looking back at my trashed desk and then at the laundry scattered at Sebastian's paws, I figured I'd better spend the afternoon putting my place in order and doling out the petty funds I still had to the screaming creditors. Then maybe I'd give Mom and Dad a call.

2

The next morning a brisk shower and a healthy dose of nervous anticipation kicked my adrenaline into high gear. I gave Sebastian a few extra ear rubs and locked the front door as I left. Although I hadn't heard from Don yesterday, I still hoped to catch up with him. With luck, I'd have a little more information by then. The morning sun blazed and almost blinded me as I headed across the driveway toward my yellow 1961 VW. So what if my family called me an over-aged hippie, I loved that car.

With no traffic to battle, I cruised at seventy-five southbound on Highway 101 toward San Quentin State Prison. Images from the newspaper cast shadows over the otherwise warmth of the spring morning. Everyone who lived nearby knew the common legends of the prison: the first facility of its kind to be built in California; the hundreds of inmates executed on the hanging stage in the lower yard in the 1800s and early 1900s; the gas chamber that had been designed and created by a pest control company. Supposedly, a pig was used to test the contraption, making sure it was suitable for executing condemned, dysfunctional humans. I doubt anyone did any tests to determine if the pig had been dysfunctional.

There had been escape attempts, suicides, stabbings, shootings, and murders, all of which the media had reported in the past. Personally, as long as its three thousand inhabitants stayed inside the walls, I'd never given the facility a second thought. Probably that's why I'd brushed aside Don's story a few weeks earlier.

But now with my curiosity triggered, I wanted to know what lurked beyond the towers that rose like periscopes from San Francisco Bay. Other than what I'd seen on television, I had no idea what to expect on the other side of a maximum-security prison. For sure, I doubted it resembled the country club-like setting surrounding the tall, black wrought-iron gates. Opposing the manicured lawns of the comfortably rich, San Quentin loomed like a giant Gothic castle—its pointed arches and steep stonewalls poking toward the gulls flying overhead. Gloom seeped into my gut.

Attached to the left gate was a tiny building. I assumed it was the guard-house when a short, fat uniformed man swung the gate halfway open and approached my car. Sweat dripped from my forehead.

"Can I help you, sir?"

I swear the guy sounded as if he'd growled instead of spoken.

"I'm Matt Belding, Special Investigator for the District Attorney's Office. I have an appointment with Warden Cooper this morning."

He made a rude sound through his lips as he thumbed through the yellow pages on his clipboard. With a snort, he shook his head, went back into the building, and picked up a phone. Obviously, I hadn't impressed him. He hung up and returned, then barked to see my driver's license.

"Yes, sir." I handed him my California I.D., which he took his sweet time to examine—first one side, then the other—before casting a final look at me. "Okay, the warden's office is in the last building on the right, just before the silver hurricane fence. Park across from the yellow and pink building."

How thoughtful. Simple instructions even I could handle. The guard waddled back to his post and opened the gate just wide enough to let me pass. Good riddance. I eased my VW toward the appropriate parking area just a short distance ahead, hardly believing the rows of Victorian houses to the right. They looked strikingly similar to those in the upper class Pacific Heights neighborhood in San Francisco where I'd been born and raised: impeccably styled buildings with yellow and pink clapboard, trimmed in white with red tile roofs. They reminded me of a crop of wild berries connected by landscaped paths—until I remembered this was supposed to be a prison entrance. Strange contrast, to say the least.

DR. GREGORY VILNER

Each house boasted a picture perfect view of the bay; a sign in one declared it the San Quentin State Prison Museum. I wondered about the kind of people who lived in the other mansions on that north hill. Who would want to live on prison grounds?

Driving on, I approached a three hundred-foot solid yellow and pink monstrous building. Next to it was an even taller gun tower, complete with forty-foot moat and quacking ducks. The black drawbridge, currently half-drawn, ended the tourist show. Just beyond view of a smaller building—the San Quentin Restaurant—were security fencing and rusty razor wire that formed a second, far more forbidding, entrance to the actual prison.

What the hell have I gotten myself into?

I parked in a visitor's spot, grabbed my trusty briefcase full of legal pads, pens, and the old tape recorder, groaned as I pushed myself out of the car and headed for—what? I didn't know. Above the wooden doors a large brass sign indicated the building held the Warden's Office, Administration Office and Personnel Office. I pushed one door open, but saw no one in the foyer. The area overflowed into a long hallway, lined on both sides with half-glass and half-walnut stained doors leading to various offices. Restrooms were at the end, according to the generic gender pictures on the far wall. Men in blue jumpsuits, whom I presumed to be inmates, meandered in and out of the offices, apparently unsupervised. They stunk of body odor, lessened only by an even worse stench that permeated every spore of air space. No guards stood watch anywhere.

Apprehension raked down my spine. Who was watching whom?

I walked until I found the warden's office, and then froze in my tracks. His receptionist could have doubled for Marilyn Monroe, exactly like the woman who had popped in and out of my teenage fantasies. Her scent rescued me from the hallway as I quickly shut the door. There was a split second of silence between us and I suddenly wondered if I'd remembered to use mouthwash that morning.

"Good afternoon. You must be Mr. Belding."

Damn lucky she spoke first. I don't think I could have found my tongue, although another muscle responded with no problem. How did she know my name? Of course, Sal had set up the meeting. I hated it when I acted like this. What can I say? Blonde hair, blue eyes, that tight blouse—they all made for an embarrassing bulge in my suit pants as she rose from her desk and led me to the warden's connecting office. The full-length view of her voluptuous body and her slender, long legs...man, I hoped I didn't sear her when she backed into me after knocking on the warden's door.

She grinned and opened the door. My temperature soared a few more degrees as my colorful imagination indulged in fantasy.

"Warden Cooper will be with you shortly."

Her breasts—perfect silky melons—made me want to forget the thousand bucks a day and lip-lock instead, with her wrapped around me in solitary confinement. No such luck. As fast as she'd ignited my passion, she closed the door and left me alone in the warden's office, cooling off with my giant embarrassment.

I tried to focus on something else. So far, this maximum-security prison had been nothing like I'd expected.

A large window overlooked the sparkling blue waters of the bay. Seagulls darted everywhere. Turning toward the large office, I counted eight matching chairs surrounding a mahogany conference table in the center of the room. The high ceiling, hardwood floor, and exquisitely paneled walls made me think the room could have doubled for a Fed's executive office in Washington D.C.

I'd never met a prison warden and my nerves made me forget the blonde—momentarily at least. If Warden Cooper could tell I'd never done anything like this before, I'd be dead meat.

The door swung open and I jumped.

"Good morning, Mr. Belding. I'm Warden Cooper." He entered the room and reached to shake my clammy hand.

"Good morning, sir." He seemed pleasant enough, not the large six-foot plus man I had imagined, with a grizzled prison face and manner. We even had similar shades of suits: muted gray, white shirts, red ties. Power clothes. He was about my height, probably an inch shorter than my 5'10", but balder and much fatter. I smiled. "It's nice to meet you."

"Please, sit down." He pointed to one of the conference chairs then reached for a notepad on his desk, picked it up and joined me at the table. "Mr. Belding, this is the list of inmates and guards Mr. Tarantino asked me to prepare for you."

There were fewer than a dozen names on it and I glanced at the warden. His brow had wrinkled and he rubbed his hands together as I turned back to read. "I'm surprised the list is so short."

"Well," he rubbed faster, then sighed and stopped working his hands completely. "We've been able to determine these people were in the proximity of the areas with direct sight over the lower yard on that day in hell. I think they must have seen an inmate stabbing another inmate with a weapon or perhaps they were directly involved themselves. However, we still don't know who gave the emergency signal 'Code Red.'"

I found it hard to believe that nobody knew what had started the commotion, but I kept that opinion to myself for the moment.

Warden Cooper leaned forward to hand me a blue index card. "If you have any reason to think the person you want to interview might be guilty of a prosecutable crime, then you must read the Miranda Rights before the interview. Do you understand?"

I nodded, looking him straight in the eye, accepted the blue card and stuffed it in my shirt pocket. Sure wouldn't use that sucker unless absolutely necessary. My job was to build these people's trust and I couldn't do that if I started spouting the Miranda Rights as soon as they walked in the door.

"Any idea when I can tour the prison? It would help me when I interview people to have a mental layout of the grounds."

He smiled. Obviously, he'd anticipated my request.

"I've already scheduled you for Friday morning at eleven if that's acceptable."

"Yes, sir, that's great. I'll be here on time, ready to begin."

The lines around his eyes deepened as his smile faded. "I'm so glad to hear that, Mr. Belding. You know, I feel terrible that this tragedy happened. I'm afraid it was my fault since I wanted the motorcycle show and concert so much. Perhaps I wasn't as cautious as I should have been."

I thought about turning on my tape recorder then mentally slapped myself.

"Even though this is a prison, I wanted to believe a little kindness—one time, as a trial—would go a long way." He frowned. "My hope to provide some fun and morale boost completely fell apart. Innocent people died for no reason. Nightmares have begun that I believe are my just punishment for the catastrophe."

Since I had no clue how to respond, I sat with my mouth shut.

"Mr. Belding, everyone here at San Quentin—especially me—wants to get to the bottom of this incident. You have my full cooperation."

"Thank you, sir. I appreciate any help I can get."

He stood, which I took as my cue to leave. We shook hands and I said, "I'd like to get started right away, even before the tour if possible."

"Fine. However, you must understand that rather complex arrangements must be made for you to meet with the inmates inside the walls of the prison. I'll need some time to set up interviews...how about beginning the first of next week?"

This was cooperation? I didn't think so.

"Actually, sir, I'd prefer to start today. Possibly by interviewing any of the guards who were on duty that afternoon."

He blinked a couple of times, but kept his authoritative air. "Well, yes, I believe some of the guards may be available. If you'll please be patient while I check to see if any can be temporarily relieved from their duties, I'll have my secretary summon you when we're ready." He moved around me and left his office in silence.

Summon me? Great. I figured I'd just pissed him off royally. Picking up the list of names, I breathed a sigh of relief that there weren't any like Machine

DR. GREGORY VILNER

11

Gun Kelly, Al Capon, Simon head of the Zebra Killers, Jeffery Dahmer, Stanley "Tookie" Williams or Charles Manson. Nearly ten minutes passed before the blonde slipped through the door. Another immediate blaze in my pants. Damn, I hoped my lust wasn't as apparent this time.

"Please follow me, Mr. Belding."

I followed all right, like a panting dog, through her office back into the long hallway, just past the restrooms and into a tiny room that smelled as if it housed brooms and mops ten minutes ago. So this was how it was going to be. The windowless room left a lot to be desired, considering all the hours I'd be spending alone with inmates.

A thousand bucks a day.

Maybe the money and the Marilyn Monroe look-a-like would make the closet more inviting. Who the hell was I kidding?

"This is where you'll conduct your interviews, Mr. Belding. An inmate will be assigned to you for any errands or other assistance you might require."

I decided to be nice. It wasn't the blonde's fault that I'd been sent to solitary. "Thank you, Ms...?"

"Kirby. Leslie Kirby." She held out her hand for a polite shake.

I took her soft skin, perhaps enjoying the touch a moment longer than I should. The fire burned again and I feared another embarrassing uprising, but she broke contact and continued her list of instructions. "When you finish today, you'll need to stop by the administration office and pick up an I.D. picture badge and a book of tokens."

"Tokens?"

"They're used at San Quentin like money since real money isn't allowed in the facility. You buy a booklet for seven dollars and then use the tokens to pay for meals at the restaurant." She graced me with a smile.

I smiled back an expression I hoped didn't look like an idiot grin stemming from an overgrown hormonal daydream.

She giggled, placing a well-manicured hand over her lips. Our eyes met.

Hers sparkled. I was absolutely fascinated.

"Thanks," I somehow managed to utter. Before I could think of anything intelligent to add, she turned and headed toward the hall, closing my "office" door behind her. I couldn't help wondering what someone with her looks was doing in a hellhole like this—this specific hellhole being little more than an 8' x 8' cell: one worn wooden desk, a broken credenza, a filthy ashtray, a grimy phone, two nicked wooden chairs, and a rank green, plastic trash can—its cigarette and sour milk odors battling in the surrounding air.

Obviously, I was the loser in that skirmish.

A thousand bucks a day. A thousand bucks a day.

If I remembered correctly, the present San Quentin site had been purchased by the State of California from notorious General James Estelle in the 1850s, but no signs of that time period were still visible. In fact, other than a half-dead rubber plant in the corner, nothing was visible. No books or photographs or magazines.

The force of the door slamming against the wall startled me. A tall, athletic, well-tanned man in a perfectly pressed green shirt, black tie, shining gold badge, tan slacks, and black leather boots spilled over from the doorway into the cramped office. G.I. Joe in the flesh.

"Are you Matt Belding?"

"Most days, yeah. Do I know you?"

"No, sir, we haven't met, but I've always wanted to meet you."

First time I'd ever heard that line. "You have? Why?"

"Remember that piece in the *Chronicle* about the Bay area commercial fishermen you wrote a few years ago?"

Uh-oh. Sure I remembered it. I loved it. Problem was I'd pissed off a lot of sport fishermen by revealing the damage sport fishing had done to commercial fishing in the bay. I prayed this guy wasn't packing a mini-harpoon somewhere in those well-creased pants. "Yes," I said, sweat slipping down my chest.

"Well, sir, my father and grandfather were both commercial fishermen.

DR. GREGORY VILNER

13

I thought your article was the best, most beautifully written tribute I've ever read. I sent a copy to each of them and we've been fans of your stories ever since."

Whew. "Thanks, man. It was one of my favorites, too. Somebody needed to point out the ugly side of sport fishing."

He nodded and stepped up to me, grabbed my hand and smiled a dashing Ken smile. I swear he should be traveling south to Hollywood instead of staying locked behind these walls. Suddenly I wondered why he did stay. Curiosity and suspiciousness...I'd need both in this job.

"Guess I better return to my post, sir."

"Well, thanks for stopping by—I'm sorry. I didn't ask your name."

"Walsh, sir. Captain Ted Walsh. If I can help in any way, just let me know."

I decided to test his sincerity. "Actually, Captain, there might be something you could handle for me."

"Yes, sir, name it." He stood even straighter, his creases peaked at attention.

"Warden said he'd send down a guard for me to interview, but I haven't seen anyone yet."

"No problem, sir. You tell me who you want to talk to and I'll see to it that he or she shows up."

Now we were getting somewhere. "Any person on this list will be fine." I handed him the paper I'd been given by the warden.

Without another word he scanned the names, gave me back the paper and headed out the door. I watched his military retreat, wondering which people I could and couldn't trust behind this concrete fortress. As much as I liked the ego stroke from the captain, so far, the jury was still out on everybody.

Captain Walsh had barely left when a smelly human—small, wiry, and scowling through a heavy dark beard—slid through the doorway.

"Name's Tuttle. I'm s'posed to help you."

I sighed. Big mistake. Nobody should take a deep breath with an inmate in the room who made trash odor seem rosy.

"I'm s'posed to wait outside till ya' need somethin'."

Tuttle's arms, covered in thick, black hair, stuck out from rolled-up sleeves. His pants were so dirty they looked like topsoil—as if he lived in the ground like a furry-legged spider. Tuttle the Tarantula—perfect description for a pest who'd be hanging out in some corner waiting to be summoned for necessary errands.

"Well, Tuttle. Thanks, but...I don't need anything right now. I'll holler at you when I do."

He grunted and slipped out the door. I was fairly certain the tarantula's real job would be eavesdropping for the warden. Pictures of the lackey guards carrying messages like scribes to pharaohs crossed my mind. The posted listener didn't surprise me. After all, I'm sure the warden's job was on the line, pending the results of the investigation.

With no guard yet to interview, I took advantage of the opportunity to head over to the Administration Office and have my picture taken. Even though I didn't see Ms. Kirby as I passed her office, I couldn't help remembering the touch of her hand. Somehow, I had to find a way not to act so stupid around her, maybe ask her out to dinner. The thought of food reminded me to buy a book of tokens. Surprisingly, it was a semi-efficient process and I soon passed Ms. Kirby's office again. Still empty.

By the time I'd set up the tape recorder and dug a legal pad and pen from my briefcase, someone stood at the open door. I glanced up to see a sullen-faced guard staring at me. Although tall, he had a thinner build than the soldier-like Captain Walsh. This man's red hair didn't give him quite the same imposing presence either. His nametag read: Sergeant Ed Eudon.

"Please come in, Sergeant Eudon. Have a seat." I gestured to the only other chair. He walked toward it, but didn't sit and he refused to meet my gaze. "I'm Matt Belding, Special Investigator with the District Attorney's Office. I'd like to ask you some questions about what happened during the riot a few days ago."

"Oh, yeah? Big fucking deal."

Shit. Just my luck some guy with a bad attitude would be first.

"Please, Sergeant, sit down." Bad attitude or not, there was no way I'd let him think he could bully me. I just hoped he couldn't tell how fast my heart was racing.

He sat and I opted for the direct approach. "Would you mind telling me what's bothering you about coming here today?"

That got his attention. His eyes zeroed in on me, like spectators on a two thousand pound bull charging toward the matador.

"For starters," he growled, "I have no time for this shit. I've got a job to do so I can go home." He slung an arm in the general direction of the door. "But instead of doing my job, I've got to come in here and talk to some know-nothing, fucking idiot!" He crossed his arms when he finished and dropped the glare.

At least he was honest. "Thanks for being so frank." I picked up my legal pad and smacked it on the table. "And you're right, Sergeant. I don't know anything yet, but I hope you'll cooperate. I need your help to find out the truth about the riot."

He snorted. "Great. I don't just get stuck with an asshole, I get one who tries that fancy motivational, psychological crap. Well, I'm not falling for it, buddy. And as for wanting the truth, you'd better hope to hell you never find out."

Okay, so maybe truth wasn't a welcome dinner topic at San Quentin.

"Are you saying you believe there was an ulterior motive behind the riot?" I shifted to push the record button on the recorder.

He flinched.

"Look, Sergeant, the only people who'll hear your responses are the Governor's legal staff." This wasn't the time to tell him the tapes could be subpoenaed.

The sergeant's facial muscles twitched beneath skin turning as dark as Napa Valley's finest burgundy. His jaw locked as he stared at the whirring machine.

"This is an interview with San Quentin Prison Guard Ed Eudon."

He exploded. "Let me give you a piece of fuckin' advice, asshole." He stayed in the chair, but one hand flew in front of my face like a pistol barrel. "Some of the boys around here get real upset when you call them prison guards. We're not fucking guards, we're correctional officers, and I'm a correctional sergeant to be exact. Got it?"

The hand dropped and I breathed again. "I'm sorry, Correctional Sergeant." I rewound the tape and started over, this time using the proper term, then continued. "For the record, Sergeant Eudon, I'm here as a Special Investigator with the District Attorney's Office. We're attempting to discover the underlying causes—"

"That's a joke," he said with a sickening chuckle.

"What are you talking about?"

"That the Governor and the D.A. really give a damn about underlying causes. Ever hear of PREP?"

I shook my head, thinking this guy might have more emotional issues than brains and I'd be much better off with a different job.

A thousand bucks a day.

"What's PREP?"

He rolled his eyes. "Look Mr. Special Investigator, the government tried some dumb ass Prisoner Rehabilitation and Education Program—PREP. They made it sound like they were sending inmates to Yale or Harvard before leaving the prison. Shit."

"So you don't think it was effective?"

He howled and doubled over, his so-called laughter gnawing at my nerves. "Oh, it was effective all right. Gave the inmates vocational training they could really use. One dude, a habitual offender who pleaded guilty to a couple of dozen counts of burglary, took the locksmith course. That came in real handy when they released him."

Was this guy kidding or stalling? I had to get him back on track. "Sergeant Eudon, can we talk about the riot that occurred on July Fourth?"

"You can talk about it all you want. I'm not saying a damn word."

"Why not?"

"Because I don't have an attorney here and couldn't afford one anyway."

"Do you think you need an attorney?" This was an interesting twist. I had hoped for mere background information and this guy acted all edgy. 'Course, this place puts me on edge, too.

"Look, man, someone screwed up here one hell of a lot that day. They need a body to blame and a low-life correctional officer is an easy target." He shook his head. "Not me, though. I'm only two years away from my pension."

The hothead made sense. Doubt if I'd give a different response in his shoes.

He pushed away from the table and stood.

"Wait, Sergeant, I have more questions..."

"My shift's over, man, and I'm clocking out of this shit hole."

"Are you refusing to be interviewed?"

His movement toward the door halted. "Let's just say I'm refusing to be interviewed by someone stupid enough to believe that the State of California really wants to know what caused the riot."

"But I'm with the D.A.'s office."

"Then you're working for the wrong people. They know what happened here that day. They know what's wrong with this place and what needs to be done to fix it." Sweat slathered his forehead. "Problem is, they don't give a damn about these inmates or us. They figure we're all a bunch of low-life scum and the only time those in charge ever get worried is when they think one of 'em might make it to the outside and tell the truth. That would mess up what those in charge are doing. Is that something you can understand, Mr. Special Investigator?"

"What are you saying exactly?"

He covered his face with his long hands then swung them away and stared me down again. "What I'm saying is those in charge punish those who get out of line."

"That's what I've been hired to uncover here, Sergeant, but I need help."

"Not from me, mister. It's dangerous and stupid. You'll get yourself killed."

Killed?

I punched the stop button as he slammed the door behind him. I don't know what makes people so damn vindictive. What the sergeant revealed was exactly what Don had tried to explain to me. Again I wondered if the money was worth the risk. On the other hand, if I died in the process, at least my life insurance would help my parents. I just hoped I'd have a chance to know Ms. Kirby a little better before I bit the big one.

Partly out of disbelief and partly because I wanted to make sure my tape recorder had worked, I punched rewind and listened. There it was... Eudon had said something about the state bureaucrats already knowing what had caused the riot. That bothered me. Or maybe it was his unmasked anger and rage that made me wonder if he fell into the same category as criminals and killers.

I needed to think. Grabbing my briefcase, I stuffed the recorder into it and headed across the windowless closet where I dismissed Tuttle who had been leaning on the wall just outside the door. For a spider, he had awfully big ears. Before leaving the grounds, I stopped at Ms. Kirby's office.

"Excuse me..."

"Yes, Matt?"

God, she was intoxicating. Torrents of blonde hair hung nearly to her hips. Her fully shaped bosom and long, red fingernails combined with that perfume made me forget what I was going to ask. I fumbled open my briefcase and randomly picked a name on the list the warden had given me. "Could you help me set up an interview with Mark Wilcox, please?"

She picked up the phone and dialed a three-digit number. While waiting for someone to answer, she smiled and winked at me—my reward for noticing her. Most definitely she wanted people to notice her. What virile man could help it? Her scent made my head whirl.

Finally, she spoke into the phone. "This is Ms. Kirby in the warden's office. Mr. Belding would like to talk with Mark Wilcox on Friday at one o'clock. Please have him contact me to confirm the interview." She hung up and smiled again. "Okay, Mr. Belding, you're all set."

Pretty lady, you have no idea how set I am. Being a male had its drawbacks. I liked this sexual picture haunting my conscious thoughts, but I felt totally out of control.

"Uh, thank you, Leslie." What a pathetic wimp I was. Didn't even have the balls to ask her out. Sometimes I wish I could've been more like Sal. He would have had her stroking his balls by now.

"*Ciao-ciao*, Mr. Belding."

Even I couldn't miss that cue to leave. Fine with me. I couldn't wait to escape this prison. The sun had already started setting when I pushed open the doors to freedom, sucking in air that had taken on its customary chill during this season around the bay area. Fog inched its way over Mount Tamalpais to descend into Marin County.

Damn. There was fresh bird shit all over my car. Even though the Italians think that is good luck, I wasn't so sure after the first day on the job. It's a good thing Ms. Leslie Kirby was part of this assignment or I might have backed out for good. She was incredible—my fantasy woman. If I didn't know better, I'd say I was in love. Problem was, I *didn't* know better. I had no clue about her or her feelings for me. Maybe she'd give me a chance with time. God, I hoped so.

I stopped at the guard gate and opened my trunk when commanded, slammed it shut when he grunted his okay, then drove away without looking back.

3

On the way home, I came inches from eating the chrome on a brand new, black Ford pickup. They shouldn't let people drive who had just been to San Quentin for the first time. I couldn't focus on anything but getting away from that idiot at the guardhouse, not to mention the "Correctional Officer" I'd interviewed. Ed Eudon had some serious baggage and issues he needed to address.

I punched in an Eagles tape and let their music work the knots out of my head and stomach. Like most residents of Marin County, I lived in an apartment that hung off the side of a cliff. The narrow, winding streets surrounded the housing complex and one driveway that descended rather abruptly into a small parking area outside my building. Backing out was virtually impossible.

When my friends visited from other parts of the country, they were always amazed to see how we locals lived. The steep stairs to garages and carports made simple tasks like toting a bag of groceries great feats of aerobic exercise. The winters, however, brought very real fears of mudslides. Entire homes had been known to slide down such hills. But the rewards of living in such potential jeopardy were the priceless, incomparable views of San Francisco, the Bay, and the Golden Gate Bridge.

Personally, my apartment provided an unobstructed view of a neighbor's red roof and of beautiful trees and the bay in the distance. The inside was a basic efficiency: a small kitchen, a bedroom with boxes everywhere, a computer desk, an eating area with four chairs and a table, and a television. All the walls were painted green with brown trim throughout, except for the bathroom, which was white.

Today when I parked, I couldn't help noticing more boxes at the bottom of the stairs. Good-sized boxes too. I got out of the car and wrestled one to view the return address. They were from Sal. I carried them up the stairs, all the while wondering what in the world was inside the heavy packages. I knew my aching back would revolt, and after I stacked them I paid the expected price...muscle spasm, big time. This made me angry enough to try kicking them through the door, but of course they weighed too much. After I hauled the last one inside, I relished in a thorough stretch while Sebastian warily checked the new stack of boxes.

One thing was for damn sure. My cramped apartment full of boxes felt like a mansion compared to the confines of the cell-like interview room at the prison. Sebastian was already bored with the cardboard, oblivious to everything except his empty food bowl. "Well," I said, while shaking Meow Mix kitty crunchies into the cat dish, "I think Sal has gotten me into something way over my head." Although I'd never admit it to a living soul, I talked to my cat constantly. Sometimes my best ideas resulted from chatting with my thirty-five pound furry friend. I checked the answering machine to see if there were any messages from Dad or Mom. There weren't any and I hoped he was feeling better, but knew he probably felt like something Sebastian might spit up. He was always in so much pain. I cannot perceive or understand how the cancer infected him—he had always stayed in great shape.

The phone rang as soon as I turned away. It was Sal.

"So, how'd it go today?"

"Awful," I said.

"I'm not surprised, Matt. It's a different world out there, that's for sure, but you'll do fine, good buddy."

Right. Always the optimist. "I don't know, Sal. All I managed to do was piss off the first guard—excuse me—I mean 'Correctional Officer' I interviewed."

"Don't worry—"

"No, seriously, I'm not sure I'm cut out to be a criminal investigator or whatever it is. Besides, it gave me a splitting headache and those boxes you sent me ruined my back!"

"So you're going to quit and not take the money that could help your parents?"

Damn, Mr. Manipulation was at it again.

"Matt?"

"I'm still here," I growled. "Yeah, of course I'm going to keep the job. I'm going back Friday for a tour and more interviews."

"Great, now stop whining about the other stuff and get busy going through those boxes." As usual, he had easily become perturbed with me, and he'd lapsed right back into the controlling guy he'd been in college. Fine, I would just ignore him this time.

"What's in them anyway? They weigh a ton."

"Everything we have so far on the riot: forensics, police reports, and witness interviews...that sort of thing. Shit, my other line's blinking. Gotta go."

Before I could fire off another word, I heard a dial tone. Gee, it only took 24 seconds for Sal to piss me off. I wasn't nearly as tolerant as I used to be. Fact was, in college I never knew when he'd show up or what he'd have in mind for me to do on his behalf. Most of the time, it would be making up lies to earn him dates with women. His actions were the major reason I parted ways with him after we graduated. He'd gone to law school while I took a job freelancing for the *San Francisco Chronicle*.

Sal was always trying to get me to join in adventures that gave him an adrenaline rush, whether racing motorcycles or hiking jagged cliffs in Yosemite. I, on the other hand, was quite content to go through life as an observer. He couldn't understand that I was happy most of the time without such challenging activities.

And I was happy...until my dad got sick. That thought sobered me back to present day, and the boxes. Sebastian had polished off his supper and was staring at me from the top box that was labeled number one. "Well, don't just sit there, use a claw and open it."

He blinked at me.

"Worthless cat." I used a key from my pocket to slice through the tape and opened the flaps. Shredded paper flitted to the carpet and Sebastian took an immediate interest, pawing and clawing at a rainbow of colored strips.

I popped the others open and realized the documentation was overwhelming—several thousand pieces of paper and pictures, some of which were incredibly graphic photos of blood and dead bodies. After separating the contents, I stacked them onto the table. Good thing I had a couple of days to myself before reporting back to San Quentin. This glut of information would take hours. And a cheeseburger. Maybe two and some fries.

After a quick run to McDonalds, I spent the rest of the night at the table, familiarizing myself with names and events that concerned the riot. When the sun hit my face the next morning, I headed outside for the morning paper. I was only gone a few minutes, but when I came back the red light was blinking on my answering machine. A voice, more polite than I heard yesterday, spoke in a low volume. "This is Ed Eudon. Please call me the next time you're at San Quentin."

Strange. My first worry was how he got my number and the second was why he wanted to talk. He sure as heck didn't give me the impression he wanted to divulge much information during our interview. Or maybe he was putting on a tough guy image because the Tarantula was listening. Whatever the reason, it was still strange.

A yawn interrupted my thoughts and sleep became top priority. I hit the shower and then the bed for a few hours. About 3 p.m. Wednesday, something wet touched my cheek and I came straight out of bed. "Dammit, Sebastian, I've told you not to do that!"

The cat sat on my pillow, staring at the wall as if studying the Mona Lisa. He must have felt hungry enough to nudge me out of my beauty sleep, but he obviously thought ignoring me would be better punishment for not feeding him before I crashed.

"Okay, okay, c'mon. I'll give you some milk before I start my coffee."

His head lolled in my direction, apparently accepting my peace offering.

I'd barely finished pouring my cup of hot java when the phone rang. "Belding, here," I said and took a sip from the mug.

"Matt, it's Don. I got your message."

Finally. "Hey, Don, thanks for calling. I'm sorry I didn't follow up with you, but my dad's got cancer and I've been out of town a lot helping him and my mom."

"Oh...I'm sorry."

"No problem, man, I understand."

"Listen, Don, is there any chance we could meet tonight? I have some questions to ask you about your last involvement at the prison."

"Well..."

Uh-oh. "What's the problem, Don?"

He sighed. "It's like this, Matt. At first, I wanted to go public with what happened to me...maybe save some other guards the same trouble I had. But after this latest riot uproar, I'm not sure I want to anger anyone else."

"What if I told you I'm working with the D.A. to clean the place up?"

"It's impossible. That place is beyond reforming."

I hated how monotone he sounded. He'd given up. I had to make him fight again. "That's exactly why I need to talk with you, Don, so I can give an accurate assessment back to my boss."

"Can you guarantee I won't have to be involved in testifying or anything?"

"I don't think you will. I just need your first-hand experience. Just like the info you gave me when I worked on the sport and commercial fishing story. I know I can trust you."

Trust was something I couldn't toss around lightly on this assignment. Don had been very helpful, giving me the inside scoop he'd heard from one of his fish and wildlife buddies a while back.

"C'mon," I prodded, "I'll buy you dinner at the Octopus Seafood Restaurant in Novato."

"Is that the one on Redwood Highway 101?"

"That's it. Seven o'clock okay with you?"

"Well, okay, Matt, I'll see you there."

Man, that did not sound like the Don I knew. Where did his "everything by the book" and "justice" attitude go? This investigation was getting murkier by the minute.

It was 5:20 p.m. when I looked at the clock again. I'd gotten sidetracked going through the stacks of information. There were so many conflicting reports and stories from the witnesses. No wonder Sal needed somebody completely objective. Too bad he thought of me first.

No, that wasn't true. Guess I should have been grateful, and I really was grateful when I called my parents to tell them they could expect a nice check from me early next week. Dad had sounded stronger on the phone, and I couldn't help but laugh at his fatherly concern when I told him about this assignment. He actually said, "Be careful out there with those hoodlums." I hung up grinning, and realized I'd be late for dinner if I didn't get my butt in gear.

Granted, I took the curve out of the parking lot a little fast, but I thought it more than a little unusual that the truck that nearly side-swiped me looked so much like the Ford from the previous night. It sped away so fast I couldn't get its license plate. On the other hand, what could I do about it? He hadn't hit me. At least I assumed it was a "he" driver. The windows were tinted too darkly to tell. Two near misses in a 24-hour period, both by almost identical pickups. Probably coincidence, but I wondered if it wasn't a "hoodlum" keeping an eye on me while I nosed around about the riot.

As usual, the Octopus lot was full when I pulled in, but I found a place to park, grabbed my briefcase and headed toward the restaurant. Don, a somewhat overweight and balding man, was waiting by the bridge next to the entrance feeding Koi in the pond.

"Hi, Don."

He turned, looked both directions before settling his eyes on me. Paranoid, definitely paranoid. Something had happened to him, that was a given.

"Hey, Matt. You look like hell."

"Thanks, it's kind of you to notice." Gee, maybe my all-nighters had finally caught up with me. "I'm glad you came, Don. I need your honest opinions about San Quentin."

He nodded. "A lot goes on out there that no one will tell you about...but like I mentioned a few weeks ago, I think other people should know about some of these things."

We entered the building and the steamy aroma of fresh cooked Dungeness crabs reminded me of being on the ocean. The resident crab cook, Vince, was extracting red-hot crustaceans from a boiling pot with a giant spoon. I moved toward him and said, "I want mine extra large, Vince."

"Hey, Mr. Belding, coming right up. There's an empty spot for you to sit." He pointed to an open table not too far away, while the hostess followed us. She asked if we wanted coffee. Don and I both said "yes" and I asked if my favorite waitress, Vanessa, was working tonight.

"She sure is. I'll send her right over." The hostess wiggled away in a way that made me temporarily forget the cracked crab. And with Vanessa as our waitress, we'd be awarded efficient service in a pretty, dark-haired, brown-eyed package. Don and I would enjoy the meal in spite of the less-than-thrilling topic of conversation. He was even less thrilled when I placed the tape recorder on the table.

"What's that for?" He scowled at the machine.

"Now, Don, you know I used one each time we talked before because of my lousy memory. Besides, I'd rather eat than take notes."

Vanessa arrived with our coffee, smiling from ear to ear. "Here are your drinks, Mr. Belding. Guess what? I just waited on Buddy Miles, Carlos Santana, and Mickey Hart from the Grateful Dead and earned a big tip!"

"Good for you," I said, smiling enough to be polite. The Octopus' motto was "From Our Boats To You" and it was typically filled with celebrities dining on fresh fish with fine wine. "I'll have the fresh cracked crab with three tartar sauces, two cocktail sauces and two orders of sourdough French bread and butter. Oh, and please bring me the crab right out of the boiling pot—I think Vince put one aside for me."

Don said he'd have the same. As soon as Vanessa left, we both went for our coffees. The restaurant was busy as usual. People talked and laughed, some in rather loud voices, all in the utilitarian atmosphere. It would have been easy to relax if I didn't have some hard questions for Don. I pushed the record button and plunged ahead.

"So, how long did you work for the California Department of Corrections?"

Don put down his coffee. "Fourteen and a half years."

"What part of that time were you assigned to San Quentin?"

"Just about every single day."

"And why did you first contact me a few weeks ago?"

Something in his eyes darkened. "They tried to kill me."

The grip on my coffee tightened. "Tried to kill you? Who? The inmates?"

"No, Matt, we could handle them okay. It's the guys in charge you have to watch out for."

"Can you be more specific?" My mind ran back over the day I'd spent behind the walls of San Quentin. Had I already made enemies? Is that what Eudon wanted to talk to me about?

"You need to understand my position. The other guys...guards I still hang out with on their off hours...they're scared. They don't want to say anything that might get back to the upper echelon. They need their jobs. And they're afraid they'll get the same treatment I did."

"What do you mean? What kind of treatment?"

"I'll tell you the specifics later." He took another sip of coffee. "First, I need you to understand why they did it. That's why I called you."

"Good idea."

Vanessa arrived with our food, but Don barely noticed. His eyes were focused somewhere else, somewhere he didn't want to be. I, on the other hand, was as eager to down the cracked crab and French bread as I was to hear what Don had to say.

"Look, Matt, the most powerful inmate when I worked there was named Clarence Redmond. Everyone calls him "Big Red." He ran all the narcotics in the prison and had all the juice there was to be had. There was also a nervous little prisoner named Ferret, Redmond's little prostitute. He needed heroin daily."

That bit of info made the sourdough a little less appetizing, but at least Don's story about Redmond was accurate. I'd seen his name in the files I studied yesterday.

"So, all is fine until one day little Ferret decides he's been butt-fucked enough. He tells Redmond he isn't going to bend over for him no more, doesn't care if he gets sick from no more heroin, and doesn't care if he dies. So Redmond smiles at Ferret and says, 'Okay, little buddy.'"

Don stopped talking and cracked apart a crab leg. He didn't eat the meat inside, just kept cracking it until it lay pulverized on the plate. I swallowed another bite and kept listening.

"So Ferret's relieved, figuring he was paid up. A deal's a deal. About an hour later, Redmond catches him walking around the yard and says, 'I can still count on you for doing other things, can't I, little buddy?' Ferret nods with a smile on his face like an idiot, saying, 'Anything you want, Big Red.' So Redmond gives him a butcher knife to hold until they get back to West Block, and Red walks away real fast. Soon as he's far enough away from Ferret, one of his other pawns starts screaming, 'Knife! Knife! Ferret's got a knife!' and inmates scatter in every direction. Ferret panics and then runs toward Redmond with the knife held out in the open. The guards on the gun post towers shoot six rounds into his pathetic little body, tearing him to shreds. He never knew what hit him."

"I take it 'hit' is the operative word."

"Now you're getting the big picture, Matt. People die up there all the time—a lot of it planned by the inmates under Big Red's leadership. He was in charge in the yard." He pushed aside the plate in front of him and swallowed more coffee. "Nobody gave a shit about that convict. The captain didn't care. He just filled out an incident report. If he classified it as a murder, he'd have to do a whole lot more paperwork and there'd be an inquiry panel and an investigation by the California State Police."

I was still unclear why Don was a target, so I let him keep talking. Maybe something he divulged would help in my investigation.

"But if a guard dies, then the ones in charge, whether they're officers or inmates, need a fall guy, so there's less heat from the outside."

"So, you're telling me the guards and inmates coordinate illegal activity?"

He nodded. "And the fall guys are the ones en route to the gas chamber. What's the D.A. gonna do? Tell them they'll die twice? Meanwhile, Big Red makes it easier on the inside for them if they'll perform his dirty work. It's all about survival, Matt."

"And murder." Suddenly I had no more appetite, either. "So did you confront your supervisors about Ferret and is that why they tried to kill you?"

Vanessa came back and frowned at our fairly full plates, but I motioned for her to take them away and refill our cups. She did and Don collected himself again.

"No, saying anything to anyone is a sure road to suicide. The only thing I can figure is that they think I misplaced some keys and that those keys might incriminate them."

"I don't understand."

"Well, neither did I at first, but one day I was at my locker, trying to put on my uniform, and the captain's secretary comes right in as I've got my jeans around my ankles, saying the captain wants to see me before I change into uniform. So, I yank up my jeans and follow her into his office. The watch sergeant, my lieutenant, and the captain were all standing there, looking like vultures. They asked me a bunch of questions about some keys from South Block—the same stupid-ass questions from the day before, so I figured they were just yanking my chain, because I tried to do things by the book and I wasn't going to take the fall for somebody else who'd screwed up the whereabouts of some keys."

"What happened?"

"I told them I didn't know anything more than I did yesterday and I was going back to the locker room. But the sergeant said, 'Hold it right there, Barrett. That's an order.' And I told him this wasn't the goddamned Marine Corps and I didn't take orders and I didn't come on duty for another thirty minutes, so if they wanted to talk to me they could wait till I was on the damn clock."

Now this was the fiery Don I remembered. He was much more recognizable than the timid man I saw outside on the bridge watching the Koi.

"But the asshole sergeant ran up behind me, grabbed my belt and pulled out the buck knife I keep on it. He said, 'Well what do we have here? Looks like we caught this boy bringing contraband into our prison. That's not very smart, Barrett.' They all knew I carried that knife with me into work, but it always stayed in my locker. That's when I realized I'd been set up and why they wanted me in there in my street clothes."

"All because of the keys?"

Don shrugged. "I guess. That's why I called you in the first place, so maybe you could help me figure out the reason. I know you like to solve things and look for clues and details. All I know is that before I could react, those goons had a hold of me and the captain got right in my face and said, 'Barrett, you fucked up big time. I can't have my guards thinking for themselves.' They pushed me up against a wall, patted me down, and ripped my clothes off, shouting, 'Strip search!' the whole time. They made vulgar remarks about my physique, and then the captain said he wanted to make sure I wasn't hiding anything."

"But your clothes were off by then, right?" I'd heard horror stories about how inmates treated each other, but if the guards' supervisors acted like this...

Don didn't stop talking, he just nodded. "The captain told the sergeant and lieutenant to stretch me out over his desk for a *thorough* examination.

Matt, that mother fucker put on a rubber glove and rammed his finger up my ass."

I winced.

Don almost started crying.

"They were fucking laughing at me when I screamed from the pain. They made me put my clothes on, then handcuffed me and dragged me out into the parking lot and threw me into a patrol car. The sergeant drove us out to the middle of the rock quarry, and they pushed me onto the gravel and rocks. They were taking turns kicking my sides and beating me with large stones that felt like boulders. See that scar?" He fingered a three-pointed line near his temple. "If I hadn't turned my head when the rock hit me, the doctors think I would have been blinded. Finally they gave me up for dead and took off."

"After you recovered, did you file charges?"

He grunted. "Sure, but my life was shattered. I had to explain what happened to the D.A.'s office, then in a civil court. Nobody believed me. But I passed a lie detector test the State of California required and the other three guys all failed it. I ended up with a very large cash settlement for damages and personal injury, but it will never erase what those bastards did to me. And Matt, there's still a lot worse things going on out there."

I wish he hadn't said that. I was glad to hear he'd gotten some money out of the horror, but I still couldn't understand why they targeted him. "And you think it's all because of misplaced keys?"

Vanessa dropped the ticket beside him, but he ignored it. "I'm not sure. That's what they asked me about, but I wonder if they think I stumbled onto something else and they were just taking me out as insurance. I wish I did have something concrete other than just the rumors about Big Red. Believe me, if I knew why they chose me, the D.A would have known. I could have used it in court."

I picked up the ticket and pulled out my Visa; glad I'd get funds from Sal before another payment was due. Something registered in my gray matter.

"Was Ed Eudon the sergeant involved?"

"Hell, no, he's one of the few people around there who attained sergeant without giving in to corruption. I doubt he's got a dishonest bone in his body. He's not like the other guys. If Eudon said water ran uphill, I'd believe him."

Well, that opinion might be important later, even if I still didn't know why Don's life had been threatened.

"So, who were the men involved?"

"The sergeant was Jack Halsey, a real hop-to-it former Marine Corps Vietnam vet. He always sounded like he was really pissed that the war was over, and he thought the prison should be run like the Marine Corp."

"Guess that's why you popped off to him about not being in the Marine Corps."

"Yeah," Don nodded, "but now that he's been fired, most of his time is spent on his ranch in Sonoma County, probably trying to keep the cows in proper formation and keep them marching in rhythm to the band."

I couldn't help but chuckle at that picture. Seemed most military guys I knew tried to handle their personal lives as if they were still on base. Needless to say, it never worked. "And what about the lieutenant? Who was he?"

"Charlie Kirschner. I thought Charlie was a decent guy before this went down. He was fired, too, just like Halsey after the suit was awarded to me, but four days later he supposedly committed suicide."

Vanessa had swiped my card and returned it at that moment. I gave her double my usual tip of five dollars and was rewarded with a grin *and* a peck on the cheek. Ahh...it would be great to have money coming in again. I needed to call Sal's office for a check.

"And the third person?"

"Captain Walsh."

"What? But he's still working at the prison!"

"Now you understand why I didn't want to talk about it, and why the other guards are scared shitless."

This didn't make sense. "But why wasn't he fired, too?"

"He covered his ass by going to the warden and ratting on the other two. That's how it works in there, Matt. No loyalty, no rules. Survival of the strongest and smartest, that's it."

The little I'd eaten was knotting in my gut. "So he walked?"

"Well, they slapped his hands, demoted him for a while, but he was raised to captain again as soon as things cooled down. People like him thrive in that system. He knows exactly what to do and when to do it. He's cold, calculating, and extremely clever."

Man, my impression of him had sure been off. Wait, my *first* impression scared me shitless until he complimented me about the article. Could that have been a red herring? Maybe something to keep me from suspecting him of anything? I'd been out of work too long. I was getting soft on noticing details and body language.

The more answers I got in this case, the less I knew, but one thing I needed to be absolutely clear about was the South Block key question. "Tell me again what you did or didn't do with the keys, Don."

He sighed. "There was a ring with keys to South Block C section. I took the keys at the beginning of my shift, like I always did. Then I hung them back on the same hook in the sergeant's office at the end of my shift. Routine stuff, you know."

"But they went missing?"

"I guess so. That's the impression I got because the next thing I knew the sergeant was furious, shouting at me that the captain had come in saying two inmates died, the keys were missing and the warden would have the captain's hide if they didn't show up. But I doubt that was true."

"What do you mean?"

"Back then our warden was a guy named Paulson who was afraid of Captain Walsh. I'm not sure what the captain had on him, but it must have been big. Walsh pretty much ran the prison at the time."

"So what happened the first day they were missing?"

"The captain and I got in this big argument. He said that I put the security of the whole prison in jeopardy, that those keys could have opened all the cells in South Block."

"You think he was trying to set you up for a bigger fall later?"

"Yep, but I'm pretty sure he had second thoughts about that after I told him off that day."

"Why? What did you say?"

He leaned back and crossed his arms. "I told him if he was that goddamned worried about the security of our prison, he ought to keep an eye on his pet inmates, especially the one he had who was working for him as a clerk. He gave that guy free run of his office."

"And that clerk was..."

"Clarence—Big Red—Redmond."

Now things were making more sense. "So Redmond used to be a clerk to Captain Walsh, who runs the joint any way he wants, and they each looked the other way when it served their purposes. How well organized." I thought I'd puke.

"Now you got it, Matt. And now you know why the guards and most of the inmates are scared all the time." He sighed again, unfolded his arms, and tossed a napkin onto the table. Standing, he said, "I'm exhausted."

I turned off the tape recorder and extended my hand. "Thanks. It took a lot of guts to be this blunt with me, Don. I appreciate it."

He returned the handshake. "No problem. But please memorize that tape and then destroy it."

"Will do." I nodded, hoping the tape would be the least of his worries from now on. After saying my good-byes to Vanessa and Vince, I headed for the nearly empty parking lot, wondering if my worries were just beginning. Even at $1,000 a day, I wasn't sure how long I'd last in that prison.

4

The conversation with Don had spooked me more than I realized. I checked every corner, every empty lot, and every vehicle to see if a black pickup was following me. Talk about paranoid. I was worn out from the facts swirling in my head and the lack of good sleep the day before. Finally, I arrived home late, drained, but thankfully with no accidents or Fords in my wake.

Thursday morning I slept in and studied the book on how to conduct a criminal investigation that Sal had been nice enough to include in one of the boxes. Sebastian enjoyed an early bowl of Kibble then stretched on the comforter at my side, purring a hundred miles an hour.

"You know, Sebastian," I said, petting his head, "this book is good for organizing, but I have to figure out a way to make the interviews work. I've got to get those guards to trust me so they'll open up. And I bet they're like police officers...they won't say much unless they consider me part of their team."

Sebastian squinted at me. I suppose this was his way of encouraging my recent line of thinking.

"So," I rambled, still stroking his fur, "what can I do to make that happen?"

He purred louder and rolled away. Obviously, I was on my own. Fine. One thing I *could* work on was making the "office" they'd given me a little more comfortable. Maybe a more casual atmosphere would negate the skepticism that most law-enforcement personalities possessed. I would take along my Eagles tapes to play when I wasn't interviewing. It would at least help clear my mind and help me relax between meetings.

Hell, it might even perk up that shabby rubber plant that looked as if it had spent time on death row. Mom always talked about how much better her plants grew if there was a pleasant mood in the house. That's why she often played classical music. She even told me that some friend of hers whose new husband played rock music was certain the gyrating guitars had ruined her African violets. Of course the Eagles were hardly Mozart, so who knew what would happen to the little rubber plant. But it was worth a shot. Something green and fresh in that drab room had to help.

Sebastian and I spent the rest of the day lounging around the house, munching and napping when we felt like it. By Friday morning, I was refreshed and curiosity had overtaken my earlier fears. I'd do my best to uncover the facts and earn a grand a day doing it. And of course, the lovely Ms. Kirby was a darned nice fringe benefit. What could be so bad?

Friday morning was foggy as I drove through the gates of San Quentin. I tried to hang on to my better attitude, but it was hard to stay pumped up when surrounded by thick, gray mist. Before I could show the guard house gorilla my new picture I.D., he waved me through and I parked in the same spot as I did earlier in the week. To add to my dismay, the lovely Ms. Kirby was talking on the phone when I walked into her office. She simply pointed a long red-tipped finger toward the warden's office and I headed there, only to discover I was one of about a dozen or so people waiting for a tour. So much for the personal exploration of the prison I'd been expecting.

From listening to their candid conversation, I detected the others must all be rookie cops, off in a little group to the side of the warden's desk. Talk about feeling out of place in a crowd. The theory I had shared with Sebastian about how these types of people interacted with "outsiders" was about to be tested.

A fifty-ish female from behind the men yelled, "The tour is now starting." I followed them, taking in the prattle of the woman leader, who overorchestrated the highlights of what we saw to the point of being sanitized.

We entered through the ground floor of the three-hundred-foot long East Wall. Death row inmates nested above us on the fourth story and our matronly guide told us they had their own private yard on the fifth story.

Double black iron gates—separated approximately twenty by fifteen feet—buzzed open, one at a time and then clanged closed behind us before allowing the next one to open. My first glance on the other side didn't reveal the ominous gloomy atmosphere I had anticipated. Instead, it resembled an outdoor college campus.

We stood beside a well-kept, thriving multi-colored flower garden in front of the chapel. Here the sweetly smiling leader explained how inmates fill all the jobs and do all the work required for San Quentin to function on a daily basis. Our so-called guide even joked about an escape attempt in progress as she pointed out "trustee" inmates who came and went as they pleased from the captain's office. After Don's insights last night, I wondered if there might be any truth to her remark.

We were allowed to stick our heads into the legal area beside the captain's office where lawyers met with their inmate clients. Next we stepped into a rotunda, a big hollow area with armed guards on a gun rail near the ceiling. The guide informed us that this was North Block. The only elevator in all of San Quentin was here, and it was the only way up to Death Row. Condemned prisoners passed through this rotunda just minutes before being strapped into the gas chamber and executed. I tried not to think about that.

Actually, it wasn't too hard. I was more worried about the prisoners who were right in front of us. Were those guards above us really sufficient? I had expected everyone to be locked up or in full restraints. My earlier "what could be so bad" attitude now sent shivers up my back. As if on cue, our guide's verbiage shifted toward security issues. She pointed out every gun tower and gun walk within the facility.

"The three-story building on our left is an extra-security area called the Adjustment Center—it's a prison within a prison, which has double-barred cells." Her voice was a dull monotone, like the steel bars we passed. Then suddenly she smiled and in a brighter, almost proud voice she said, "This is also the place where Charles Manson and Simon, the head of the Zebra Killers, are housed." The cops *oohed* and *ahhed* at that bit of trivia. I wanted to puke.

We followed like baby chicks as she pointed out the upper yard. I asked about the three separate, fenced-off enclosures, each about fifty-feet square that separated the Adjustment Center from North Block.

"Oh," she said, shrugging a little, "those are the exercise areas for white, black, and Hispanic inmates. The viciousness of the gangs forced these separations years ago. It helped cut down on confrontations, stabbings, and murders."

I shuddered. We kept walking through the chapel across from the Adjustment Center before moving further into the prison. Just as we passed the circular guard post in the center of the yard, the loudspeaker blared: "Escort! Escort! Escort!" The cops moved instinctively, and the matronly guide slammed me against a concrete wall. She pointed to a Manson look-alike in full body and leg chains, accompanied by four guards armed with nightsticks, as she told us the tower and gun walk guards above us had their guns aimed and ready.

Everyone in the upper yard had moved to the walls and were frozen like ice sculptures, their eyes pointing away from the procession. Mini-14s and 870 shotguns, trained on the escort, made my bowels feel like they'd let loose at any moment. After the escort passed, our guide again put on her phony smile and moved us toward the movie theater as if this happened every day. These things *did* happen every day and I seriously questioned again the thousand bucks a whop wages.

After the movie house, we stopped at the main dining room where the majority of inmates ate their meals. I was amazed. The place bustled with prisoners cooking and other kitchen workers making the final preparations for lunch. Everything was scrubbed spotless and looked almost as professional as a well-supervised restaurant. My stomach growled at the aroma of some sort of beef and potato offering just as my back started aching. I almost wished we could stop to take a break from hiking across San Quentin's cold stone floor. The guide, however, herded us to the next point on our tour.

The only cellblock we were allowed to visit was West Block, the trustee honor unit. We entered through the solid steel door, which was open and unguarded. This was the only way in and out. I was surprised to see the shower room located at the entrance, just inside the door and to our left. It had a wide, open row of showerheads and seven naked inmates ignored us as we passed. Their lack of embarrassment and interest reminded me of what I'd read in a book about prison life. Incarceration removed all modesty because prisoners never had any semblance of self-control or modesty. Those bare asses sure embarrassed the heck out of me, though. The cops in the group kept faces of granite.

We moved forward, seeing inmates lurking all over the place. There were three small rooms with hard cement floors and three windowed doors to our right. One was the lieutenant's office, one was the sergeant's office, and the guards used the third room for their lunch breaks—and it was a mess. Scattered across a table were bits of leftover food, chip bags, and cups.

Farther on, five tiers of cells went straight up through the middle of the building. The place stunk worse than an outdoor privy. Iron stairs served as the only access to the upper levels; fifty cells were located on each tier. Under the same roof was another similar structure, which made the guide boast, "For a total of five hundred cells!" I couldn't figure out why she was so puffed up with pride—five hundred in this small of an area seemed awfully cramped.

Next we noticed the two gun walks, nearly fifty feet above, with armed guards patrolling their length along each wall. There was nothing but air between the walks and the cells, preventing any contact between guards and inmates. The matron gave us a serious look. "If a guard on a gun walk sees an incident between inmates, his only recourse is to fire a warning shot, then fire directly at the perpetrators if they continue."

Maybe it was because of these severe consequences that each cell door was open. Inmates gathered in two and three in some cells, while others leaned over railings, chatting with those above and below them. Some were simply sleeping, reading, or exercising alone. Since so few inmates were readily visible the guide explained that most were working at their various jobs in the prison. I held back from the group of cops and slowly looked around before catching up to the others.

While it was noisy, with radios playing and people talking, there seemed to be a peaceful atmosphere among the men. No obscenities could be heard, cells were neat, and all things considered, the place appeared civil. Although it stunk to kingdom come, it didn't seem so bad. The thought of gazing into a human zoo entered my mind, but just then I heard a murmur and a chuckle behind me. Someone whispered, "Look at that fat ass, four-eyed motherfucker." Cages or no cages, I hurried back to the group, suddenly glad I was touring with cops.

Just as I caught up, the guide said, "We're running a little behind schedule, so we'll have to postpone viewing the hospital and hurry on to lunch." As we passed by the two sections of Bravo Block that separated the rotunda leading to the hospital, I asked if we could take a quick look at the South Block, known as "the hole." It supposedly had the worst and dirtiest San Quentin offered. Everyone on the outside had heard rumors that food and human shit stuck to the walls there.

She shook her head and frowned. "No, no need to. That unit is exactly like this one. Hurry along now and please stick together."

Right. Just like this. Hmm...she sure didn't like my questions.

Much quicker, the guide took us past the prisoners' canteen in the upper yard where they purchased supplies. From there she pointed to the East Block, telling us it housed the new arrivals and then pointed to the North Block, which housed the main population. The size and confines of it all started to get to me. I'd definitely lost interest in seeing much more, especially when the guards came to meet us, shaking our hands and laughing a little. None of this added up to what Don had described, nor did it account for the way Ed Eudon had talked about the place.

The tour ended in San Quentin Restaurant, located outside the walls in a round, yellow cinderblock building with a view of the bay that rivaled some of the finest eateries in Sausalito and San Francisco. We were fed a hearty meal of turkey, mashed potatoes, peas, cornbread, choice of coffee, tea or milk, and apple cobbler.

All during lunch, the rookies cracked jokes about the carefree prison atmosphere. "Man, maybe I ought to hold up a liquor store" or "My wife doesn't cook this well," gained the most laughs. I didn't see anything funny. Maybe the skeptical reporter in me was on alert, but I figured this whole tour was a facade for the public's approval.

By the time I politely separated from the group, I couldn't wait to get to my dingy office and track down Sergeant Eudon. I headed toward that end of the prison and hoped that this time Ms. Leslie Kirby would be available for a little chat. Before opening her door, I straightened my jacket, sucked in my gut, and tried to look macho. What a sorry effort. Who was I kidding? I was Columbo. Even so, she greeted me with a warm smile and a coy flip of her long blonde hair. I took this as a good sign. That flirty flip was definitely beyond the requirements of a professional greeting. When it finally sunk in that she could be coming on to me, my hormones raged. All discretion and common sense walked the plank. She smelled so good... good enough to nibble.

"So, Mr. Belding. How was the tour?"

I didn't think telling the truth would be in my best interest just yet. Ms. Kirby may be luscious on the eyes—and she was even more luscious in my fantasies—but she still worked for the warden. Instead, I said, "It sure isn't the Hilton."

Her laugh was incredibly sensuous.

"Ms. Kir—"

"Please," she interrupted. "You can call me Leslie. And do you mind if I call you Matt?"

Perfect. First names were first base, as far as I was concerned. And how I'd love to move up to the plate for a grand slam homer.

"It is, Matt, isn't it?"

Damn. I doubt she'd have anything to do with me if I came across as an idiot. "Uhh, yes, of course. That would be great." Her eyes mesmerized me and I suddenly forgot the legitimate reason I'd come to her office. Definitely she was coming on to me, no doubt about it.

"Did you need something, Matt?"

"Uhhh...yes. I'd like you to call Sergeant Eudon for me so I can set up another interview with him. The sooner the better." I hoped that sounded convincing.

"I can do that for you, no problem." A manicured hand moved across the pages of the duty roster and she dialed three digits. "Sergeant Eudon, please." A pause ensued and we smiled at each other. She turned her attention back to the call. "Sergeant Eudon? Yes, hold just a moment, please."

My hand touched hers as she passed me the phone. Immediately I pictured us entwined in my bed, minus clothes. She must have felt something, too, because her nipples rose to attention beneath her sweater. Heat swelled again in my pants. I worked to clear my throat and caught a glimpse of her seductive smile.

"Eudon, this is Matt Belding. I'm ready for our follow-up interview. Can you meet me tonight at Melody's on Lincoln Avenue in San Rafael?"

He agreed, thank goodness, because I wanted to focus all my energy back on Leslie. She had left no space between her leg and mine when she handed me the phone and the increasing warmth caused a growing stir below my belt. She noticed and grinned. As I returned the receiver, I took a chance and kissed her long fingers.

"Why Matt...how sweet of you." She seemed genuinely moved.

I held her soft skin a little longer, feeling myself grow a little longer. "Tell me, Leslie, would you consider having dinner sometime with a lowly public servant, such as myself?"

She giggled and stared at me. Damn. "Another night, maybe?"

"Maybe," she said, squeezing first my hand, then my thigh it rested on. She lingered there a few seconds then leaned down, brushing my index finger with ruby lips. "But right now I have work to do and so do you." With a quick move of her tongue, she licked the end of my finger and gave it a tug with her teeth, then pulled away so fast I seriously questioned if I had imagined the whole sensual scenario.

Work? How could I think of work with a hard on as big as that turkey leg I just chomped?

"You're right, of course," I barely managed to say. I took a couple of quick breaths and asked, "Who is the first person I'll be interviewing this afternoon?"

"Correctional Officer First Grade Mark Wilcox."

I nodded, backing away in a courtly gentleman's bow, hoping to cover the raw passion protruding within my pants.

5

I'd barely stepped through my office door when a voice thundered behind me.

"Correctional Officer First Grade Mark Wilcox, sir, reporting as ordered!"

I turned and nodded. "Thank you for coming, Mr. Wilcox. Please sit down." I did the same and placed the recorder where he could see it. He sat stiff-backed in his chair with both hands on the table, ready and waiting further instructions. To test my theory on gaining trust and cooperation, I started with gratitude. "Mr. Wilcox, I greatly appreciate you coming so quickly. Do you know why you're here?"

He nodded. So militarily correct, I thought. I took out a new tape and put it in the recorder. "Good, then let's get started." I pushed the record button. One thing I'd definitely learned with Sergeant Eudon was not to draw any further attention to the cassette player than was necessary. "Please state your full name."

"Mark Allen Wilcox."

"And your present rank?"

"Correctional officer first grade."

I noticed his hands had started to tremble a little and sweat beaded on his brow. Hmm...I wondered why Mr. Military fretted with just a name and rank routine. Maybe I made him nervous with the formalities. I'd try a different approach.

"May I call you Mark?

"Yes, sir."

I smiled. "Thanks. Tell me, Mark, how long have you been with the

Department of Corrections?"

"About three years," he said. The muscles in his face softened and his posture eased somewhat.

"And where were you working on July Fourth, the day of the Rock and Roll Riot, as it's now being called?"

The starch and endurance abandoned him and he slouched, like air had suddenly left his balloon. "Rock and Roll Riot? That's what they're calling it? What's the deal? Is someone still trying to prove that the rock and roll was a bad influence?" He shook his head, confusion wrinkling his face.

"Yes, that's what some press people are calling it." I frowned a little, then looked back at my notepad. "Do you remember where you were working?"

"Oh, yes, sorry sir. I was in Tower Two."

"Mark, do you mind if I ask you some questions about your background?" Maybe I could figure out what made this simple guard tick, or if it even mattered.

"What do you mean? What kind of questions?"

Uh-oh...he sure turned paranoid quickly. "Basic things, like where you were born, where you went to school, maybe why you chose to become a correctional officer."

"Oh, well, okay. I was born in Fresno." His nose actually turned up at the word. "But I got out of that town fast."

"Why?"

"Well, my dad died there when I was in high school and I sure as hell didn't want to die in Fresno, too."

Understandable, I thought. Not many people like the city. "So what did you do?"

"Joined the Marines and asked to be stationed somewhere it wasn't one hundred degrees in the shade. They shipped me off to the Naval Air Station in Iceland. Nothing but ice, rocks and Navy flyboys in that camp."

Marines. That accounted for his mannerisms and maybe his current job choice. "And what was your assignment?"

"They trained me as an MP. Those Navy boys thought they were hot shit with their wings and college degrees—oh, excuse me, sir."

"No problem, Mark. How'd you like it?"

"Well," he grinned, "I brought a few of them down to size."

"And after your Marine duty?

He frowned. "I tried to hire on at the California Highway Patrol, but I couldn't make it because they require people to be six foot tall. I'm only 5'6"."

"So you became a correctional officer?"

"Yes, sir. My cousin was working as one out here and he told me they had some openings. Of course, they always have openings. Most guys who get on out here realize they've stepped in a bucket of shit and they try to get out with their lives still intact. I guess I thought I was a little tougher. Plus, I believed in that duty and honor stuff we swore to as Marines."

"Did you have to go through some kind of training after you applied here?"

"Oh yeah," he rolled his eyes, "and it was something else. They give tests and ask lots of stupid questions, but the truth is they were trying to fill as many vacancies with as many warm bodies as possible. Too bad I bought their little game, hook, line, and sinker. I thought I was giving my time for a higher calling...especially when attending the State Police Academy."

"So would you say that working in San Quentin with these prisoners has had an adverse effect on your life?"

His face aged suddenly and he stared into the desktop. "That all depends. I guess not, if you don't consider alcoholism, wife abuse, or divorce."

Now we were getting somewhere. "Do you think the Academy helped prepare you for this job?" His answer was crucial—it was important to find out if these men had a realistic understanding of the conditions and situations they'd find themselves in as correctional officers.

"No way. They taught us the basic stuff...restraint techniques, take down holds, the State Penal Code, first aid. That sort of stuff. The firearm training was about the only relevant help considering what we face in there."

He scratched his shoulder and I found myself sniffing, remembering the odors from the tour.

"What could they do differently?" I scribbled on my pad, hoping he'd believe I was ready to jot down his suggestions.

"Not a damn thing."

I looked up. "Nothing?"

He shrugged. "If they told us what really goes on, nobody would graduate. They're so misleading."

"What do you mean?"

"For one thing, the manpower shortage is a major problem. My first day I was assigned to Gun Tower Two and believe me, after working there many times since, I can tell you nobody should be put up there on their first day."

Encouraging a relaxed setting with Wilcox was paying off. At least his story was meshing with what Don had divulged, although it was far removed from the image the guards at lunch had tried to impose. "Why? What happened to you in the Gun Tower?"

He sighed. "Well, I was walking up three flights of decaying wooden stairs, I wanted to use the handrail, but knew I'd have a palm full of splinters if I did. When I reached the top, I pushed up on the trap door, which is part of the floor of the tower. I expected at least a decent work area, but the place was covered with old food wrappers, cigarette butts, ashes, half-eaten food and a toilet in the middle of the floor. It stunk like a dumpster. And the windows wouldn't budge because they were painted closed."

"Did the guard you relieved give you any idea what to expect?"

Mark chuckled a sick laugh that sounded more like a whine. "Hardly. He didn't say a word. I'm not so sure he could talk."

"Huh?"

Mark shook his head, spread his hands on his knees and leaned back in the chair. "Mr. Belding, the guy was ancient. He looked like maybe the tower had been built around him and he smelled like that was the last time he bathed, too. He handed me his rifle—a mini 14—then pointed to the twelve-gauge in the corner, and disappeared down the stairs. I was too shocked to even get a question out before he was gone."

Good Lord, if this was the kind of training these guards got, it was a miracle San Quentin didn't have a riot every week. I was sure Sal and others in the D.A. office would be interested in this morsel of insight.

"So what did you do, Mark?"

"Well, I looked around to get an idea about what I should do. I closed the toilet seat because there was shit splattered everywhere. There were inmates in the yard inside the wall, below my tower outside the walls, and on the roads surrounding the prison wall. I remembered from the Academy that there was supposed to be a printed job description at each post with orders, but there sure wasn't one in that garbage heap in Tower Two."

"What about communication? Was there a phone or did you have a two-way radio?"

He nodded. "My thoughts exactly. After finding the phone and prison directory, I called Tower Three. The guard there laughed at me when I told him it was my first day, but he did finally tell me what my duties were."

"And what are the duties of an officer assigned to the towers?"

"According to the guy I talked to we're supposed to 'watch for stabbings or problems between the inmates. If something happens, we fire a warning shot or shoot the inmate if he's trying to swim away."

"You're kidding."

"Nope. That's exactly what he told me."

Geez, if that's what the kid learned on his first day, it sure didn't speak well of on-the-job training.

"I didn't see anyone trying to swim away, but I did see a whole lot of gulls. Watched them all day long and kept fighting off sleep."

As he talked, I got up to stretch and gave the rubber plant a drink from the water bottle I'd brought with me. "Why? Were you tired starting out?" I used my handkerchief and wiped dust off the plant's leaves. Maybe it was my imagination, but I think the little green guy looked healthier.

"No, sir, but as the hours wore on I spent a lot of time walking in circles. I never thought standing in one place could be so hard. Since then, I've learned that the shifts last at least eight hours, but sometimes sixteen to twenty-four hours straight."

"What?" That got my attention. "How can they do that to you guys?"

He shrugged and I sat back behind the desk.

"Do you mean to tell me that there is no break—no relief guard on those long shifts?"

"Yes, sir, and that's why we end up daydreaming. I'm telling you, Mr. Belding, sometimes nobody's watching what's happening on the grounds. My first day I ended up working a sixteen-hour shift. No food and no breaks."

The Tarantula was back. I heard him shuffle outside the door after Mark's latest statement. He'd report this conversation back to the warden for sure. Anything negative would be sent back faster than satellite communication.

"And," Mark sighed, "it was like that for the next two weeks. I started taking garbage bags up with me to clean the place when I was bored. And we don't have a choice about being stuck up there. Once, my sergeant called me in the tower and told me I had to pull an extra shift. I told him I couldn't because I had promised to go with my wife to her parents' house for a birthday party."

"He didn't understand?"

"Hardly. He told me I had to work the overtime, and then he hung up on me. I called back to his office, but he hung up again as soon as he found out it was me. I was so mad I climbed down the tower stairway and rattled the gate, trying to get the guard to open it up and let me out, but he just shook his head and walked away."

"So you couldn't leave even if you wanted to?"

"Right." The color left his face and he asked to be excused.

I clicked off the recorder. "Sure, Mark. Thanks for your help. I'll call you back if I have any more questions." I'm not sure he heard my last words; he was out the door before I finished speaking.

Interesting. Mark was so spit and polished when he'd arrived. Now after remembering his first feeling of "locked up," his guts had given out completely. Poor kid. He had even tried to make a difference when he signed up for the Academy. I wondered if many of the guards had the same high ideals when they started, or if they just hired on because they needed a job and there were always jobs available here. Lots of overtime, too, from what Wilcox had said. Trouble was, it wasn't always voluntary overtime.

I shuddered. It would take a gritty kind of man to choose to be locked up day after day. And a healthy salary. My first check flashed through my mind and I found myself disgusted at the same moment.

The Tarantula poked his head in the door. His tiny black eyes darted to each corner of the room, as if he were checking for spots to spin a web. I hoped none of the men I'd interviewed would be considered meals for this human arachnid.

"Need anythin' Mr. Belding?"

I shook my head. "No, thanks, and I'm finished for today. You can go."

I wanted to tell him to hit the cement and never come back, but I knew his presence was a certainty while I worked at San Quentin. I'd darn sure keep my tapes with me, though, just in case his furry legs decided to carry anything away to his master.

And speaking of legs, it was time to find Ms. Leslie Kirby. I needed a reality check before leaving for the day to make sure I hadn't misread her earlier attention. Unfortunately, when I reached her office the lights were off and there was no sign of her, just a note on the door with my name on it. I opened it, hoping for some sordid message, but it was only a reminder about my first meeting on Monday.

At least I had a night of enjoyable fantasies ahead of me. But before I let my imagination fondle Ms. Leslie, I had Sebastian to feed and another session with Ed Eudon over dinner.

6

Sebastian licked his paws after dining on the can of Banquet Tuna. "Good kitty," I said, patting his head. He sneered as he purred, a response I've come to learn means he really did appreciate his vittles, even if they weren't homemade. I sure as hell didn't have time to grill him anything special before I met Eudon for dinner. I did, however, wish I had a few extra moments to call Mom and Dad, but that would have to wait until later.

Melody's always reminded me of the bar on *Cheers*. I used to live up the street from the one in San Rafael and whenever I stopped in, there was the usual mix of blue-collar types and yuppies. It was a homey place without any of the pretentiousness of the other Marin County nightspots. The snacks they served made for an ample late-night fare. My favorite was the round butter crackers served with baby-smoked oysters. On Friday nights, Melody's was quiet until around seven-thirty or so. Tonight was no different.

"Going Through Them Changes" was playing on the jukebox and a threesome played billiards in the side room as I walked in. Four men in suits sat at the bar, entertaining two "blondes" they'd probably just picked up off the commuter from San Francisco. Finally, I saw Amy. She was the best waitress Melody's had on staff and I loved her smile as much as I enjoyed Ms. Leslie Kirby's hot breath on my hand.

I waved at her then pointed to my usual corner booth in the back. She saw me and nodded. Less than a minute later, Eudon came in and sat across from me. Amy arrived to take our orders.

"Hey, Matt, what can I get for you and your friend?"

Her easy manner always gave me unexplainable warmth inside. Not as hot as Ms. Leslie made me feel, but definitely more genuine. Didn't know if I liked admitting that or not.

"Hi Amy," I said. "How about bringing us a couple of drafts to start?"

"You got it."

She hurried off and Eudon opened the menu. "Thanks for meeting me, Mr. Belding. I know I came across kinda rough in your office the other day, but you gotta understand where I'm comin' from."

Frankly, I wasn't eager to give him a second chance. Melody's food was what appealed to me. On the other hand, when I had treated Mark Wilcox with a little compassion today, he had opened right up. Of course, the main question was if Eudon even had anything worthwhile to add to what I'd learned so far...which was damn little. I sighed.

"Please, Ed, call me Matt. And forget about the office visit. After taking the tour today and listening to another one of your fellow correctional officers, it's easy to see you guys have one shitty job description."

He grimaced. "That's for sure." He frowned when I pulled out the tape recorder. "No way, man, what I gotta say can't be on record."

I eyed him for a second and decided to chance my memory. Maybe I'd learn more important info if I quit pulling that thing out of my pocket. "Okay, Ed. Tell me what's on your mind."

"Well, like I said, when we talked earlier I was still pretty stressed over this Kenny Boyd thing...wondering if maybe they'd try to pin what went wrong on one of us guards."

"I thought you wanted to be called Correctional Officers?"

He smirked. "I really did give you hell, didn't I?"

"Yeah, which makes me not trust you too much right now, so get to the point."

"Okay, that's fair." He moved a napkin toward the end of the table where Amy was hovering with our beers. "Thanks." He smiled and the sincere gesture surprised me.

"You're welcome." She turned to me. "What do you men want for dinner? The place is filling up so you better put in your order now."

"Just bring us the usual appetizers, Amy."

"Sure thing, Matt."

She took off, shaking that little butt of hers for all it was worth. And it looked like quite a treasure trove from my vantage. Amy was right—the place was packed. The spicy barbeque aroma mingled in the air with a hint of stale beer odor. I gave Eudon another of my serious looks and played hardball. I hoped this would be my last meeting with him.

"So, Ed, you were worried about being used as a scapegoat. What's changed since we talked earlier?"

"Nothing, except I think because of this investigation and the fact the D.A.'s involved, maybe you were right. Maybe something good might come out of it for all of us. But if everyone was as scared like me to tell you the truth, then nothing will happen. The same shit will keep going on every day, worse on some days depending on whether the inmates are in charge or the captain's in charge." He took a long pull on his beer and kept talking. "Maybe your report might get some of Kenny Boyd's bleeding-heart liberal friends to raise enough money to make a difference in that place."

"Money? What's money got to do with it?"

He rolled his eyes, shook his head. "Matt, money is always part of these kinds of problems. We guards get a guilt trip every payday and about the supplies we use or the discounts we get at the canteen. Far as I'm concerned, they can keep their piss-poor food and supplies. I think they're just messing with our minds. Trying to keep us in our place."

"Could be, I suppose." I drank my beer, savoring the cool draft.

"Anyway, most people they hire aren't too bright, you know what I mean? They're pretty easy to intimidate. Some of them end up suicidal and it's because there's no support from the administration about how to deal with the stress that working in a place like that brings on."

His language may have been a little rough, but the man was making sense. I waved at Amy to bring another round of beers, just as Ed took the last swallow from his glass.

"But we need money." He pulled a piece of paper out of his pocket and handed it to me.

"What's this?"

"Just read it. I took it from my Prisoner Transportation Manual."

I glanced at the paragraph he'd underlined: *The general public pays the bill for protection through law enforcement and should receive this service at the lowest possible cost to taxpayers.* "Maybe I'm dense, but what's the connection?"

"They throw that bunch of crap at us every time they want to cut expenses. That phrase is why prisons are understaffed, why we're paid less than what it takes to live in our cities, and most important, it's why some officers can be easily enticed into...well, let's just say, more lucrative money-making activities that the prisoners offer because of their contacts outside. It's why some inmates have control. It's why others are served immense cockroaches cooked into their food."

I guzzled the last of my beer, trying to wash that image out of my mind and throat. "So you're saying that money—or lack of it—set the riot into motion?"

He nodded. "Either directly or indirectly...like, maybe a build-up of something bigger that got way out of hand that day."

Amy brought our next round of beers along with our food. The steaming buffalo wings and smoked oysters put the riot on hold for a few minutes as Ed and I both devoured a fair share of the food.

The money problem could be related to the riot, but it sure as hell wouldn't be easy to track. What was worse, the more credence I gave to Ed's statements, the more I worried about tracking down proof that would back up his position. After all, anyone benefiting from illegal activities would certainly do all they could to keep any connection away from the D.A.'s office—including messing up my investigation.

DR. GREGORY VILNER

55

Shit. The black Ford came to mind. Okay, I had to get as much information as possible, now that this had just taken a more personal twist. "Tell me what you know about the warden's involvement, Ed."

He chomped down another buffalo wing before answering. "Well, he's new, so a lot of the confusion that day could be part of the problem. Don't get me wrong. I think he's a decent guy, but maybe a little too trusting. Some of the officers think he's stupid, though, and they take advantage of that, because he's easy to manipulate. He doesn't understand how the cons operate and that gets him in trouble."

"What do you mean?"

"Well, he's always talking about his daughters and how he hopes the men working for him are upstanding so their families can be proud of them... that sort of thing. Hey, I got a daughter, little Heather, so I can relate." He fumbled in his hip pocket until he produced a wallet full of pictures.

The youngster was definitely a beauty. "Great looking kid."

"Thanks." He stuffed the wallet back into place. "Anyway, the warden thinks each and every con could be reformed into the kind of guy he is. Problem is, when he put some changes into place he did some good things the wrong way."

"Now you've lost me again."

"Okay." He slurped his beer then folded his hands on the table. "Like when he found out about the drug problem, he launched an investigation to find out how the drugs were getting in."

"And did he?"

"Yeah, of course. Anyone who's been there a couple of weeks knows all the secrets. A guy's old lady hides it in her mouth and passes it during a kiss, or maybe she picks a more personal place and he retrieves it when they're having relations. We strip search them before and after of course, and we find a lot, but some of it gets through, depending on which guards are on duty and where their real loyalties are."

"Is that the only way drugs make it into the prison?"

"Nah," he shifted in his seat and picked up a cracker. "Another five percent or so comes in packages delivered to inmates. We're supposed to check all packages for contraband, but their friends on the outside are pretty creative...and..."

"What?"

"Well, Matt, this is really off the record. Because we're so understaffed, the captain picked a detail of kids—that's what we call the captain's pet inmates—to search the packages. They knew that the smart thing to do was to turn in to the warden a few things they found at first: knives, joints, stuff like that. They earned his trust immediately and, of course, the warden thought his drug problem had been solved."

"I can't believe the warden would let inmates search packages."

"Hey, after they turned over the token trinkets, the warden was elated. Gave the whole program his blessing." Eudon snorted. "He even gave the captain some damn commendation for coming up with the idea, for 'developing an innovative program while saving the taxpayers' dollars.' What a joke."

"So what do the inmates inspecting get out of it? And how did they choose whose contraband to turn over?"

Eudon smiled. "Now you're getting it, Matt. They only reported contraband from inmates who wouldn't pay them off. Those who did pay didn't get their stuff confiscated. Wasn't long before those mail inspectors were the wealthiest inmates in the place. Their cells soon had color TVs, stereos, and Penthouse magazines."

"You're kidding!"

"Wish I was," he said, shaking his head. "We're just damn lucky some idiot didn't send in a gun or a worse kind of weapon. Thank goodness the warden noticed that drugs again were easily available and he figured it out. Shut the inmate inspections system down."

"But there are still drugs inside, right?"

"Of course. Some of the inmates who manufactured on the outside find what they need on the inside. We know better than to assign them to the pharmacy, but they're smart. One guy kept bugging us to be assigned to the sewer plant. He was so happy and we soon found out why...he had everything necessary to make tons of methamphetamine tablets."

"That's disgusting."

"No shit." He smiled at his pun then took another swig of beer and I did the same.

Somehow my usual appetite at Melody's had been severely curtailed tonight. The amount of drugs bothered me, and of course, it served as a major money operation that no doubt carried major power inside San Quentin.

Eudon tore into another wing and said, "But about 80% of the drugs come from the other correctional officers and prison officials."

"What? Is everyone there corrupt?"

"No, Matt, that's not what I said. But a powerful few regulate the majority of operations. Got it?"

"Yeah, I understand. And you think the main reason is to enlarge their wallets."

"Right."

"How do they get it inside?"

"Depends on their rank, mostly. Higher the rank, the cleaner the operation. Nobody questions them much. The regular guys bring it in their lunch pails or duffle bags...but some stash it right in their pockets."

"Wait. Back up a minute. You said the higher the rank, the cleaner the operation...what's that mean?"

He swallowed another gulp of beer and I motioned for Amy to bring us a final round.

"Well," he said, "there was one time the captain got to be chummy with Joseph Carlotti—you heard of him?"

I nodded. Everyone knew he was a big name in organized crime. Drug connections all up and down the restaurants he owned in Fisherman's Wharf, not to mention his import/export shipping yards in the city.

"Anyway, Carlotti donates heavily to the mayor's race and lots of charities. Most of the S.F.P.D. looks the other way at his import/export business. Problem was when the captain at the prison had Carlotti start supplying food to the prison kitchen. Twice a week one of Carlotti's trucks delivered ten cases of canned artichoke hearts and ten cases of canned asparagus tips."

"Pretty fancy food for the inmates." I tried to remember the last time I had artichoke hearts or asparagus tips. I grabbed a wing instead and munched as Ed continued.

"Exactly. One of the captain's kids always unloaded the cases, but nobody ever ate anything from those cans."

"So they were full of drugs?"

"You catch on quick."

Okay, maybe I was slow, but he didn't need to be rude, especially when I did such a good job at making sure Amy kept us in brew. She arrived with our new supply, which gave me time to cool down before I said something I might regret to Eudon.

"Thanks, Amy." I smiled at her and she winked back at me. Two flirtations in one day. Not bad for a Columbo kinda guy. "Yes, Ed, I do catch on quick, but I have to have some kind of proof to believe the senior administration officers orchestrated a major drug traffic job inside San Quentin."

"Fine," he said. "Look it up in the records. A formal report was filed in the Sacramento office of State Department of Corrections."

"What caused the investigation?"

"Carlos, the trustee inmate in the prison kitchen saw these cans coming in and none of it ever showed up on the menus he was supposed to serve."

"An inmate called for an investigation?"

Eudon rolled his eyes. "No, Carlos found the cans of artichoke hearts and asparagus. He opened one up and reared his head back only to get a mouthful of heroin. He died within a couple of hours."

"Oh."

DR. GREGORY VILNER

"That ain't the half of it. Of course, the warden was royally pissed. He had people following his officers and he clamped down on the operation, fast. Man, we had so many inmates in withdrawal and detox, it was a mess. Dangerous, too. The inmates fought constantly...we were in a perpetual state of lockdown. It was a nightmare."

"And this had something to do with the Rock and Roll Riot?"

"That's what I'm trying to tell you." He took a quick pull on his beer then straightened up and moved his plate to the side of the table. "See, the drug bust started everything. If the warden hadn't stopped the drug flow, there wouldn't have been any Rock and Roll show."

"You just lost me."

He gave me a look that said he wished I would get lost, but he settled in and explained further.

"Okay, I'll make it simple for you. Drugs are the inmates' money. They use them to get what they need. It might be simply a kid who acts as a runner to the big drug guys to support his habit, or it could be one of the big guys using a major drug pay-off as an incentive to get a guard or another inmate to kill somebody. Drugs are money, money is power—both inside AND outside."

The light bulb finally went on. "Got it. So when the warden shut down the system it caused more than just the turmoil with the inmates. Let me guess. A major player outside wanted the Rock and Roll event so a new supply could get in and return the flow of money and power."

"Give the investigator a cracker."

"Very funny. Now, who's the outside connection?"

"A biker from Sonoma County. One day he calls the warden and says how a lot of guys who get locked up used to be bikers and he's heard the morale is real low and maybe he and his biker buds could come on out and spend some time with the guys in the lower yard."

"And Warden Cooper isn't suspicious?"

Eudon shook his head. "Like I said, he thinks everyone is basically good.

WHO'S WATCHING THE TOWER?

6 0

And besides, if Big Red's on the outside now, he must be reformed, right? Just wanting to give the guys on the inside a day of fun, that's all so he said. Matt, the warden's the one who came up with the idea to have a band play on the same day. He really thought this concession on his part might help the inmates out of their problems with depression."

Something still didn't make sense. I took a final drink of beer and dropped a couple of twenties onto the ticket Amy had just set down the last time she passed. "So, let's say your theory's true...it still doesn't account for the shooting and why the riot started."

"Not exactly, no, but I bet the reason someone started shooting is drug related because of Big Red and his connections. That's your job to pinpoint it. I just wanted to give you a realistic background about why there was a concert in the first place."

I thanked him as we unfolded from the booth then headed our separate ways. I thought about all he told me as I drove home. True, the pieces fell closer into place if I believed him—too bad, because it also meant that I couldn't confide my findings to anyone. And I really hated being suspicious of every dark colored truck that passed me on the road. Seemed there were quite a few between the restaurant and my apartment. Or maybe my mind was playing tricks on me. I sure hoped so.

7

Friday's fog had turned to rain by Saturday morning, so Sebastian and I stayed under the flannel covers as long as possible. Late in the morning…okay, so it was closer to noon, we rose and ate. I tackled a few apartment chores that I'd let slide while out of town helping Mom and Dad. When I got to the last job on my list—changing the litter box—I made a mental note to do it more often but *not* on such a humid day. Even Sebastian couldn't stay in the bathroom with me as I cleaned his privy.

Late in the afternoon the phone rang, just as I'd finally gotten a shower and settled onto the sofa with my notes and a chunk of sourdough bread. I swallowed the bite I'd just taken and mumbled, "Belding here."

"Matt, this is Don. I thought of something else."

"What is it?" I hoped that whatever Don had to say would be worth putting my bread on hold. Very few things came between San Francisco sourdough and me.

"I remembered that the missing key thing happened right after some other stuff came up missing from the kitchen."

Hmmm…the kitchen was where the supposed contraband had been hidden. I put my bread and notes down. This might be worth my attention. "I'm listening."

"I don't know what was stolen, but I do remember the captain was on a rampage about missing product and mumbling something about the female guard who wasn't doing her job down there."

"Female?"

"Yeah, she was in charge of watching the kitchen when the supplies were stolen. I can't remember her name, but I heard she was fired a few months later."

"What for? Was she caught stealing kitchen supplies?" I had to be careful not to feed Don any information about what Eudon had said about drugs being shuffled through the kitchen. I still wasn't sure who to trust or who might be trying to cover their butt.

He sighed. "No, Matt, she was fired because some new correctional officer coming on duty caught her being gang-banged by four or five inmates."

"What?" Just when I thought I couldn't be surprised any more...

"Yes, inmates. She was hot and heavy with one of the convicts and he was a sicko who liked to watch her being fucked by his pals. She was also allegedly supplying him with drugs, but she wouldn't say how she got them. It happens a lot out there."

I couldn't believe this. From trafficking drugs through the kitchen to free-for-all gangbangs of the guard's choice...San Quentin had it all. "You sure you can't remember her name?"

"Sorry, Matt. All I know for sure is that my buddies say she was incredible to look at. Used to drive them all crazy, especially Wilcox."

"Mark Wilcox?" That's an interesting tidbit he didn't mention in our interview.

"Right. She was living with him when she got busted. Can you imagine what it must have been like to have your girlfriend fired for supplying pussy to inmates? We found out later she'd been arrested twice for prostitution before she was hired. So much for background checks, huh? Anyway, it must have been one hell of a blow for Wilcox to hear she went to live with an inmate after he was paroled."

"Are you saying the administration doesn't do background checks at all?"

He sighed. "What I'm saying, Matt, is that they don't care who's hired. They just need warm bodies to fill vacancies, so they run 'em through the Academy, put 'em in green uniforms, give them a badge and gun and maybe, if they get the time later, they might do background checks."

His disgust was easily heard in every word. I didn't know how the pieces

DR. GREGORY VILNER

fit, but I definitely needed specific information if I planned to investigate the episode. "I wish you could think of the female guard's name."

"Ask Wilcox. I'm sure he'll never forget her. Anyway, Matt, that's what I remembered and I thought it might be helpful."

"It might, Don. Thanks for calling."

I hung up and chomped another healthy bite of sourdough. One thing was becoming clear—as the issues became more complex they would lead me to the heart of the story. It was inevitable.

Grocery shopping was also inevitable if I planned to feed us for the rest of the week. I finished the bread and temporarily put the forensic notes on hold. Sebastian eyed me from his spot on the couch as I grabbed my umbrella.

"I'll be right back with more Kibble, Your Majesty."

He blinked, dismissing me for the moment.

Rain poured in bucketfuls by the time I left Safeway and splashed a path to my little VW. The asphalt was slippery and I should have been paying more attention to where I was headed instead of the facts bumbling around in my head. I darn near slipped and broke my neck while slowing down to fish the car keys from my pocket. Rain pelted my head and streamed down my shirt collar.

The roar of an engine caught my attention. I turned in time to see a blur zoom past, almost knocking the bags out of my hand and thoroughly drenching me from head to waterlogged toes. The noise was like a waterfall crashing against rocks and I first thought the driver must have been blinded by the rain. Then I noticed he drove a black Ford pickup. My legs wobbled. It was an intentional near miss. My hands shook as I hurried to unlock the car and tossed the soaked grocery sacks onto the passenger seat.

By the time I fumbled the key into the ignition and plowed through the lot in hub-high water, I couldn't see the truck anywhere. Even with the wipers running full power it was hard to see at all. The sky had darkened with the rain, and as evening approached, the eerie feeling of being followed crept down my back again. I strained to see each passing car, hoping for anything besides a black truck. The headlights around the parking spaces played havoc on my sight. I gave up and drove home. By the time I reached my apartment, I was exhausted and still dripping—as much from scared sweat as from the rain.

I abandoned the sacks on the dining table and took a quick hot shower. When I came out, Sebastian was browsing through the damp bags, purring over the one that contained a package of hamburger. Earlier, while filling the shopping cart with kitty kibble, fresh fruit, a stack of frozen fare and drinks, my first thought had been to pop in a pizza for dinner and call it a day. But Sebastian's purring worked its magic on me and soon I was frying burgers, trying to forget that someone had tried to waste me in a Safeway parking lot.

The pickup had to be related to my investigation. Maybe someone who knew one of the men I'd been interviewing—and if so, he or she had to have been following my every move this past week. I went to the window and peered into the darkness. Sebastian meowed and I returned to the kitchen in time to rescue our beef before it burned to a crisp.

I put my burger on a toasted slice of sourdough, and I crumbled Sebastian's into a bowl and let him eat with me at the table. Lately we'd been missing a lot of our quality time together. It was hard to eat and not go back to the window. The phone rang and I suddenly wondered if it had been bugged. "Belding, here."

It was my mom. How ridiculous for a man my age to feel safer with his mom on the phone. I didn't care. I was just glad to hear her voice.

"I wanted to let you know your dad said for you not to come this weekend."

"But I don't mind, Mom. I can drive down in the morning and come back tomorrow night."

"No, he's not feeling well and he just wants to sleep."

"I can be there for you, though."

"That's sweet, dear, but stay put. I don't need anything, and the weather's atrocious."

If she only knew. "Well, okay, but I'll send you a check first thing Monday. Call if you need anything."

"I will, dear. Bye."

Damn, I hated being so far away. I hung up the phone and then picked it back up. I wouldn't know what a listening device looked like to save my life. That reminded me. I needed to call John Corbin.

John was a buddy of mine who worked at the *San Francisco Chronicle*. His ability to uncover little-known information had been invaluable to me over the years. On his computer, he could dig up almost anything about anyone. And before I started interviewing the inmates, I wanted to know more about them—like what crime they'd committed. I called John and left a message asking for background info on inmate Joseph Hawk. He'd be my first appointment on Monday. Sometimes ignorance was bliss, but I had a feeling the more I knew, the better chance I had of living a few more years.

After hanging up again, I took my spot on the couch with a Pepsi and the forensic notes. No way could I sleep with thoughts of black pickups dancing in my brain. I studied the report of the initial investigation by the state police. There were half a dozen photos of each of the five men who were killed and there was a drawing of the lower prison yard. The glossy prints lay scattered over my coffee table. Although someone had made a painstaking effort to try to identify and trace every bullet, so many had been fired that no conclusive findings had been documented.

The witness interviews were worthless pages filled with comments from "I didn't see anything" to "I don't know." Apparently nobody used their senses that day because not one person mentioned seeing, smelling, touching, or hearing a single thing. They were just a long string of dead-ends.

Somewhere in the middle of the night, I found myself agreeing with Eudon. It was a stupid idea to schedule a motorcycle gang visit the same day as a rock concert. Maybe the warden's ideas for inmate reform would have worked in a smaller prison, but it backfired big time in one the size of San Quentin.

I stood and stretched, then went back to the window. Rain was still pouring, but many of the house lights were off in the neighborhood. A dark pickup at the end of the street eased into the shadow and around the corner before turning on its lights and driving away.

My heart thudded double-time, and I leaped back from the curtain. The people I'd pissed off with my questions weren't taking any chances that I might reveal any answers. I didn't really think someone would try to kill me—that would be too obvious to the authorities. Not that the authorities were worth a whole lot of protection. I figured the truck tail was a subtle threat not to go too far or ruffle too many feathers—just turn in a report similar to the one the state police did—something the captain could use to slap a couple of hands before getting everything back to normal.

Trouble was, normal kept getting people killed.

I moved to the kitchen and put on a pot of coffee, then poured cup after cup as I spent hours analyzing the paperwork Sal had sent earlier in the week. Before I knew it, I had dozed off and sunlight was streaming in the window. My fax rang and I awoke to see Sebastian standing beside the machine, his tail flicking in time to the scroll of paper shooting from the dinosaur Panasonic.

I smacked the sleep coating from my lips and blinked a few times before I could focus on the pages. It was the background I needed about Joseph Hawk. "Thank you, John," I mumbled and Sebastian shot me an annoyed squint. This was his prey and he didn't appreciate me eyeing the scroll lapping down the desktop. "Sorry, Buddy," I told him as I ripped it off after the machine groaned and beeped its final segment. "This one's for me. You can have the next one for sure."

He immediately curled up on the desk and turned his head away from me.

"Fine. Pretend you don't care. See if I cook you any more burgers."

I poured the last of the warm coffee into my empty cup and read what John had sent. It wasn't good news. Joseph Hawk had been a very busy man—he'd been arrested for a triple murder, had a history of armed robbery, and seemed to enjoy crimes that involved a great deal of creative violence and well-inflicted pain before the actual murder itself. Without the benefit of a photograph, my mind conjured a picture of a snarling, hardened, brutal killer. Not exactly the best way to start a Monday.

I looked at the note Leslie had handed me when I left on Friday, which I had placed on the refrigerator. *Your next interview is with Joseph Hawk, Monday at 10 a.m. in South Block/D-Section. Stop by here first because you'll need an escort.*

I sure hoped they gave me an armed-to-the-hilt, brute-of-a guard.

8

Having a rock concert in a maximum security prison was hard to fathom by itself, but combining it with the guest appearance of a motorcycle gang, as far as I was concerned, was nothing but sheer stupidity. I turned on my tape player and listened to my interviews with Ed and Don. The common content of their stories disconcerted me even more. Individually, their tales were dubious, but there was no denying that their stories added up to the same thing—the correctional officers and inmates at San Quentin are both prisoners of the system. Assuming that Don's injuries at the hands of his supervisors had been exaggerated, I kept coming back to the same question: Who's keeping whom at San Quentin? I found the answers shocking and incredibly unnerving.

By sunset, my dread of the next day had become too big a beast to ignore. I went to the kitchen and made some coffee. I was finally going to get a look at the real San Quentin without a tour guide.

I sat in the chair next to the table with illustrations of the riot everywhere; I was trying to figure out who shot whom, but nothing made sense. I was exhausted. I stretched out on the couch and was shocked to awake at 9:30 the next morning. All I could say was shit, shit, shit! Since I had to be at the prison by 10:30, I ran around my apartment like a chicken with its head cut off and flew out the door in record time.

I made it to the prison in thirty minutes. Leslie wasn't at her post outside the warden's office when I arrived, but Captain Walsh and the Tarantula were waiting in my interview room. I was a mess and I didn't look happy. The captain, I gathered, was going to escort me to the South Block area from the Administration Building for my talk with inmate Joseph Hawk. I looked at him differently from the way I had a week ago when he was praising my commercial fishing article. He also looked different dressed in an impeccably pressed captain's uniform with every crease perfect. No matter how hard I tried, though, I couldn't picture him almost killing Don, but I certainly wasn't going to ask about it while I was locked in the bowels of his prison. Sometimes things are just better left unsaid. We walked toward the East Wall.

"Well, Matt, have you been inside yet?" he asked as the big black iron gate buzzed open for us.

"Yes. I toured the facility last week with a group of police officers." I kept my opinions to myself. As we walked, I noticed that he continually surveyed everything in view. He nodded to inmates and correctional officers alike.

"Have you found it hard to work here, Captain?"

"Please, call me Ted." We made eye-to-eye contact. "I guess it takes a special kind of personality. A lot of the guys quit in their first few weeks when reality sets in. This isn't a country club. We have very strict rules: regulations, standards, policies, and procedures that we have to meet every day to protect inmates and correctional officers, and some people can't live with that. Security and safety come first around here, so there isn't much room for individuality. My motto is, 'working together everyone achieves more.'"

"But, Ted, it must be hard being locked up with the inmates five to seven days a week."

Leaning toward me he said, "You get used to it, just like anything else." Walsh certainly wasn't going out of his way to be talkative.

"Ted, I've heard that a lot of the correctional officers have problems with alcohol and violence outside of work. Is that true?"

"I don't think it's a lot, but there is some. Correctional officers aren't much different from other law-enforcement officers; they're California State Peace Officers, too. We try to screen out the ones who look as if they have violent tendencies when they first apply and then we screen them again at the Academy."

"Are the new correctional officers pretty well trained when they start their first day here?"

"For the most part, the Academy teaches them what they need to know, but like in any job, nothing takes the place of hands-on experience."

As I walked through the upper yard with Ted I was scared shitless. I felt a little bit better when I looked up and saw the correctional officers on the gun walks armed with semi-automatic rifles and shotguns. I noticed inmates walking everywhere. The captain reassured me this was normal inmate movement. We had to go all the way to South Block across the entire upper yard. The solid green steel door to D Section was closed and locked. Much to my surprise, Captain Walsh took out a huge mass of brass keys from his hip pocket and pounded them loudly on the door.

"I have every key to this block except the one to this door. The keys are separated for security reasons," he stated while banging the keys on the steel door again and again. After a minute or two, he added, "Sometimes it takes a while to get the correctional officer's attention." He pounded even louder.

"You mean this is how you have to get into these blocks?"

"Ridiculous, isn't it? Were you expecting something high tech—maybe a doorbell?" Ted was becoming furious. He grumbled, "They better open this door soon..."

"I expected electronic controls or something."

"Not at San Quentin," he laughed. His voice dripped with anger as he said, "It was built in 1853. I think they plan to let the place crumble away just like Alcatraz. That's a park now. One day, this will be an exclusive housing development!" He started to bang on the door again, even louder than the last time. His face was turning purple just as someone peered out the tiny window at the top of the door. I heard somebody yell from the other side of the iron door, "Captain Sir, I'll have the door open in a second, Sir."

When the door finally opened, I followed the captain in and the officer immediately locked the door behind us. The captain rebuked, "What in the Sam Hill took so long?"

I felt trapped like a rat in a tiny cage. Although similar to the cellblock I visited the other day, there were significant differences the guide had neglected to mention. For starters, the stench was nauseating. Humane officials closed dog kennels that smelled less acrid. A cat litter box that hadn't been cleaned for six months would be a breath of fresh air compared to the disgusting odor. Food and human waste stained the walls beneath the catwalk, which was directly across from the inmate cells. Cockroaches scampered to avoid being crushed underfoot. Other vermin searched the walls for their next meal. Male voices echoed loudly through the hollow interior. Their yells were punctuated by the clanging of metal doors and various items being drummed on the metal bars. Music blared from at least twenty different radios all tuned to different stations. There was movement everywhere. My head pounded from the deafening noise and the overpowering stench of human body odors. I felt sure my stomach was preparing to give up the last vestiges of my frozen pancake breakfast. I wasn't sure if I would survive an hour in South Block.

While I had always believed that convicted felons should pay for their crimes, I couldn't believe what I was seeing and hearing. Two hundred and fifty human beings actually lived there day and night. I couldn't fathom how any person in their right mind could spend eight hours a day, five or six days a week, in a place like this.

The correctional officer who had opened the door for us pointed back to one of the small offices across from the showers and said, "Wait in there." I was surprised that he had no interest in searching my briefcase or me. I could have brought in a gun or narcotics. Steam billowed from the hot water running from the ten showerheads, yet no one was in the showers. The white tile walls were caked with soap scum and mildew. The chrome fixtures were rusty and decrepit, and the drain screens were barely visible under wads of hair. The cement floors were coated with fungus and mold.

I felt that I would sooner die than take a shower there.

I walked into the office where I was to wait. A small wooden table was in the center of the office with one wooden straight chair at each end. An ashtray filled to the brim with cigarette butts was on the table. Although the walls were clean in comparison with what I had just seen, they probably hadn't been washed or painted for twenty years. I couldn't tell whether they were yellow, green, or brown. A refrigerator that wouldn't stay closed and an ancient microwave oven seemed to fit in perfectly. Bits of leftover lunches, presumably belonging to the guards, were scattered around the cement floor near an overflowing wastebasket. I accidentally kicked a half-eaten spoiled sandwich over and noticed small white maggots on it. With the end of my shoe, I pushed it back over and fought to control a wave of nausea. Flirting with death, I was frightened as I waited. It seemed morals didn't exist in San Quentin.

I didn't have to wait long for inmate Hawk to arrive. Sergeant Eudon brought him in the office. Eudon nodded but didn't speak a word. Just knowing he was nearby made me feel a little less terrified. Hawk's appearance stupefied me. Six-feet tall and tipping the scales at about 350 pounds, he looked angry as hell—no shirt, balding, fat and loaded with prison tattoos. He didn't swagger, didn't take a swing with his body at Eudon, and didn't even spit on the floor. He just walked in obediently like a well-trained dog and sat down. I easily believed the overgrown Hawaiian was guilty of the heinous crimes he'd been accused of committing. Still, I felt the tension in my jaw release a bit when I realized that the shackles would remain around his feet and hands.

"I'll be right outside, Mr. Belding, if you need anything," Eudon said as he shut the door. The closed door barely diminished the din echoing throughout the cellblock. Nausea still passed over me every few minutes, and my heart was still pounding to the throbbing rhythm in my head. I had to focus all my energy on inmate Joseph Hawk to keep from passing out.

"Hawk, I am Matt Belding, special investigator with the District Attorney's

Office. My job is to figure out what caused the riot."

Hawk nodded and scanned the room not muttering a word.

I turned on the tape recorder then placed the briefcase on the floor near my feet. "The following is an interview with San Quentin prison inmate Joseph Hawk."

Hawk stared blankly straight ahead. I didn't think he had heard a word I said. You could hear the noise from the vents: *hissssss*. I wasn't even sure he was seeing me, although I was sitting directly in front of him at the other end of the table, no more than four feet away. I brought in some cigarettes hoping to use them as a bargaining tool. I put them in my shirt pocket for him to see.

"Mr. Hawk, I'd like to know a little bit about you before I ask some questions regarding the riot. Would you tell me, first of all, why you were sent to San Quentin?"

"First turn off the damn tape and give me a cigarette, mister."

"Mr. Hawk, what you tell me is confidential. No one but the Governor's legal staff can hear these tapes without a subpoena. Nothing you say will get back to the prison officials, trust me."

I reached inside my shirt pocket, pulled out the full pack of cigarettes, then ripped the top open. I took one out and handed it to him across the table. He raised his handcuffed hands to take it but hesitated, as though he was waiting for me to do something.

"A light, please."

I took a book of matches out of my shirt pocket and leaned over the table just enough to light his cigarette.

Afterward, Mr. Hawk stated, "I don't talk into machines and my friends call me Uncle Joe. Take it or leave it."

I decided not to press the issue, so I turned off the recorder. He seemed to be narrow-minded and stubborn, but I wasn't about to call him Uncle Joe. "Why are you in this place?"

"You know food tastes better if you cook it yourself?"

WHO'S WATCHING THE TOWER?

He looked like he could down a 10-pound turkey all by himself in one sitting. Ignoring his attempt to change the subject, I asked him again.

Hawk took a long drag off his cigarette while he decided whether he would humor me with an answer. He finally smiled and said, "Three life sentences for armed robbery, aggravated battery, and three counts of first-degree murder."

"Is this the first time you've ever been in a prison?"

"Nah. I've been in and out of Hotel California since I was thirteen. My first rap I served two years in the juvenile justice system for stealing a car. It wasn't the first time I stole somebody's car or the first time I got caught. It was just the first time I got sentenced."

"Why did they sentence you then?"

"I didn't play their stupid fuckin' game."

He changed positions in the chair and tried to cross his legs. I lit a cigarette to calm my nerves. It tasted like shit. "What do you mean, Mr. Hawk?"

"Well, if you promise to plead guilty, they don't have as much paperwork to do. You plead guilty and pay a fine, they clear their case and give you a suspended sentence, sending you right back out on the streets again."

"So, what happened? How come it didn't work for you?"

"I was charged with an auto theft that I didn't do. Like a dumb shit, I pleaded not guilty. So, they locked my ass up for forgettin' the rules of the game."

"I don't understand."

"See, if you plead not guilty, the case has to go to trial. They have to do a lot of paperwork. That pisses 'em off, costs tons of tax dollars, so they make you pay for it. You can get away with just about anything, as long as you don't beat up old ladies, kill somebody famous, or plead not guilty. They'd probably rather have you beat up old ladies than refuse to cop a plea."

"Cop a plea, what's that?"

"Say I go out and hold up a store. The guy behind the counter gives me some trouble. So, I want to put a little fear in him. I take a pair of pliers, stick 'em up his nose, squeeze real hard and give 'em a good twist. He seems to need a little more fear, so I beat him over the head a few times with the butt of my shotgun, see? But not so much that he can't open the register and give me what I came for. Like a dumb-shit, the old fucker has a heart attack and almost dies on me before he can open the cash register. Now, I'm looking at a murder rap in addition to attempted robbery. The District Attorney could care less about attempted robbery. But if an old guy croaks, the heat's on, and they got to hang somebody out to dry. Now, if you think you're gonna take a fall, you do everything you can to strike a deal."

"How do you do that?"

Inmate Hawk leaned forward and made eye-to-eye contact with me for about two seconds. My knees started shaking.

"You make a phone call to the cops and tell them that they ain't never gonna catch you. You be quiet and then say that you can save them a lot of paperwork, but you're not taking a fall for murder just because the old geezer had a bum ticker. Tell 'em they've got one hour to make the deal. If they can't put it together by then, you're on your way out of state. You call back in about an hour and sure enough; they got a deal for you, no murder rap as long as you promise to plead guilty so that they don't have to go through the trouble or expense of a jury trial. Even though they'd charge me with attempted robbery, aggravated battery, and first-degree murder, I'd plead guilty to simple assault and I'm serving a six-year sentence."

"I find that hard to believe, Mr. Hawk."

Inmate Hawk slouched back in his chair, "Fuck you, asshole! I don't care what you believe. Look mister, there are one hundred million people in prison today, one hundred and sixty thousand of them are women. Seven out of every one hundred children have one parent in prison. Do you know why we have this problem? Let me tell you mister big shot, we need population control, we are running out of jobs, food, and resources and that's why the government developed the AIDS virus. This is the government's only means to take control of the population. The government created it all. The government is doing away with the middle-class people and in the near future we will have the rich and the poor class only, just like it was back in the Roman days. Can't you see it?"

He started turning red and changing positions in the chair, then looked outside the office.

"If you don't believe me, go ask the guys on Death Row how they pleaded and what they think of the government. Every one of 'em will tell you 'not guilty and the government sucks.' You won't find anyone who pleaded guilty up there. Nothin' up there but men who were dumb enough to make the District Attorney's Office take the time, money, and effort to prove they were guilty. They'll stick it to ya for that every time!"

Inmate Hawk was an evil-minded person who was full of himself and his knowledge of the criminal justice system and government as he saw it. The handcuffs attached to his waist limited his movement, thank God, so instead of gesturing with his hands as he talked, he bounced his left knee. The more excited he got, the faster his knee moved. I wanted to keep him talking, so I offered him another cigarette. In prison, free cigarettes are a great motivator.

Temperamentally, I asked, "What happened to you? If you understand the system so well, why are you in here?"

"I screwed up. I was robbing these folks, and they really made me mad, ya know what I mean? After I took everything they had, I tied them to some Eucalyptus trees in their backyard and threw battery acid on 'em. They wouldn't stop fuckin' yelling and screaming. They were foolish people, so I had to kill 'em. It was pretty ugly, pretty bloody, so it got a lot of media attention. That's the only reason Charles Manson's still here—you know what I mean? The press really loved the shit he was doin'. He didn't just kill people, he killed famous rich people, and he did it in a way that sold newspapers, books, and magazines. There are a lot of guys out on parole who make Charles Manson look like a baby Cub Scout, but they didn't give the press a hard-on." He took a long drag from his cigarette and exhaled the smoke out his nose. "There's one good thing about this place, there's no hard labor here, mister."

"Well, Mr. Hawk, I find it extraordinary that you're serving three life sentences. You don't have to spend much time worrying about parole, do you?"

"Shit, I'll be the fuck out of here in another six months, twelve tops." Hawk pushed his chest forward like a cocky little bandy rooster. "What time is it?" I asked since my watched had stopped and I had noticed his gold watch.

"It's whatever time you want it to be, mister."

I didn't bother to ask for the time again. Inmate Hawk was a smart ass. "How is that possible—six months, twelve tops?"

"That's the way the systems works. They give you sentences that sound like you'll never smell fresh air again, but that's for the benefit of the public, you know, the taxpayers. You see, Mr. Investigator, if they charged you with three counts of murder and sentenced you to six years, everybody will be screaming bloody murder. So, they give you a sentence that's ten years longer than the world's going to last. Then they take somebody like Manson, and say, 'See, we're protecting society. We're never gonna' let this animal out into society again.' But every day, they let guys out who are just as bad, or worse, they're just not as famous as Charles Manson. I'll get out, don't you fuckin' worry."

"So, what will you do when you get out?"

"Some bullshit job. Probably work my ass off for nothin' until I can't stand it anymore and wind up back here again to see my old buddies. You can't get a decent job if you're an ex-con. People on the outside treat you the same way they treat dog shit on their new shoes. After a while you get so pissed, you want to find somebody wealthy that's got everything going their way and make them hurt as bad as you do."

"In your mind, what would make things better for ex-cons?"

"The state ought to find a decent job for 'em, maybe help 'em set up their own business, give 'em training, buy 'em a decent car and give 'em a house, maybe a repossession that they could fix up. But that ain't never gonna happen."

I got up and started laughing at him thinking he was joking, but the stone cold look on his face told me otherwise. "Well, that would be pretty expensive, don't you think?"

Hawk was so pissed off his face was cherry red. Sweat began dripping from his forehead when I laughed at him. I realized that if he broke out of the shackles, he would kill me without blinking an eye. I panicked at my expense, felt the sweat dripping from my armpits. He had to be the most emotional, foolish and temperamental person I had ever experienced or encountered in my life. He was definitely an insane blemish on society.

Suddenly, Hawk yelled, "Bullshit! You Motherfuckers! Bullshit!" He scared the shit out of me. Sweat plastered my clothes to my body. Thank God he calmed down quickly. "I know it would cost a lot less than lockin' people up in here for the rest of their lives. Do you know what they spend on someone locked up in this hole?"

"No, tell me."

"The State of California says it costs between $48,000 and $125,000 a year. If the state had any sense, they'd strike a deal and pay me $35,000 a year to stay out of trouble and then they could keep the rest of the money."

This time I laughed to myself. Since my knees were still shaking, I didn't want to piss him off again. "How long do you think you'll stay away when you get out this time?"

"Who knows? Maybe six months, maybe a year. People think ex-cons come back 'cause they're hopeless cases. I think we come back 'cause, as lousy as this place is, it beats the hell out of trying to live with people who treat their dogs better than you."

"That sounds very strange coming from someone who poured battery acid on people and then killed them."

"Tell me, Mr. Big Shot, how is pouring battery acid on someone and killing 'em ten minutes later any worse than locking someone up in this hole, forever? Listen, I've spent six years in an eight-by-ten white concrete box, I've been raped at least once a week since the first year I was incarcerated. I've been stabbed nine times and shot seven. I freeze during the winter and burn up during the summer. The food I get is always cold and usually I don't have any idea what it is. If I get lucky, it doesn't have dead roaches or flies cooked in it. I haven't done anything as natural as hold a woman in almost six years, and I don't even know what my seven-year-old son looks like. Personally, I think I'd rather have the battery acid."

"Mr. Hawk, let's talk about—" My train of thought was interrupted by a loud commotion outside the door. A group of inmates was entering the showers.

"I want another cigarette, Mr. Investigator."

I nonchalantly handed him one, then placed the pack of cigarettes on the table and continued. "As I was saying, Mr. Hawk, let's talk about the riot." He leaned forward, waiting for me to light his cigarette. I complied. I didn't want to anger him again.

"I've got nothin' to say 'bout that." He focused his eyes on his cigarette and concentrated on blowing circles as he exhaled smoke. He didn't move a muscle. I lit another cigarette and started puffing—it still tasted like shit. I got up and emptied the ashtray into the garbage can next to the refrigerator. Feeling sick, I crushed my cigarette. I wasn't a smoker.

"You were in the lower yard when it started."

"Yup, I was."

"As a matter of fact, Mr. Hawk, you were injured. You were hit by a bullet in the thigh."

"Yup, I guess so."

"According to my records, you were standing near the stage, less than five feet away from Clarence Redmond when he was killed."

"Yup, I sure was."

"You must have seen something!"

"No. I didn't see a goddamn fuckin' thing." His knee started bouncing up and down like a piston in an engine and his eyes rolled back in his head. The sweat from his forehead was starting to drip onto his hairy chest. He took another puff from his cigarette then flipped ashes onto the floor.

"Mr. Hawk, please, the purpose of this investigation is to find out what really happened that day, to attempt to pinpoint some of the causes, so that the State of California—"

"The State of California?" He leaned back and forth and said, "What do I care 'bout the fuckin' State of California?"

"Look, Mr. Hawk, there's a possibility this investigation, because of the attention this particular incident has received, might be instrumental in making some desperately-needed changes around here for you guys."

"And I'm supposed to think that's important enough to die for in this place?"

"Don't you think you're being paranoid, Mr. Hawk?"

"How long have you been around here, Mr. Investigator?"

I sat back down. I was getting nervous again. Looking at the floor, I quietly replied, "One week."

"You've been here a fuckin' week, and you haven't learned jack shit about this place, have you?"

"I'm just asking you to tell me what you saw that day, Mr. Hawk."

"No, you're asking me to fuckin' die. Let me tell you a little bit about how this fuckin' place works. If you want to just do your time and get out, you don't see or hear anything in this fuckin' place. If I tell you what I saw, it goes in a report, it gets back to the warden, and suddenly I disappear in some type of mysterious accident. The last guy who went to the warden told him that some of the prisoners were getting drugs from the outside and selling them to the inmates. He told the warden that the captain was in on it and he had proof. Do you know what happened to that little snitch?"

"No, tell me."

"The warden goes to the captain, and the two of them have a big laugh about what these assholes are gonna think of next. The captain says he'll take care of it. Couple hours later, the captain and two of the guards walk into the guy's cell. The captain says, 'We heard it's your birthday today.' The inmate is real confused because it isn't his birthday. The captain says, 'Sing "Happy Birthday" to him, boys.' All three of them start singing just as loud as they can. While they're singing, one of them holds the inmate on the floor, the other two jump up and down on his hands, breaking all of his fingers and hand bones."

"Did you see this happen?"

"You can't see from one cell to another unless you have a mirror, but I didn't have to see it to know what was going on in that cell."

"Mr. Hawk, would you be willing to testify to that in front of a grand jury?"

"Are you out of your fuckin' mind, Mr. Investigator?"

I started to pace back and forth. I didn't know what to say.

"I can guarantee that you will be protected once I leave here."

"You can't guarantee shit."

I was silent.

"Are you gonna write something good in my record for the parole board? Do you want to know who turned over drugs to the captain? Ask the captain's kid. The inmates run this place." Hawk started to jiggle his chains. "The guards are nothin'. They gotta pick up our shit, bring us clean clothes, give us our food, stick their hands up our asses every time we leave and return to this block, and watch us in the showers and our separate yards. What kind of a bullshit job is that? The state couldn't pay me enough to do that kind of shit job! Besides, I don't know anything. I was asleep when all that happened."

"I don't believe you, Mr. Hawk."

He was pissed again, his knee going a hundred miles an hour as his face turned cherry red. "You can believe whatever the fuck you want, but I'm not sayin' another word."

I sat back down. I didn't know what to do. I was at a loss for words.

"Mr. Hawk—"

"Fuckin' forget it, man. I can sit here and keep my mouth shut for the next six months. I've got no place else to go. How 'bout you, Mr. Big Shot?"

We were done. There was no doubt in my mind that Hawk wouldn't be saying another word. I got up and tapped on the door's window to signal Eudon that we were finished. Hawk stood and turned to go, but not before snagging the pack of cigarettes I had left within his reach. Stupid me. Oh well, I guess I didn't need them.

On his way out the door, Eudon said, "Wait here, Mr. Belding. I'll be back in a few minutes to escort you out of the facility."

I hoped the few minutes he promised were indeed only a few. I'd had enough of South Block to last a lifetime. There were four men in the showers as I turned to pack my briefcase. There was a lot of truth in what Joseph Hawk had said, and it disturbed me. I found him disturbing. I found the whole damn place disturbing.

I put my briefcase on the desk as I sat to wait impatiently for Eudon's return. I had an unobstructed view of the showers, and I wondered if anyone knew I was watching them. The four men were talking, gathered around a single showerhead. Although there wasn't a guard in sight, I assumed one was in the next office supervising the showering inmates.

My thoughts turned for a moment to Eudon. No matter how hard I tried, I couldn't picture him coming to work day after day in this hell-hole and then going home to his sweet little girl to be the perfect daddy. Spending so much time in such an evil place had to take a toll on a man's soul. South Block could easily be the Biblical house of the devil. The only things missing were the red-hot fires of hell.

Suddenly, my eyes focused on the shower again. As I crossed my legs, three inmates pinned back the arms of another inmate and shoved something white in his mouth. Another inmate repeatedly rammed something into the struggling man's upper body. I couldn't believe my eyes! The sight of bright red blood spurting from the trapped inmate jolted me from my stupor. Blood shot out each point of penetration as his heart pumped harder and harder, clinging to life. I was witnessing a murder!

My God, where the hell were the guards? The scream that emerged from me seemed to go unheard as the prisoners froze for a split second. Despite my terror, I instinctively took one small step toward the showers. My movement started an avalanche of activity—the three murders became like the Keystone Cops, practically tripping over each other to escape the crime scene. The victim had fallen to his knees and was staring at a shiny object protruding from his chest as if he could not believe what he was seeing. He slowly raised his head and our eyes locked. He opened his mouth, moving his lips silently. He was begging me to relieve him of his pain. Out the door, I stumbled toward him, the steam from the showers fogging up my glasses, my heavy feet moving by their own power, as my mind screamed at me that any effort to help would be fruitless. He suddenly toppled forward.

I will never forget his cries of agony as his upper body hit the cement floor, plunging the instrument of his pain deeper into his chest. Somehow, he found the strength to crawl toward me, like a dehydrated man in the hot dry desert crawling on the sand toward an oasis of water. I ran through the steamy mist and sank to my knees. I put my glasses in my shirt pocket then cradled his head in my lap as though he were a fallen child instead of a convict. He kept trying to tell me something, and I frantically tried to understand his mumblings. I knew he had to have whispered the names of his attackers—or maybe some last words for a family member. It was important that he not be allowed to die before leaving that message. I frantically tried to make sense of the different sounds he was mumbling and instead of any number of phrases that I might have expected to hear, the last words from his bluish lips were "tell Kimble there's a contract on him, and we'll burn in hell together." He slumped motionless to the floor.

I don't know what shocked me more—the murder or the fact that he chose to make a threat with the last words he would ever speak. I didn't know who Kimble was, but something warned me not to share this with anyone until I was sure what it really meant.

All of a sudden, an ear-piercing horn started to sound every few seconds. Short, single tones and repetitive loud blasts filled the air. Eudon and a half-dozen other guards descended onto the crime scene.

"Did you see what happened, Matt?"

I nodded, but when I tried to speak, I vomited uncontrollably. The horns blasting were piercing my ears and head. All I remember is everything going blank.

When I came around seconds later, Eudon had stretched me on the floor in the officers' room. I could hear the banging on the steel door to the unit as more guards descended to the area in response to the crisis. Over the loudspeaker a voice repeated, "Lockdown! Lockdown! Everybody back to your cells! Lockdown! Lockdown!" All I could think about were the walls closing in on me; it was getting harder and harder to breathe. The taste in my mouth was overwhelming.

"I've got to get out of here!" I all but screamed as I tried to stand. Eudon helped me up but held me at the same time.

"You can't leave now, Matt, we're in lockdown." Eudon spoke calmly but firmly. "You have to stay right here until the alarm stops." The tone of his voice made me understand that I had no choice.

The shower floor was dark red. Blood was everywhere. The guard squatting over the body tried to find a pulse, then shook his head no. Outside the office, someone shouted, "Inmate Browning's dead. Good riddance to bad rubbish."

"Can you talk?" I could barely hear Eudon over the horn blasts even though he was just inches from my ear.

"I think so." I shut my eyes, trying to shake off the dizziness.

"What happened?"

"They were in the shower. The next thing I knew they pinned the guy's arms back, shoved something in his mouth, and started stabbing him over and over again. Where were the guards, Eudon? Wasn't someone watching them?"

"Someone should have been watching the shower area. Things happen around here and a minute later, someone's dead." Eudon shook his head.

"How can you think with all this noise? When will they turn off those damn alarms? My head is killing me."

"As soon as everyone in the entire institution is locked down and accounted for—it usually takes about twenty minutes."

Correctional officers were starting to file out past the door of the little office to return to their posts. Technically, South Block was under control. Personally, I doubted it was ever really under control.

"You know," Sergeant Eudon continued, "the worst part of this job is that damn alarm system. When it goes off, you have no idea what the problem is. You just drop what you're doing and run like hell to respond. It could be murder, rape, stabbing, or a take-over. You just don't know. It could be your last few minutes on the face of this earth. When this happens, your adrenaline starts flowing. You get sweaty and clammy. We'll all have our share of nightmares and cold sweats tonight."

"What happens now?"

"Internal Affairs will be in to do an investigation. The San Rafael coroner will come to pronounce him dead and remove the body. San Quentin has its own burial ground across the highway in Marin County."

"They were in the shower, Eudon, naked. What could they have stabbed him with?"

"Most likely it was a shank, a shiv. That's a flat piece of metal—probably made in the auto shop. The cons have ingenious ways of hiding weapons and passing them around until they get them to where they're going to be used. You can be sure this was well planned."

"But, it was so...silent. I thought I was imagining the whole thing. The steam, all I thought was this can't be really happening. I don't know how you do it, being locked up in here, day after day, night after night."

"You just do it, that's all." Eudon was quiet. I was staring out the door of the little room that had been my cage for almost two hours. During all the excitement and confusion, someone had turned off the water in the bloody steam-drenched showers. The victim was alone. Face down. Dead.

The alarms finally stopped. South Block was still filled with the shouts of inmates, the sound of clanging metal, and the din of a multitude of radios. Except for the ringing in my ears, it seemed almost quiet to me. Eudon helped me walk to the open area just outside the steel doors. I couldn't breathe deeply or fast enough. Even though we were still well inside the walls of San Quentin, I felt as liberated as an animal released from a cage into its natural habitat. We didn't say much as we crossed the upper yard in the bright sunlight and headed for the big black iron gates of freedom. He seemed as relieved as I felt, although he didn't say it. We shook hands at the gate and I left.

The sound of the gate closing and locking behind me was the nicest sound I had heard in several hours. Fresh air never smelled so good. The gardenias, the redwoods, the Bay breeze, the brightness of the sun, the silence and beauty of all I could see brought me back to reality. The horrors of the South Block had been beyond my wildest nightmares. I wasn't sure whether I would ever stop smelling it. If I never went back there again, it would be too soon.

Although it was lunchtime, the thought of food was revolting. The memory of the murder raised the hairs on the back of my neck. As I drove away from the San Quentin grounds, I rolled down all the windows and sped as fast as I could toward the open highway.

It was only a few minutes before I was one of many cars heading north on the five-lane highway. The congestion of San Rafael gave way within minutes to the more open road around Novato. I left the steep, forested hills of Marin behind as the highway narrowed into two lanes and started its trek through the rolling hills of Napa Sonoma County and toward the flatness of the Santa Rosa Plains.

Twenty years ago, open pastures with stands of old oak and eucalyptus trees surrounded each of the towns north of San Rafael. Now, industrial parks had begun to replace the pastures. The miles between Novato and Santa Rosa were starting to blend into one long stretch of indistinct towns connected by business parks and shopping centers. I hoped the Sonoma County fathers wouldn't let this country go the way of Silicon Valley and the peninsula south of San Francisco, where open space is non-existent.

The sun shined on my face, the wind in my hair, and the idyllic views of the farms, green hills, and vineyards began to restore my sense of life and freedom. The fresh smells of the countryside were slowly replacing the stench of death and fear. The mental image of the victim's blood flowing in such quantity had suddenly illuminated the fine line between life and death. For the first time, I became aware of how close I might have been to my own death. I witnessed the attack! I could only imagine what would have happened if one of the murderers had seen me watching. I could have died.

After forty miles of high-speed driving, I finally began to unwind. I left the highway just north of Santa Rosa and turned around in the Chateau De Braun Winery parking lot. After a peaceful stroll through the gardens and several moments of resisting temptation to pick up a bottle of wine for the ride back, I slid behind the wheel for a leisurely trip south. It occurred to me on the way back that I should have waited for the investigator to arrive at the scene since I had been a witness. On the other hand, I wasn't in any shape to be interviewed and I had told Eudon everything except inmate Browning's last words. There was no way I could identify the perpetrators. All I could say with any certainty was that three naked men had killed a fellow inmate in the shower.

One minute he was alive, the next he was dead.

9

It was three o'clock when I returned to San Quentin. The fresh air from the bay smelled wonderful. I hadn't arranged for another interview, but I was hoping one of the guards on my list would be available. The trauma of witnessing a murder was beginning to cause the muscles in my neck and back to feel like pieces of rope that an experienced sailor would use to teach an advanced class in knot-making techniques. I was a nervous wreck and felt empty. I was in no mood to waste any time.

Since Leslie wasn't at her post when I entered the lobby, I went to my interview room and set up my tape recorder, knowing she couldn't have gone far. The rubber plant seemed to be drooping more than ever, so I went to find some water for the poor thing.

I heard a sexy female voice down the hall ask, "Mr. Belding, when are you going to interview me?"

I hadn't thought about interviewing the warden's secretary. She wasn't even on my list of key people. But I've always believed that when an opportunity arises, only a fool would ignore it. And I wasn't a fool! With all the negative events of the day, she would be the perfect cure from my illnesses. I wanted her so bad I could taste it

"Right now would be just perfect, Ms. Kirby." I was not wasting any time. My enthusiasm was undeniable as she followed me into the little room. I could smell her perfume. I felt as if I were floating in a scent of passion. My mission was solely to get a date. I was as flustered as a teenaged boy who'd discovered a beautiful woman. I managed to knock my brown chair over backward, which in turn knocked over the rubber plant. I slowly and deliberately righted both before I turned to apologize for my clumsiness. This time I knocked over the full cup of coffee that was to be my lunch. As she helped me wipe up the mess, she leaned close enough that I could again smell the scent of her hair and view her perfect breasts. I decided that I'd better sit down and start the interview before my hormones caused me to make a fool of myself.

"Mr. Belding, what happened this morning must have been quite a shock for someone not used to dealing with violence. Are you all right?"

"Actually, Ms. Kirby, I've got the beginning of a real tension headache. Any chance I could get an aspirin without having to report to the prison doctor?" The last thing I wanted was to look like a wimp to her. On the other hand, if I hoped to score a date, I was going to have to be able to relax enough to let my personality overwhelm her.

"Poor baby. Sit right there and relax. I've got some in my desk. I'll be right back."

I was treated to a great view of her long legs and rear when she turned and walked out the door, then she rewarded me with an even better shot of her cleavage when she returned and leaned to hand me the aspirin and a glass of water. She rubbed the top of my head and started to purr, "There, there, this will make you feel better, Matt." She was teasing me. I thought I was going to crawl out of my skin.

"Thank you. I'm sure this will do the trick. Ms. Kirby, I have a number of questions I want to ask you. First, I've got to get something off my chest. You are a very, very attractive—actually a stunning—lady." She smiled coyly as I added, "I hope my saying that doesn't offend you in any way."

With a Southern drawl and undisguised pride, she replied, "No, it doesn't offend me at all. But I hear it often. The prison tends to magnify every woman's femininity."

"I just can't imagine why a beautiful woman like you would work in a place like this!"

"I believe that life is what happens to you while you're making other plans." She laughed. "If I told you all the details of how I got here, it would make perfect sense to you, but let's just say that after working with Warden Cooper in Sacramento, the thought of working for someone else just didn't appeal to me. So, when he came to San Quentin and asked me to come with him, I did. We've been working together for eight years. I've been with him through three promotions, his marriage, his divorce, his battle to get custody of his daughters, and his open-heart surgery. I'm not about to leave him just because I don't like the neighborhood his new office is in."

I leaned back in my chair, confused by her answers.

"Some people might get the impression...from what you just said, there's more to your relationship with Warden Cooper than just work. You know how gossip is..." I only wanted to hear that she was single.

"Some people get that impression no matter what the truth is. So, I don't worry about them. Warden Cooper says it gives him an ego boost. Let them have their fun. We both get a good laugh out of it now and then, and it keeps the guards from hounding me. The truth is—well, I was born and raised in Rocky Mountain, North Carolina. It's a very small town, very old southern white society. I'm afraid that even if I wanted to have a serious relationship with Warden Cooper, I doubt if I could overcome my strict upbringing. Older men and younger women are not to be seen in public. We work very well together and that's as far as it goes. I have a great deal of respect for him, but deep down, I still have limits and boundaries."

"Listen, I'm sorry. I didn't mean to get so far off the subject." Her scent was making me melt like ice cream in the sun.

"Don't give it another thought. I have to deal with it all the time. After a while, you develop a certain sense of humor about it or you go stir crazy."

"You said that it keeps the guards from hounding you. What did you mean by that?"

"The male guards hassle the women around here all the time. They're always propositioning them, making lewd remarks, and then asking them for a date. They can't understand why the women here won't go out with them. They make jokes about the differences between male and the female guards. Some of them, especially the macho types, like to believe that the women can't shoot, can't handle prisoners, aren't capable of separating their emotions from the job."

"Is that just because female guards are relatively new to San Quentin?"

As she leaned forward, she gave me another terrific shot of her beautiful cleavage. I yearned to suck them.

"Well, it's a case of—what would you call it? Transference, I guess. The white guards used to say the same things about the black guards. Since the women have come into the picture, at least the black guards and the white guards agree about something."

She leaned back in her chair and crossed her legs, tighter than a vice. The motor between my legs was going full speed ahead like a tugboat moving a ship.

"Is there any truth to what they say or is it simply prejudice?"

"That's hard to tell, Matt. I know a lot of these guys have military backgrounds, so of course they can shoot a rifle better than most of the women. They weigh more than the women do, so they have an easier time handling the bigger prisoners. On the other hand, I've never heard of three or four women starting a fight with an inmate just to prove how tough they are. Maybe it evens out and maybe it doesn't. Either way, I personally don't think the women should be here in the first place."

"That surprises me."

"Well, Matt, in my opinion, it's only okay in the administration and personnel departments." She rubbed her right leg with her hand, slow, soft, sensuous strokes. "Please don't get me wrong, Matt. I'm not one of those Southern belles who think women should have to stay home, cook, clean and have seven kids, if that's not what they want. But I do feel that women have a different emotional makeup. Women are designed to bring new life into this world. They're not made to stand on the top of gun towers and put bullets through an inmate's head. I think it does something detrimental to women to see people locked up in cages like animals in the zoo. I know when I come out from the captain's office inside the prison walls, it takes a few days for me to get back to normal."

"There are allegations being made that some of the female guards and some former female guards are living with former inmates. Do you know anything about that?"

"Oh, I hear rumors just like everybody else. I don't know. I can see how that might happen, though."

I thought I heard the Tarantula outside the door. I leaned back in my chair and crossed my legs, almost falling backward. I felt like a clumsy idiot.

"Matt, some of these girls are young and very impressionable. They come to work here and the first thing they encounter is the incredible amount of hostility that the male guards, supposedly their co-workers, have for them. The men harass them, get them drunk, and take advantage of the situation. They get frustrated and quickly become disillusioned with the entire system. Then one day, walking back and forth on that gun rail, they start talking to the prisoners in their cells. After the way the guards have treated them, the inmates don't have to have a silver-tongue. All they have to do is act like decent guys. If they are nicer than the people she's working for, she starts to question whether she's on the right side of the fence or the wrong side. Good grief, I'm starting to sound like a psychology major. I'm sorry, Matt." She laughed, an incredible tinkling sound that drove me nuts. Then she flipped her hair back, pushing her scent through the air between us. She knew what I had on my mind.

"No! By all means don't be sorry. Go on. It sounds as if you have a better understanding of this facility than anyone I've spoken to."

"Well, I'm just speculating. I don't really know anything."

"You sound like you know a great deal. Please, go on."

"No, let's talk about something else, Matt. I thought you were here to talk about the riot."

"You're right. Were you in the office the day that Big Red and the warden

DR. GREGORY VILNER

93

discussed the details for the motorcycle show and concert?"

"Yes, I was. Warden Cooper asked me to come into his office to take shorthand on everything that was said between Big Red, Captain Walsh, and himself."

"Are you telling me Captain Walsh was in the meeting, too?"

"Oh, yes. In fact, he really surprised me. I thought he would throw a fit over the whole thing, but he was very calm, almost congenial."

"I don't understand, why did that surprise you?"

She changed positions in her chair and so did I. My lower back and neck were starting to hurt again and my head was still killing me.

"The captain's such a—well, he doesn't like anything that's out of the usual routine. If he had his way, he'd keep the inmates locked up all the time. Well, whenever anything out of the ordinary happens, he gets really nervous and upset. He's not a bourgeois type of man. It was quite a surprise to see him sit there, not interfering with the plans that Warden Cooper and Big Red made that day. Everything was going along just fine until the warden told Big Red that his people should be at the west gate two hours before the concert so the bikes and riders could be searched. Big Red was really upset and started pacing the warden's office like a caged tiger. He said that his people weren't going to stand for having their bikes handled and maybe dismantled by guards looking for contraband, so he started to walk out the door."

"Big Red couldn't have thought they'd just ride in, could he?"

Leslie shrugged. "Well, Matt, I figured that was the end of it. Captain Walsh would get his wish and everything would go back to normal. But Warden Cooper stood and said, 'Hey wait a minute, Clarence. I think we can work this out."

"Wait a minute, Leslie. Who's Clarence?"

"Oh, I'm sorry, Matt—Clarence is Big Red's real name. I think the guards used to call him that, just to make him mad, but that's his real name, Clarence Redmond."

Wait a minute here. I sat back in my chair confused about all these people!

"Clarence Redmond, Redmond, Clarence, and Big Red are the same person?" I was stunned, wondering if my headache had gotten the best of me.

"Yes. Why, of course, they're the same person."

"I keep hearing all these stories thinking they're about four different men. Damn. This guy must be an evil monster." I could not believe how narrow-minded I'd been. I felt foolish.

"Not really, Matt. Not what I saw of him anyway."

Leslie flipped her hair back. She was surprisingly gorgeous, definitely a stunner. I wanted her so badly. She would definitely cure my headache. I had to ask her for a date. I felt the dampness of my clothing—sweating wasn't a good sign.

"Well, anyway, Warden Cooper says, 'Clarence, I think we can work this out so that everybody will be happy. Will your men let you search their bikes?' Clarence looked indignant but said his men would do whatever he told them to do. Warden Cooper went on to say if Clarence would personally search each and every person including their motorcycles, and give his word there is no contraband of any kind on the men or their motorcycles, he would accept the deal. Well, I looked over at Captain Walsh because I just knew that he was going to come out of his chair and go right through the ceiling, but that didn't happen. He just sat there sweating, turning purple, and nodding his head, like he thought it was a great idea. That's when I thought something was really fishy. I couldn't put my finger on it, but I knew something was out of whack."

"Did you have any theories, Leslie?"

"Oh, sure. I had a thousand of them. But now, with Big Red and all those people dead, only one of my theories holds any water. See, I figured—I mean, I know—that Captain Walsh didn't agree with the way that Warden Cooper did anything. So, I think that he was going to let the warden make a big mistake and then get rid of him once and for all so he could take the warden's position."

I waited and listened for more but she just sat silently and stared at me with those big, beautiful dark blue eyes.

"Well, thanks, Leslie. You've been a big help." I was amazed that I stood without making a fool of myself. The tension in my neck had disappeared. I didn't know whether it was the aspirin or just that I had lost myself in our conversation, but it didn't matter. I prepared to make my move.

"Glad to be of assistance, Matt. How's the headache?" She moved close to place a cool hand on my forehead.

I was about to say just fine, when I realized that there might be more to be gained by lying. I have yet to meet a woman, no matter how tough on the outside, who doesn't respond to a little human weakness in the opposite sex. I decided to press my advantage.

"Actually, not much better, Leslie. I was thinking of kicking back and closing my eyes for a few minutes, but I hate to cut my time short with you. I do appreciate your input, but even more than that, I've enjoyed talking to you as a person. You're a beautiful woman." This was it. Time to pop the question. I was sweating big time, my armpits were soaked. It was now or never. "I know I already asked once, but I'd really love to have dinner with you out on the bay some night. There are boats with live music, cocktails, and dinner. I promise you'd have a great time."

"I'd love to, Matt! I don't have much of a social life and obviously, in this job I don't have much of a chance to meet any interesting men. San Quentin State Prison is not a great place to meet eligible bachelors." She winked and treated me to that sexy laugh, and then she suddenly turned quiet.

"I'm sorry, Matt, I'm rambling on, while you're sitting there in so much pain. Why don't you just lay your head back, close your eyes, and let me see if I can get rid of some of that tension." She moved behind me, and placed her hands around my neck. Her thumbs began to knead my neck muscles, and I started to melt beneath her fingertips. Her talents were being wasted—this woman's fingers should never again touch anything as inhuman as a typewriter or keyboard. I closed my eyes, imagining what she looked like as she touched my flesh. The moment was so intense that it did not even seem strange when she loosened my tie and unbuttoned the top buttons of my shirt while rubbing my tight neck muscles. She continued her sensual massage down my back. For a moment, I was more than content to follow in whatever direction we were headed. Without a word, she bent forward, letting her hair spill over my face. The bulge in my pants was growing with every second.

As if I were dreaming, she kissed me on my mouth, long and hard. We touched lip to lip and then tongue to tongue. My God, I was most definitely in love. She took my glasses off, placed them on the table, then reached between my legs and grabbed Willie, who was like a Marine Corps general at attention. Even in my greatest fantasies, I had always been the aggressor—it had never occurred to me that if I were lucky enough to make love to this woman, I might be the one who was pursued!

She lightly rested her hand on my zipper, creating an emotional rush that made my heart jump. I was breathing hard, thinking about making love to her right then and there. As the blood pulsed through my penis, she seemed lost in her own sensual world. For the first time, I found the strength to move. Something told me to be careful. I sat up, and while I wanted to unbutton her blouse, I didn't. Her eyes shot open. They looked fiery with lust, but looked also hard as blue flint. She smiled again, and freed one beautiful breast from its nesting area. She leaned over and placed her swollen nipple inches from my mouth, while starting to stroke my thigh with her other hand. Suddenly, I remembered something that she had said, about San Quentin magnifying a woman's femininity. If I went any further, my assignment there would be history. I knew I had to stop, so I would not be seen as her pawn, or as the laughing stock to any of her confidantes. I quickly decided that there would be plenty of time to date Leslie after the investigation.

When we heard somebody outside the door, I stood and blurted, "I think we better wrap up the interview now. I'd still like it if we could have dinner, maybe after I've finished this assignment." Leslie didn't answer, but her smile turned to a tight-lipped frown. She slipped her breast back into her bra and strolled to the other side of the desk.

The door flew open so fast it bounced off the wall, as if someone had planned to surprise us. The Tarantula stood there with a broom, a mop, and a half-assed grin on his face. I grabbed my glasses and put them back on. Leslie scowled at the Tarantula and walked out the door without a word. If she could play it cool, so could I. I glanced at the inmate and said casually, "Go ahead and clean up. I'll take a break." I heard the Tarantula crack his knuckles as I followed Leslie to her office.

"Leslie, I—"

"Wasn't that a hoot, Matt? I've got lots of work to do and you probably need to call it a day. Do I need to schedule any appointments for you tomorrow?"

Jesus, did this woman have ice water in her veins or what? An hour ago, I thought I had to handle her with kid gloves in order to get her to go out with me. Now, she practically rapes me and dismisses the incident as if it were a minor interruption in her schedule.

"Uh, could you ask Captain Walsh if he would meet me tomorrow morning about ten?"

"Sure. No problem." She winked at me and said. "Bye, bye for now."

I replied back, "Chow, chow." I wondered if I looked as confused as I felt.

Mark Wilcox was just coming through the black security gate as I was walking to my car. Thousands of seagulls were raising hell on the bay. My car had fresh white and green bird shit all over it again. The fresh ocean bay air smelled fantastic. I was flying high with a smile from ear to ear. I had made it to first base with Leslie, the woman of my dreams. I had to shake myself back to reality. The perks of this assignment might just compensate for all the anxiety it generated.

I yelled, "Hey, Mark, do you have a second?"

Wilcox looked at his watch and then looked back at me. "I have to be someplace in a few minutes. What do you want?"

Mark kept walking toward his car and I followed. He looked very tired. "I just have a couple of questions about a female guard that you dated and supposedly lived with last year."

"I don't want to talk about her. That's a part of my past. I was younger then, maybe I didn't use good judgment at that time, nobody's gonna hang my ass for what she did."

"Mark, you're not under any suspicion. There were allegations made that a female guard had a prior record of prostitution. Don't you feel that we should make certain the state only hires people who are qualified for their jobs?"

"Well, I guess so."

"Would you please answer a few quick questions about her?"

"Well, I guess... I can tell you... what I know... I guess."

"First of all, what's her name?"

"Nikki Buckner."

"Did you meet her at San Quentin?"

"Yes. She was walking around, confused like everybody else on their first day at work. She asked me where the officers' locker room was located. I gave her directions, and then I decided to escort her personally. God, you would not believe how incredibly beautiful that woman was. Anyway, she was really friendly. A lot of the women who come in here act tough, but she was different."

I leaned against Mark's car.

"How so? What do you mean by 'different'?"

"Well, she was the kind of a woman most men only dream about dating. When she said she would like to go out with me, just like that, I couldn't believe my ears. We went out that night and got really drunk and I nailed her. I had so much fun with her."

"What did you talk about?"

Wilcox stared at the birds in the bay as he replied. "I asked her about her first day. I remember her saying that the only thing that upset her was the tour of the facility she took with the other new officers. All the inmates were yelling, 'Hey, baby, you got beautiful ass. Baby, come over here and let me fuck you.' I started laughing and she got really upset. She said she didn't think the inmates should be allowed to talk like that. I was laughing so hard she could barely understand what I was trying to tell her. I explained to her that they weren't talking to the female guards. They were yelling at the new male officers. I turned red in the face. She thought about it for a second, and then she started laughing, too. We had a great time together, she was funny."

"Did she tell you anything about her past?"

"Thinking back, in light of what I know now, she told me a great deal. But I was either too naive or too starry-eyed to catch on to what she was saying at the time."

"What did she tell you?"

"She said that she just wanted to get away from her old man and make a new life for herself. I thought she meant her ex-husband or her father, but now I realize she was talking about her pimp."

"Can you tell me anything else about Nikki?"

"Yeah, there was one thing about her that I just couldn't understand. I mean, she was stunning. When we walked into a bar at night, half the men in the place would almost fall off their stools. But she didn't see herself that way at all. It was like someone had convinced her that she was ugly. Anyway, we dated for quite sometime and she moved in with me. Then things started to get really weird."

The sun was beating down on us and it was hot.

"What do you mean by weird, Mark?"

"Well, everything started falling apart. We were getting along really well when she first moved in with me. I did everything I could do to make her happy, but she started fights for no reason. She seemed to need that type of tension in her life, as if a happy relationship would strangle her. That girl loved to fight, and I don't mean just with words. I'm still eating off paper plates because she broke every dish in my house. One day I asked her if I could borrow five dollars. When I opened her purse, I almost had a heart attack. There must have been fifteen bindles in there."

"Bindles, what are bindles?"

"They're like pieces of paper rolled up with drugs inside, about the diameter of a cigarette. It's one of the most common ways to get drugs to a large number of inmates."

"Did you say anything to her?"

"No, I didn't know what to say. I didn't know whether she was using drugs herself or smuggling the drugs into the inmates. Either way, I knew it was bad news."

"Well, what did you do next?"

"I called my cousin at the prison who was working Internal Affairs, you know, the one who got me the job in the first place. He said he'd been trying to reach me for two days— he told me to get rid of her. If she wouldn't leave, I should move out immediately, because they had been watching her and she was going to be busted. He said unless I wanted to take the fall with her, I should kick her out of my house that very second."

"And you did, of course?"

"You bet, Matt. I told her to pack her shit up and find another place to live. I threw all her crap out on to the lawn with the help of a friend. I quickly changed the locks on the front door. She was pissed—I'd never seen her so mad. I figured she'd get busted and I'd go down as an accessory, since she lived in my house and we'd both end up looking out from the wrong side of the prison bars. Let me tell you, she was gorgeous and she was great in the sack, but she wasn't worth goin' to prison for."

We were both wiping the sweat off our foreheads. "Was she arrested by the police?"

"Not right away. She got into some other scrapes first."

"Like what?"

"She was up on the gun rail with Sergeant Fernandez on third watch. They started doin' it right there on the gun rail. The lieutenant was checking all the gun walks and gun posts with a new infrared scope one night, one of his favorite toys. He spotted them while they were goin' at it. Nikki got a two-week suspension without pay; Fernandez got demoted to correctional officer."

"Did she come back to work after that?"

"Yeah. I saw her a couple of times after that. She seemed rude, really surly, and smart-assed, if you know what I mean."

"Mark, you said she got into trouble a couple of times."

"Yeah, there was an inmate named Downing. He used to write her poetry and stuff. The watch sergeant caught her giving him a knob job through the bars, but she stopped him from turning her in by doing the same for him. Both of them were charged with misconduct because some of the inmates got jealous and complained to the captain. He got a two-week suspension and hers was three weeks because it was her second offense. While she was on suspension, they charged her with supplying her inmate poet friend with drugs. They had photographs and everything, so she was finally fired. She went to the local newspapers to tell them about some of the things going on out here, but nobody believed her. It helps them sleep better at night if they refuse to believe the truth. If anyone realized how bad things are in San Quentin...Someday they're going to have a very rude awakening."

"I'd say the Rock and Roll Riot was a rude awakening, wouldn't you, Mark?"

"You've gotta be kidding me. That'll be nothing compared to what's going to happen one day in the near future. We still don't know who called the Code Red lower yard on that day of the riot. Picture this, three thousand inmates held back by one hundred and forty underpaid correctional officers, some of them not sure whose side they're really on. We can't even protect the inmates who are just trying to do their time from the animals in this garbage dump. One of these days those convicts are goin' over the wall in force—then you'll see a real riot. These guys will be runnin' all over Marin County and San Francisco doing what they do best."

"Do you really think there's going to be a mass escape?"

"It's only a matter of time if things stay the way they are."

Given what I experienced that day, I tended to agree with Mark. "Let's get back to Nikki. Do you know where she is living now?"

"Well, it's my understanding she's living in Sacramento with a former inmate from this facility—the guy who used to write the poetry."

"Mark, do you think she'd talk to me if I could locate her?"

"Maybe, but I doubt it. She's probably all caught up in drugs and only God knows what. I doubt that her new boyfriend would appreciate her talking to an investigator hired by the District Attorney's Office."

"Why's that?"

"He's not a very nice fella. He's into all kinds of bad shit. He was with the bikers at the prison the day of the riot—one of the Hell's Angels. He thought he was a good friend of Big Red's, but I don't know whether Red felt the same way about him. I heard a rumor that he was one of three bikers involved in a rough power struggle to see who's going to take Red's place as the leader and president of the Hell's Angels."

"Have you seen Nikki since she was fired?"

"No, Matt, I'm not that crazy."

"Can you think of anything else about Nikki? Please, think hard, Mark."

"Talk to the warden's secretary. She and Nikki were real good friends for a long time. Real good friends, if you know what I mean..."

"No, I don't know what you mean."

I moved away from Mark's car and shielded my face with my hand to block the sun.

"Oh, I figured by now you would have heard. Leslie is known to prefer pussy, although I hear she can suck the brass off a doorknob. I hear it also depends on her mood. Anyway, I don't know whether they still see each other or not, but they were really close friends at one time."

"Wait a minute, wait just a minute, Mark!" This was too much to absorb at one time. "Look, you're telling me that Leslie and Nikki were lovers? I can't imagine them even being friends!"

Mark shrugged. "Listen, Matt, they used to work together on the gun rail in the East Block. Leslie would have been out of a job herself if the warden hadn't taken a shine to her. I guess he decided that her disciplinary problems were due to the fact that she wasn't suited for the demands of a correctional officer. So he took her on as a secretary before she got in very serious trouble."

"Leslie Kirby was a correctional officer?" So this was the woman of my dreams! I felt sick to my stomach. I became depressed and sad. She lied to me. She fuckin' lied to me.

"Yup, she sure was." Mark looked at his watch again. "Listen, Matt, I've really got to run."

"Thanks, Mark. As always, you've been a big help to me."

The guards wouldn't be the only ones having nightmares tonight.

.

10

I drove home slowly that day—crushed from my discovery about Leslie and upset about my father's condition. When I got home, I flopped into bed. I couldn't eat or sleep. Sebastian woke from his nap and licked my forehead to announce that he was hungry. I pulled myself together long enough to fill his bowl with Kibble before heading back to bed. I finally dozed off around 1:00 a.m. and was rudely awakened by my alarm at 8:00 sharp.

I had no desire to go to the prison that morning but I had no choice. My stomach ached. I wasn't looking forward to interviewing Captain Walsh. I thought about what he had done to Don Barrett in the rock quarry. I wondered again about Barrett's credibility. When Eudon talked about the corruption of the upper administration, I could only assume that he was including Captain Walsh. I knew there were plenty of civil servants hiding their crimes of malfeasance behind long service records, firmly entrenched in their positions of authority without fear of removal or punishment, than any of us care to imagine. It didn't seem possible that the Captain Walsh I had met and the one Barrett described could be the same man. Captain Walsh must have several personalities.

The fat guard at the Main Gate recognized me and waved me through. As I rolled into the now familiar parking lot, I was immediately overpowered by the buildings' colors of pink and yellow. My jaw had tightened to the point where I feared my teeth would crack. After yesterday, I was thankful that I wouldn't have to go any farther than the Administration Building.

I heard the Tarantula cracking his knuckles as I approached my office.

Leslie was not in her office as I passed. Unfortunately, Captain Walsh was waiting in the interview room, chatting amicably with the Tarantula. There was no doubt in my mind that he was listening to Tarantula's opinions of my interview with Leslie. I hoped he had the decency not to mention it.

"Hi, Matt." He stood to shake my hand with a funny grin plastered on his face. His grip was like a vice. My hand was throbbing when he let go. I was sure he was trying to send a message.

"Good morning, Ted." I wondered whether he or the Tarantula had been snooping around my office. I glanced at the desk to see if I had left any notes that could have been of interest to them.

"Matt, are you getting the kind of cooperation you need from the prison staff?"

"I have no complaints, Ted. In fact, things are moving along nicely."

I threw the briefcase on the floor, turned on the tape recorder, and sat down. "Shall we get started?"

He sat and splayed his hands flat on the table. "I'm ready whenever you're ready."

"For the record, Captain Walsh, I'm here as a special investigator for the District Attorney's Office to uncover the problems and conditions that contributed to the event now known as the Rock and Roll Riot. Are you willing to discuss these issues with me?"

"Shoot. Let's go for it." He uncrossed his legs, leaned back and put his hands on the back of his head.

"Ted, how long have you been with the California Department of Corrections?"

"Eighteen great years."

"Were you assigned to San Quentin during that entire time?"

"Yes, sir. You bet."

"When did you acquire the rank of captain?"

"1972, it was a great year."

"How did you happen to become a correctional officer, Ted?"

"Let's see now. I grew up in Ross, that's a little town just west of here. I went to school there, and then I joined the Army and served in Vietnam. After my tour, I moved back and got this job with the Department of Corrections. I've been here ever since."

"Do you have any theories about the so called riot—how it got started, how it could have been prevented, or who called the Code Red in the lower yard that day?"

He leaned forward and put his hands back on the table.

"It's obvious how the whole thing could have been avoided. Warden Cooper should never have let those bikers in this facility."

Walsh not only avoided the question, he blatantly and squarely blamed Warden Cooper for the riot. He must have seen the surprise on my face. I was in total shock.

"It's no secret around here how I feel about Warden Cooper. He just isn't qualified to be a warden, not at San Quentin anyway."

"Well, Ted, how did the bikers happen to get in here to begin with?"

"Well, the first time I heard about it was when Warden Cooper told me to come to his office for a meeting with Clarence Redmond. At first, I thought he was kidding me. We were as glad to get rid of Redmond as he was to be rid of San Quentin. Anyway, when I got to the warden's office, Redmond wasn't there, just Warden Cooper and his secretary. I knew that he'd lost all his marbles when he said Redmond was coming in to discuss a motorcycle show for the inmates."

"Were you were against the idea of a motorcycle show?"

"I'd have been against a Sunday sermon if it involved Clarence Redmond!"

"Ted, did you voice your objections and opinions to the warden?"

His fist hit the table and jarred my tape deck. The noise scared the shit out of me. I didn't need this. It was too early in the morning for emotional problems.

"You better believe it! I told that idiot it was the stupidest idea he'd ever come up with. He got pretty angry and said that we couldn't run a prison like some sort of medieval torture chamber. Well, I've seen him before when he would get on that soapbox of his, so I just clammed up. About that time, Redmond came strolling in. They discussed their motorcycle show and the concert. I just sat there biting my tongue. They got into a discussion about how the bikes were going to be searched. Clarence said there was no way anyone was going to search his buddies' motorcycles. I figured that would be the end of it, but the warden got the bright idea that if Redmond searched his people and the motorcycles and swore to us that there was no contraband on them, he'd take Redmond's word for it. I couldn't believe what I was hearing!"

"Why didn't you speak up, Ted?"

"I started to, but I changed my mind."

"Why is that?"

"I figured that Warden Cooper was about to demonstrate to the world just how incompetent he really was. I didn't want to stand in his way."

"Weren't you concerned that people might be hurt or even killed?"

"I've got to admit that I was shortsighted there. I never thought it would turn out the way it did."

I changed positions in my chair to relieve the growing pain in my lower back. "What did you expect to happen?"

"I figured we could turn it to our advantage. I knew Redmond wanted to get his motorcycles and men in here to fill some long-overdue narcotics orders. So once they were inside the prison walls, we only needed to find one piece of contraband on them. The warden gave me his word that if we witnessed one illegal transaction, we could take them all down. That's what I was waiting for."

"What *did* happen that day, Ted?"

He leaned back in his chair and I could barely hear what he was saying. The Tarantula was outside the door cracking his knuckles. I couldn't wait for this interview to end. I was starting to feel sick again.

"Matt, most of what I know is second-hand from the reports. I wasn't in the yard when it started, but from what I gathered, it was pretty bad. My men had instructions to act on the first altercation they observed. They were all told to intercept the first illegal transaction and quickly separate the inmates from the bikers, then lock down everything and everybody. The bikers were supposed to be segregated, then searched and charged with the applicable offenses. That's it, but it didn't quite work out that way."

"When did it get out of hand?"

"As soon as the concert started, one of the boys in the towers saw three officers in the yard being held at bay by Redmond with a gun. I believe they called the Code Red lower yard. The officers reacted very quickly. They fired at Redmond and killed him. Then all hell broke loose. From that point on, it's impossible to tell who did what."

"Do you know who fired the first shot?"

He stood and started to pace. "Matt, I'd rather not say."

"Captain, let me remind you that this is an official investigation."

"I'm sorry. I have a tendency to be a little protective of my men."

He nodded. We made eye-to-eye contact.

"I believe it was Officer Kimble."

Our eyes met again. I was shocked. Alarms went off in my head. *Kimble!* Could it be the same Kimble that the dying inmate whispered in my ear about a contract killing? Could the same Kimble have fired the first shot? If so, my instinct to keep quiet was probably right on the money. I hoped that my facial expression did not reveal my excitement. I felt my armpits getting wet. I forced myself to conceal my inner thoughts and concentrate on Captain Walsh.

"It's a damn good thing he was in the tower that day. If it had been some-one else, someone who wasn't an expert rifleman like Kimble, it could have been depressingly worse. There were lots of people in a very small area. It was a difficult shot to take out Redmond and not kill anyone else. There are very few guards here who could have done it."

"What happened after that?"

Ted sat back down. The alarms continued to go off in my head. I couldn't stop thinking about Kimble. I was going nuts. I was sweating like a fat man in a steam bath. I needed fresh air.

"Well, Kenny Boyd was shot immediately after that. It looks like he was shot by one of the bikers, maybe by Redmond after he was hit. If the bullet that killed Kenny Boyd hadn't passed right through him, we could have used ballistics tests to confirm which gun shot him. There were so many guns down there at that time, it was impossible to figure out exactly where the shot came from."

"I don't understand. How could Redmond have shot him?"

"Real-life shootings aren't like the ones you see on television. Even with a high-powered rifle, men don't just fall down and die. They often have time to fire a shot, but they don't always aim very well. Redmond was standing right in front of the pink stage, near the spot where Hendrix was singing. It's possible that Redmond's last reflex fired the shot that killed Boyd after he'd been hit. Once Boyd went down, it turned into total confusion. Most of the inmates ran toward the walls, you know, for safety. From the time Redmond was killed until the time it was over was maybe thirteen seconds, no more. It wasn't much of a riot in the usual sense of the word, but it sure was destructive for the time that it lasted."

I had to stand; my back and neck were killing me. "Thirteen seconds?"

"That's it. Things blew up very quickly, and then it was over. Most of the inmates didn't want anything to do with it. Once we surrounded the bikers and everyone threw down their guns, it ended."

"Do you know how many shots were fired?"

"We recovered all the weapons and expended shell casings, eighteen in all."

"Eighteen shots were fired?"

Walsh nodded.

"It's a miracle that only five people died!"

"There was so much confusion, a lot of shots were fired into the yellow walls of the prison or the grass. Thank God for the National Guard."

"What do you mean?"

"They were called to help control the incident."

"But you said the riot ended very quickly."

"In a place like San Quentin, you never take things for granted—especially when the prisoners have just had a little taste of the better life."

I nodded. "Captain, there's something else I would like to ask you about. It concerns the incident you were involved in three years ago with former Correctional Officer Don Barrett. You don't have to talk to me about it if you don't want to."

"How did you hear about that?"

I leaned against the wall next to the rubber plant to ease a cramp in my left leg. Ted ran his hands through his hair as I said, "I know that it doesn't involve the riot directly, but it has brought up a number of questions concerning your influence and position within this facility."

"You talked to Barrett, didn't you?"

"Yes, I did."

"He's somethin' else, that one."

"What do you mean by that?"

"Well, you see, Barrett's one of those guys who's always got a conspiracy on his brain. He looks for all the right reasons in all the wrong places. He never feels like he's capable of stupidity, which couldn't be further from the truth."

"What is the truth, Captain Walsh?"

"First of all, you've got to understand how I feel about that particular incident. It was, without question, the most deplorable thing I've ever done in my life. I should never have allowed myself to get so angry, but I just couldn't handle my feelings about his stupidity and carelessness. Barrett came in with a bad attitude that day. It was like, 'Hey, what's the big deal?'"

"What *was* the big deal?"

"Two inmates lost their lives because of his carelessness!"

"What did Barrett have to do with their deaths?"

"Well, let me tell you, we had these two inmates sharing a cell in South Block B section. One inmate was in for forgery and the other for carjacking. Both of them were model prisoners, they just wanted to do their time and get the hell out of prison. Right after Barrett's shift, the guard who relieved Barrett said he couldn't find the brass keys to the cellblock. Barrett was supposed to take them off his gun belt and hang them back in the sergeant's office. I told the third shift officer I'd have the sergeant bring them to him as soon as we located them. I left to find Barrett. About five minutes later, another guard came running down the corridor screaming that B-33's on fire! We had to stand there helplessly and watch the two inmates burn to death because we didn't have the keys to let them out. They were screaming, yelling, and crying as they burned to death. There was nothing we could do for them. I felt so bad."

Ted shook his head from left to right several times. "We were helpless without the keys to that unit. When I went back to the sergeant's office, the brass keys were hanging on the board next to the microwave—right where they belonged. My inmate clerk said Barrett had just come in and hung them up. I was furious. Sometimes incompetence makes me crazy, you know what I mean? I called the front gate to try to stop Barrett before he got out of the east gates, but the gate guard said he was already gone. I called his house about twenty times that night. I even sent a patrol car to his house but he never showed."

Walsh began to pace around the small room much like a caged lion. He wiped the sweat from his brow with his sleeve.

"I asked the warden's secretary to tell him that I wanted to see him immediately, if not sooner, the next day. When he finally got his butt into my office, he acted like he hadn't done a single thing wrong. He had a real bad attitude. He turned his back and started to walk out of the office. When the sergeant told him to stop, that little jerk started talking about how he wasn't in the Army, and how he didn't have to take orders from anyone, and all that bullshit. He made me furious—I went through the roof. When I spotted his damn hillbilly silver buck-knife on his belt, I couldn't believe that even Barrett was stupid enough to carry an eight-inch knife into the prison. I lost my mind right there—completely blew a fuse."

Ted slammed his fist on the doorframe and scared the shit out of me again. I was getting tired of his emotional reactions. "Those two inmates were screaming at the top of their lungs, Matt. I still hear their voices. I just couldn't take Barrett's attitude for another second. What we did to him should never have happened. I'm sorry to say it, but we acted like a lynch mob. After it was over, I realized how wrong it was. I went to the warden. I figured I'd be fired anyway and lose my pension, but because I came forward first and told the truth, he spared my job. He warned me that it better not ever happen again. The other two, the lieutenant and sergeant, sat there on the stand and denied it ever happened, which cost them their jobs. I kept mine because I didn't lie. I'm very lucky I'm not serving time for assault and battery. There were no other motives behind that incident, Matt."

"It wasn't your intention to kill him?"

"God, no! But we were just damn lucky we didn't. It makes me sick to think about what we did to that boy. But his attitude made me crazy with rage! He acted like, 'so what, assholes? Two inmates burned to death, but who cares? Who really gives a shit?' Well, Matt, I have to live with it."

"Ted, I guess that just about does it. Thank you for being so candid." I turned off the tape recorder.

Ted smiled as he turned to leave. "Are you sure there's nothing more I can do to help?"

"No, thank you anyway. I just need to get Mark Wilcox back in here to finish where we left off yesterday."

"I hope you brought a bunch of extra cassettes with you. That boy can talk!"

We laughed without meeting each other's gaze. "That's why we ran out of time during the last interview."

"I'll send him right down, Matt. This bureaucracy moves slower than most. Most of them are just inefficient. Ours is inefficient and security-conscious."

"Thank you." We shook hands one more time. He squeezed my hand like a vice again, sending another silent message.

As I sat waiting for Mark Wilcox, I decided to wait until I got home to try to connect the two dead prisoners to the man Ted said had fired the first shot. I caught myself staring at the rubber plant. Taking pity on it again, I poured a large cup of water into the pot and watched it slowly begin to seep into the hard soil. My thoughts turned to Officer Barrett and Captain Walsh; I had no doubt that Walsh and his cronies had beaten up Barrett. But after talking to Walsh, Barrett's accusations seemed far-fetched. Leaping to conclusions had always been a major flaw of mine. Although I hated to admit it, my lack of objectivity had interfered with my work on more than one occasion. My interview with Captain Walsh reminded me that I needed to keep my emotions in check during this assignment.

Mark Wilcox startled me when he appeared at the door; I hadn't heard his footsteps or any noise for that matter. It had only been five or ten minutes since Walsh had left. Obviously, Walsh was the man to call if I ever needed to get something done in a hurry.

Wilcox, always the soldier, sat at attention. He had a shiny gold badge, shiny shoes, and perfectly ironed clothes.

"Mark, are you ready?"

"Yes, go ahead."

I turned on the tape recorder.

"What was your assignment the day of the riot?"

"Wall Post five."

"Were you alone at that post?"

"No, that day there were two of us in each tower and wall post."

"Who was with you?"

"Sergeant Eudon was with me. Have you met him yet?"

"Yes, I have."

"He's pretty unique around here and he's really smart. Not just book smart. He's really talented. He paints and he writes."

"What does he write, Mark?"

"Poetry and stuff, music, country songs and things like that. That's really what he does best."

"Mark, I need you to think about what happened during the riot--even the smallest details might be important. Who called the Code Red lower yard?"

"Okay, give me a minute here." He adjusted his body in the chair.

"When were the first shots fired and who fired them, do you remember?"

"I don't know that it was really a big surprise. I remember we were expecting trouble that day. I thought we were prepared for it, but the first shot still came as a surprise. All I remember is that I heard a shot from a mini-14 and it hit Kenny Boyd in the head. I remember the blood gushing from his mouth before he hit the floor of the stage. Almost immediately, the second shot hit Big Red. All of a sudden, there was gunfire everywhere. It's really hard to say what happened."

"Please back up, Mark. You said Kenny Boyd was the first to go down, the first to be shot. Are you sure? Don't you mean Redmond fell first?"

Mark leaned forward in his chair, put his hands on the table and looked me in the eyes as he said, "No...That much I *do* know. That day I was using my binoculars to get a good look at the Band of Gypsies. I was looking right at Kenny Boyd when that first shot hit him in the head."

"The gunfire was from a mini-14?"

"I know it was one of the mini-14's. They have a very distinct sound, but I'm not sure where it came from."

"Do you realize what you're saying?"

"Trust me Matt, the first shot that was fired that day was definitely from a mini-14." Mark paused for a minute. The perplexed look on his face mirrored his contemplating mind.

"Do you understand what you are saying, Mark?"

"Yes, I do, why?"

"Well, then someone wearing a green uniform is responsible for killing Kenny Boyd."

Sweat began to glisten on his face as Mark shook his head.

"Matt, I thought a lot of Kenny Boyd. Here you have a guy who used to be a convict right here in this place. He does his time, gets out, and hits the big time with music. I think that's something special."

"Kenny Boyd was a San Quentin inmate?"

"Yeah, he used to sit in his cell at night playing his guitar and writing songs in West Block. Occasionally Sergeant Eudon would bring his guitar to work and the two of them would play together for hours. I used to love to sit up there on the gun walks and listen to them. The music they played was great. It made the time pass quickly."

"What kind of inmate was he, Mark?"

"He was a model prisoner. He never should have been in here to begin with. He spent most of his time trying to protect himself from the other inmates, trying to keep them out of his life, but they wouldn't leave him alone, especially Browning. That nut had a crush on Kenny like you wouldn't believe. He used to pant after him like a dog in heat, but Kenny was straight all the way—you know what I mean? He should have done twelve, maybe eighteen months in here at the maximum, but he had to fight just to protect himself. He ended up doing an extra three years because of the write-ups."

"How often does that happen, Mark?"

Mark sat back in his chair, yawned, and stretched his arms.

"All the time, we get guys in here who are halfway decent, just trying to do their time and get out. If they go along with the inmates with the juice, running drugs, getting involved in the prostitution and corruption, they'd be out in no time. But because they try to stay clean, they end up doing more time than the animals. That's the way it was with Kenny—he had to fight to be left alone."

WHO'S WATCHING THE TOWER?

116

"Mark, are you absolutely certain that Kenny Boyd was the first person killed that day and not Redmond?"

"I'm positive. It's like I said, I was watching the band through the binoculars. I could also see Redmond, because he was standing beside that asshole Browning, right in front of the stage down on the grass."

"Did you see a gun in Redmond's hand at that time, Mark?"

"If I had, I would have been shooting at him, not watching Boyd through a pair of binoculars."

"Thank you, Mark, I don't want to keep you any longer."

I turned off the tape.

"Okay." As Mark headed toward the door he said, "Captain Walsh says I talk too much." We both chuckled as he started to leave.

"Hey, Mark, would you ask the captain to send Greg Kimble down?"

"Sure."

He left quickly.

Captain Walsh was sure Redmond was killed first. Mark swore he saw Boyd go down first. True, the shots were fired so closely together that either was possible. If Boyd were hit first, though, as Mark claimed, the repercussions would be catastrophic. Maybe Browning had been a fanatic Kenny Boyd fan and had made the threat because he believed Kimble had killed his idol.

As I was thinking, Greg Kimble knocked quietly on the door.

"Officer Kimble here, sir."

"Yeah, come on in."

Greg Kimble was not the typical picture of a correctional officer. His uniform was rumpled, in sharp contrast to those of the other officers I had seen in the facility. Greg seemed run down. His reddish tousled hair and fair skin made him look almost anemic. He couldn't have been more than twenty-four years old. His demeanor did not fit the profile of what I had pictured to be a man who elicited threats from a dying convict. I decided not to mention the threat on his life until I had a handle on him.

"I'm Matt Belding, Special Investigator for the District Attorney's Office. Thanks for coming down so quickly. Please sit down." Without making eye contact, he walked over to the chair and slouched into it. I turned on the tape recorder and proceeded with the interview.

"Sir, would you please tell me your full name and rank?"

"Yes, sir, Gregory Arthur Kimble. I don't have any rank. I'm just a correctional officer."

"How long have you worked for the Department of Corrections, Greg?"

"About three years." Kimble finally looked up and our eyes met. "I didn't start that riot, you know."

"What do you mean?"

"A lot of the guys around here are saying that it was my fault, but it wasn't. It's like Captain Walsh says, it was the warden's fault."

"Greg, first of all, we need to know exactly what happened, how the riot got started, who did what, when, where and how. Secondly, I would like to see if any of the conditions that contributed to the riot are from some of the other incidents of violence that have occurred here in the past. I would like to see things improve at this facility to make sure that this doesn't happen again."

"Well, if you got rid of the inmates for starters, that would be a big help and my job would be much easier," Greg laughed.

"It wouldn't be much of a prison if there weren't any inmates."

He leaned back in his chair and almost fell over. "I think that's a matter of opinion."

I needed to gain control of the interview. Greg seemed troubled by his role in the riot. He was highly defensive and his strong odor permeated the room. He smelled as if he hadn't taken a shower in weeks.

"Greg, let's back up for a minute. Can you tell me a little about yourself?"

"Like what do you want to know?"

"Where did you grow up?"

"Bakersfield mostly. My dad worked for the Union Pacific Railroad, so we moved a couple of times. But we always went back to Bakersfield for some reason."

"Did you attend college?"

"Yeah. Four years at U. C. Berkeley."

"What was your major?"

"Criminal Justice."

"Did you want to be a police officer?"

"No, that never entered my mind. I just chose a major I found interesting."

"How did you happen to become a correctional officer?"

"Well, one of the guys in my class said he was going to work for the Department of Corrections. He boasted that they were going to pay him seventeen thousand dollars a year. It sounded like my kind of job, just sitting around doing nothing, so I applied."

I had to stand, my leg was falling asleep and my lower back was on fire. "Did you feel prepared for this job after you graduated from the Academy?"

"Yeah, pretty much. There wasn't much they could teach us in a classroom, I guess. Some of it was really stupid stuff. One instructor told us, 'If you see a guard kicking a prisoner, shoot the guard.'"

"So you don't feel that prisoners need to be protected from abusive guards?"

He nodded. "That's not what I mean. It's wrong for a guard to beat up on a prisoner, but under California law, punching someone or kicking them would be simple battery. That's a misdemeanor, and I don't think impressionable recruits ought to be instructed to shoot a fellow officer if they observe him committing a misdemeanor. Besides, maybe the inmate's got a knife or a gun, who knows?"

"Do you like working at San Quentin?"

"It's okay, I guess." Greg hesitated for a moment. "Except for the jokes the other officers play on me."

"Don't you mean the inmates, Greg?"

"No, I mean the correctional officers. They play stupid jokes on the new officers."

"Are you often the target?"

"No, not any more than anyone else, I guess. I fell for one or two jokes, but that's just a part of paying your dues as a new employee. You're called a fish for the first nine months of employment by the old timers."

I wasn't so sure Greg really believed what he was saying, because he seemed so nervous. I was certain something was bothering him.

"What kind of things have they done to you?"

He sat up and looked around.

"The first one I fell for was really embarrassing. Someone called down to my tier and said they hadn't gotten my fire extinguisher report and that the lieutenant was pissed. So, I said no one had told me about this report, but that I'd get right on it. Well, I ran through the whole cellblock, up and down five flights of steel stairs, counting all the red fire extinguishers as I went up the stairs. Then I re-counted them on my way back down the stairs. When I called the lieutenant and told him there were twenty-seven in the unit, he said twenty-seven what? So, I told him that there were twenty-seven fire extinguishers in the East Block. I guess he figured out what was going on and said, 'Kimble, East Block has twenty-eight fire extinguishers. You had better count them again.' I spent about three hours running around the cellblock looking for that one goddamned red fire extinguisher. One of the inmates finally said to me, 'Hey, boy, is this your first day in the cell block?' I told him I couldn't talk to him until I got something cleared up. So he said to me, 'You gotta count the fire extinguishers, right?' I said, 'No, I've already counted them fifteen times. I gotta find the one that's missing!'

"Well, there were about twenty inmates that were within an earshot and they all started laughing hysterically. The one that was talking to me said, 'don't let 'em mess with your head, boy. There isn't no missin' red fire extinguisher you idiot. They're just seein' how long you'll run up and down them steel stairs before you drop dead, that's all. They got ya, didn't they?' I was really embarrassed, especially since all those inmates knew what was going on and I didn't have a clue."

"It sounds like that was a relatively harmless prank."

"Yeah, most of them usually are, but some of them are downright dangerous."

"Can you give me an example of a dangerous one, Greg?"

"You bet. Well, we had this inmate in the Amusement Center. He was—"

"The Amusement Center?" I hadn't heard of such a thing in San Quentin.

"Sorry. That's what I call the Adjustment Center. It's for the convicts who are a bad influence on the guys on Death Row, you know what I mean?"

"I've got the picture."

He stood and put his hand on the table.

"Well, one of the watch sergeants told me to take this one inmate to the showers. He said I just needed to put him in handcuffs, not full-body chains. So, I went to the guy's cell and took a good look at him. This guy was over seven feet tall and must have weighed 400 pounds! So, I went back to the sergeant and asked him if he was sure the guy didn't need leg restraints and a double escort. The sergeant looked at me real disgusted-like and said, 'Are you afraid of an inmate, Kimble? 'Cause if you are, I'll get someone who isn't such a candy-ass to handle him, maybe one of the female officers.'"

"What did you do then?"

"I went back to his cell and told him to turn around and to stick his hands through the tray slot. I put the cuffs on him and opened the door to his cell, but he wouldn't come out. He just sat on his bunk and said, 'I don't feel like takin' no goddamn fuckin' shower!' Everybody was watching, so I grabbed him by his ear and jerked him out of the cell. He was so mad that his face turned bright red. This guy was African-American. I'm not kiddin', his face turned purple, then red! The whites of his eyes got huge and real bloodshot. I thought they were going to pop right out of his skull. The look in his eyes went all the way through me. I thought I was dead. I never felt that way before—not from Charles Manson, not from Simon head of the Zebra Killers, not from Jeffrey Dahmer, not from anybody. He said to me, 'I'm going to kill you, you fuckin' little bitch. I'm gonna chew your guts up and spit them on your momma's grave.'

"I said, 'You aren't gonna do a goddamn thing. I've got you handcuffed. You're gonna get your filthy, stinkin' black ass down to the showers right now.' I was really getting mad. I kneed him in the nuts, but he didn't even flinch. He just smiled. Then he brought his hands out from behind his back—and dangled my handcuffs in front of my face. He was double jointed, an escape artist! No one had ever been able to keep him in any kind of restraint. He just stood there, grinning at me. Then he bends over and puts his face right in front of mine, eye-to-eye. I was scared shitless. His spit flew in my face as he said, 'If I didn't know that those motherfuckers over there put you up to this, you'd be dog food in a heartbeat. Don't you ever fuck with me again, you hear me you little motherfucker?' He walked back in his cell and slammed the cell door behind him. I remember feeling sick and shaking in my boots."

"Greg, what would have happened if he had grabbed you?"

"That's what makes me really mad. That watch sergeant knew this guy was bad news. If he had grabbed me, the guards up on the gun rails would have killed him. When he leaned down and put his face in mine, I heard them pulling the bolts back on their rifles.

"The second time was when we were having the election for the Teamsters Union. The guards who were not for the union were in for a surprise. This big shot from the union, D. I. Roberts, went home after work one day during the elections and made homemade fudge brownies with walnuts and 170 adult doses of Ex Lax. He brought them to work the next morning for the guards who are against the union. Well, as soon as he sets them down on the table outside the sergeant's office, everybody starts grabbing them. Before you know it, the huge tray of brownies is empty, but D. I. Roberts forgot to tell the union officers not to eat them. The union pigs ate every one! The inmates and the non-union guards laughed their asses off—it was a very explosive day."

"How often do things like that happen here?"

"A couple of times a week."

"That must make it really hard to work at this facility."

"I just try to do my job and stay out of their way."

"Greg, you said that some of the guards feel that you were responsible for starting the riot. What have they said to you?"

"Stuff like. . .you know. . .I guess it's just their way of kidding around, but I didn't fire the first shot and that really gets to me."

"Where were you assigned that day?"

"Gun Tower three."

"Why did you fire into the lower yard?"

"Because Redmond had a gun in his hand, and he was holding three guards at bay in front of the pink stage. Someone could have been hurt, a guard—actually three guards—if I hadn't."

"Greg, Captain Walsh says that you are one of the finest marksmen in the system."

"I think I do okay for myself."

"But that had to be an incredible shot from Gun Tower three, that's more than two hundred yards!"

"Well, the mini-14 is a really accurate weapon."

"I know, but that's still quite a shot from that distance."

"It was nothin' special."

He sat back down. I didn't want to challenge Kimble with the details of the riot, at least not yet. He had admitted to killing Redmond and corroborated Walsh's story almost word-for-word. For the moment, I felt it was best that he think I believed him and accepted his story. I wasn't ready for him to tell Walsh that I had heard another version of the shooting.

"Well, that about does it. Do you want to add anything else?"

"No. Can I go?" Greg looked visibly relieved.

"Yes, you can go. We're done for now." I held out my hand as I stood to shake his, but he was already out the door. He never even looked back.

I needed to talk to Mark Wilcox again, but I remembered his comment about Walsh saying he talked too much and decided it would be best to keep our next meeting informal. I made a mental note to watch for him in the parking lot.

When I left the office, I was surprised to find that the Tarantula was not at his post as I expected. I assumed that he had just wandered off. However, as I rounded the corner, I spotted him and Walsh huddled together at the end of the corridor near the entrance to the building. Was the Tarantula reporting to Captain Walsh instead of the warden as I had suspected? The Tarantula nervously cracked his knuckles and rubbed his hands together as he talked. Am I overreacting—could their conversation be about something else? I slipped back into my office without being seen. I spent a few minutes straightening the two chairs and papers. If the Tarantula was supposed to be assigned to me, he was going to keep the office cleaned and water the plant. When I left five minutes later, both men were gone. I decided the Tarantula and I were going to have a little talk about his job duties.

I saw Eudon coming out of the warden's office as I was leaving the building. The smell of the fresh bay air started to calm my nerves.

"Hi, Matt!" Eudon's greeting was genuinely warm. "How ya doin', my good friend?"

"Much better than the last time I saw you! By the way, thanks, Eudon."

"Thanks for what?" he asked.

"Thanks for taking care of me yesterday when that inmate was murdered in the showers."

"You handled yourself pretty good, all things considered. Don't worry about it. It's cool."

"Listen, I heard Kenny Boyd was once an inmate here. Is that true?"

"Yup, he did a couple of years I guess."

"Something very strange and confusing is going on here. Captain Walsh says Redmond was shot first, but Mark Wilcox swears Boyd was hit first."

Eudon looked surprised. "If Wilcox says Boyd went down first, then he did. That kid wouldn't lie if his life depended on it."

"That's what I thought. Do you agree with him? Was Boyd hit first?"

"I don't know, Matt. It happened so fast. I've got to run. I'm on duty in two minutes, you know," he replied before bolting across the lot.

"Hey!" I yelled. "What time does Mark Wilcox get off work?"

"He's usually out of here by four."

I shouted, "Thanks! Take care."

As I watched him disappear behind the walls of the prison, my gut tightened. I needed more time to talk to him.

11

I jumped into my car, confused as hell about what had actually happened. The drive home, as usual, proved fertile time for thought—more questions than thoughts, actually. Why was Ted Walsh so sure that Redmond had been killed first? The question was particularly perturbing, given that Mark Wilcox had witnessed the shooting with his binoculars and swore to a completely different scenario. Wilcox had nothing to gain from lying. Walsh, on the other hand, was a suspect. Leslie had hinted at a grudge between Walsh and Redmond, yet that didn't explain the discrepancy in the two stories. Where did Kenny Boyd fit in? And why would Walsh want him dead? Granted, he had once been a prisoner, but from Mark's description, it didn't sound as if he had gotten into the power struggle or had enough juice to have given Captain Walsh a reason to kill him.

I was jolted back to reality when I was forced to swerve to avoid a head-on crash. A black pickup, traveling much too fast for the steep, winding, narrow road, had been in my lane. I couldn't see who was driving it because of the tinted windows. I tried to tell myself that it must have been a new neighbor, or a visitor, since they always took the road a little too fast; at least until they had a close encounter with the unprotected narrow shoulder of the road or another car. Yes, it was a reasonable assumption—and had it been anything other than a black pickup, I wouldn't have given it another thought. But it was a black pickup. I tried to tell myself that it was just a coincidence. I found myself checking my rearview mirror, just in case.

I parked and practically sprinted up the stairs. There was a note on the front door of my apartment. It wasn't very large. In fact, I almost missed it the way it was shoved between the doorframe and the door. However, its message made up for its lack of size. It said,

> Drop it while you still in one pieace and quit playin Serpico!!
>
> Keep asken questions and yore a dead man!!
>
> Stop the investigation right now or you will be dead by tomarrow!!!

The note was hand printed in black ink on a piece of a paper bag. In spite of the bad grammar and the child-like writing, I got the message. What bothered me more than the note was the fact that it had been shoved between my doorframe and front door. Someone had taken the time and effort to find out where I lived. My gut told me that the driver of the black pickup had left the note—probably only a few minutes earlier.

I had only received one other threat during my career as a reporter. I had stumbled across a drug lab and received an anonymous call at the *San Francisco Chronicle* about the wisdom of publishing an article. Thank God, the Federal Bureau of Investigation had apparently been one step ahead of me. The culprits were arrested before my story broke. Nothing ever came of the threat, although I convinced myself at the time to buy a handgun.

However, this was a different situation altogether. Neither the Federal Bureau of Investigation nor anyone else was working on this case. I was the only one treading too closely to the truth—I just wished I knew *which* truth was endangering my life. I could only suspect that Ted Walsh was behind the note. I put it in a sandwich bag, being careful not to handle it any more than necessary to preserve any fingerprint evidence, then slipped the baggie into my briefcase.

I couldn't settle down. I tried to read, watch television, get Sebastian into a game of find-the-mouse, but nothing worked. Even Sebastian seemed restless. Every few minutes I paced and peeped out the curtains to see if I could spot any unusual activity. I checked the windows one at a time. They were locked—which I already knew since I'd been checking them all evening.

Just before the Channel 8 news came on at ten o'clock, it dawned on me that I had seen a black pickup truck on other occasions. One had been outside Melody's the night I met Eudon. I felt certain it was the same truck that had almost sideswiped me at the Octopus Seafood Restaurant parking lot when I met Don.

I was going nuts! I needed protection. It took me a while to find my gun. I knew it was in a shoebox on the top shelf in the bedroom closet—I'd put it there after my sense of security had returned two years ago. Given my proclivity to store things in boxes, it took almost an hour to locate the right box. I finally found it behind a column of brown file boxes, sandwiched between old college textbooks that I had once thought would be valuable sources of information. Luckily, the ammunition was in the same box. I loaded the clip with the thirteen golden bullets that the gun shop's owner had given to me. Hearing the clip snap into place did little to restore my confidence or stop me from shaking. All I knew was the 9mm Smith & Wesson was ready to go. The same fog and terror I had felt in South Block engulfed me as I sat on my bed holding a loaded weapon, praying it would be a quiet night.

It was after three a.m. before I finally stopped looking out the windows. I wedged the back of my desk chair under the front door's brass doorknob even though I knew it wouldn't prevent a determined person from getting inside. Even so, it was comforting to know I'd have fair warning of an intruder. Certain everything was secure, I placed the gun by the lamp on my cardboard box nightstand. I didn't have to turn off any lights because I had done that several hours earlier. I had no intention of sleeping, but with Sebastian curled beside me, it wasn't long before I dozed.

I bolted upright at the sound of the first noise. Half asleep, I thought I must have been dreaming until I heard the noise again. I quickly put on my glasses and tried to focus. My hands were sweating as I slowly and quietly reached for the gun. I was shaking and clenching my teeth tightly to swallow my screams of fright. I was certain the person in the black truck was going to kill me. The curtain moved outward ever so slightly as though caught by a breeze—but I was certain I hadn't left the window open. *Oh fuck, somebody was coming through the window!* Without hesitation, I squeezed the trigger. The blast of gunfire shattered the silence. *Meeeoooow!* filled the air as Sebastian shrieked and leaped from the windowsill, flattening across my face as we collided in the dark. I grabbed him before he fell to the bed. There was no sign of movement at the window. Nothing. I waited several minutes, clutching Sebastian with one hand and the gun with the other. All was quiet. I must have killed the person trying to break in through the window. Cautiously, I crept around the bed to the window. I could hear the light rain hitting the roof. My neighbor's back light had just come on, providing enough illumination for me to clearly see that there was no one at my window or on the roof below it. I checked the glass thoroughly. The window was still locked, just as it had been when I fell asleep. The only difference was the bullet hole in the center of the window, inches from where Sebastian had been sitting behind the curtain. Shit, how was I going to explain this to the proprietor? I won't tell him. I'll call a glass company to come out and replace it at my expense.

Oh my God, I almost killed my cat! Sebastian was a wreck. I was a wreck. Both of us were shaking uncontrollably. I slid to the floor under the window, dropping the gun. Sebastian's claws remained attached to my body. Neither of us moved until it dawned on me that I should check him. I carried him down the hall and I turned on the bathroom light. As I rubbed my fingers over his shaking body, wads of hair collected and fell on the floor. Even though I was covered with cat hair, he was okay. On the other hand, our collision had left me with a long, bloody scratch on my left cheek. Sebastian's stare could have been apologetic or annoyed—it was impossible to tell.

Sleep was out of the question. It was too dangerous and I was too nervous. Instead of sleeping, I retrieved the large boxes of forensics that I had stacked by my desk and tried my best to go through them very methodically, page by page. The previous day's events had made me more determined than ever to get to the truth, but the reports seemed impossible to decipher. I made coffee and cleaned my glasses, then attacked them again. This time I discovered a very troubling photograph, a picture of the gun that was found on Redmond—a snub-nosed revolver, barely two inches long. Kimble couldn't have seen such a small gun from his post two hundred yards away even if he had been using binoculars like Wilcox. My hands started shaking. The notation on the back of the photo said that it was found in Redmond's left jacket pocket. The weapon had never even been drawn.

It was six-thirty in the morning. I had to talk to Wilcox before I saw Kimble again. After a hurried shower and breakfast, I raced back to San Quentin hoping to catch Wilcox before he reported to work.

I couldn't believe my luck. Mark Wilcox was coming up the stairs from the lower correctional officers' parking lot just as I parked in the upper lot. The calmness of the early morning fog was a stark contrast to my raging emotions.

"Mark!" I shouted. He looked up and waved at me as he climbed the stairs.

"What happened to you? You look like hell!"

"It was a rough night." I wasn't about to explain the scratch on my face—he could think whatever he wanted.

"Listen, Mark, I didn't want to officially call you to the office. I think it's better Captain Walsh doesn't know we're talking."

Mark's expression was both puzzled and confused.

"I've been told that the first shot was fired at Redmond and that it was fired by one of the top marksmen in this facility, Officer Greg Kimble."

"Kimble? One of the top marksmen? You must be kidding! Or joking! He's afraid of guns! We called him Tremble Kimble in the Academy. He used to get the shakes so bad during target practice that we were afraid he'd shoot one of us!"

"Is it possible that the first shot came from Tower three?"

"Yes. It's possible. *Anything* is possible."

"Mark, are you absolutely sure Redmond didn't have a gun?"

"He might have had a gun, but it wasn't in his hand. The captain had told us to keep a real close eye on Redmond, so I'm sure I would have noticed a gun if he had pulled one." Wilcox started laughing hard. "Kimble might have seen a gun, but I don't think so!"

"What's so funny, Mark?"

"Kimble! God, on top of being a lousy shot, the man is a certified space cadet and he can't see too well. The glasses he wears are about a half-inch thick. Matt, I remember on several occasions there were always these seeds lying around his gun tower after I relieved him. I spoke to the lieutenant about my concerns and he figured Kimble was just feeding the seagulls birdseed. On a hunch one day, I took some of those seeds and had them tested by the goon squad. Lab tests proved the birdseeds were *marijuana* seeds. That idiot was sitting in the gun tower getting stoned on duty! I probably shouldn't tell you this, but we played dirty tricks on him all the time."

"What kind of tricks?"

"Have you heard about the Amphibious Assault?"

"No, what is it?"

"One of the guards called Kimble's tower one night and didn't identify himself. He just said, 'Hey, Kimble, this is me. Look out there on the bay. Do you see those bubbles?' There was a long silence before Kimble said, 'It would be rather difficult to miss them.' The other guard said, 'We have a report that there are about twenty frogmen launching an amphibious assault on San Quentin to free the inmates from West Block. Make sure they don't set foot on dry land.' Kimble said, 'You can count on me, sir,' and hung up. The next thing we heard was about thirty rounds of automatic weapon fire. Kimble fired all thirty rounds of ammunition he had into the bay. When he ran out of ammunition, he panicked. He called the captain and started yelling, 'We have an amphibious assault on the southeast corner of the prison!' Everybody was sent out in the dark to combat the invaders. Someone who was running with an eight-seventy shotgun tripped and discharged a round. That was all it took. It sounded like the shoot-out at the O.K. Corral. Even the gunmen inside the building were shooting out the windows into the bay just to get in on the action. Two patrol cars responded to the emergency with their lights off and crashed head on into each other. It was insane! Kimble was so proud of himself when he went home that night. We didn't have the heart to tell him the truth. And by that time, we were afraid that if anyone found out how it got started, we'd all be fired."

"Do you think Kimble fired the first shot?"

"Well, he probably did fire the first shot, but I can't imagine why. I guess Kimble could have hit Kenny Boyd if he was shooting at Big Red. That I'd believe. But there was no reason to shoot at either one of them that day, as far as I can see."

"You say you were in Gun Post five. Could you see who was in Tower Three with Kimble?"

"No, Matt, the way the towers are constructed, you can't see who's in the other towers."

"Thanks, Mark."

"Sure. You're serious about this Kimble thing, aren't you?"

"I'm very, very serious."

"I don't know. It just doesn't make any sense to me."

Mark was right. It didn't make any sense. Nothing about San Quentin made any sense.

We talked as we walked, then parted near the drawbridge to the armory. I went to the Administration Building while he went through the two black iron gates to work. The Tarantula was not at his post. Within seconds of opening the door to my so-called office, I knew it had been searched. Not that it was ransacked, but things had definitely been moved around as if the office had been cleaned. Since the garbage and the ashtray full of smelly cigarettes were untouched, I doubted that the Tarantula had read my mind and added light housekeeping to his list of chores. I quickly checked to see if I had left anything behind that would have been of interest to anyone. My habit of relying on my tape recorder for notes had paid off again. Rarely did I write anything down during my interviews. Whoever had searched my office had left empty-handed.

I found Captain Walsh's direct number where I had stashed it in my briefcase and dialed it.

"Walsh, here."

"Ted, this is Matt Belding."

"What can I do for you?" He sounded bothered. I guessed I was wearing out my welcome.

Doing my best to sound nonchalant, I said, "I need to finish with Greg Kimble. Just a few loose ends, you know how it is with these reports. Is there any chance I could see him now?"

"Yeah. No problem. I'll send him over there in a couple of minutes. Is there anything else you need?"

"No, Ted. Thanks. Not right now."

Just as I hung up, the Tarantula knocked on the door. He entered immediately, cracking his knuckles as he asked, "So, like, got anything for me to do, Mister?"

If he were eavesdropping, I really didn't want him outside the door while I interviewed Kimble. "Yes, Tuttle, as a matter of fact there is. I need a rough sketch of the layout of the inside of the prison. Nothing too fancy. Take this notepad, stand right outside the door to this building and draw a picture of what you see."

"Yes, sir. But I can do that from memory. I've been here almost twelve years."

"I'll feel better if you're actually looking at the layout of the facility while you draw. Accuracy is very important."

"I can't."

"I told you—it doesn't have to be a good picture—just accurate, okay?"

"No, I mean I can't 'cause I don't have anything to write with."

After sending him on his way with three sharpened pencils and a legal pad, I waited impatiently for Kimble to arrive. Walsh said it would be a few minutes. Twenty minutes later the Tarantula was back with a crudely drawn diagram of the facility. Three minutes after that, Greg Kimble arrived. The timing made it obvious that someone didn't want me talking to Kimble without a spy outside the door. Maybe the extra time had been spent being coached by Walsh. Or perhaps threatened was more like it.

Greg was noticeably nervous and even more disheveled than the last time I had seen him. He looked and smelled as if he were in the throes of a hangover.

"I thought you said we were done. I don't have anything else to say to you. I told you that," Greg snarled and stared without saying another word.

"I know, but I'm a bit confused. Sources have told me that they doubt that you could have made that kind of a shot from where you were stationed that day. Some of the officers said you barely passed the firearms training course at the Academy."

"I do a lot of target practice on my own, sir. My shooting has improved since the Academy. I'm as good as any of the others now."

"Who was in the tower with you during the riot?"

"No one, sir."

"But there were two people assigned to each tower that day."

"Maybe every other tower, but not mine. I was alone."

"Greg, I have reason to suspect that the first shot fired didn't hit Clarence Redmond."

"What?" He looked up, obviously surprised.

"I have information that Kenny Boyd was hit first."

Greg stood and shouted, "That's fuckin' bullshit, man."

"Look, Greg, one of your fellow officers was using binoculars to watch Hendrix while he was singing. He says that the first shot struck and killed Kenny Boyd."

"That's not true!" he shouted several times, his faced growing redder by the minute.

"I have no reason to think the other officers are lying. Did you see a gun in Redmond's hand?"

"Yes or I wouldn't have fired." I took the photograph of Redmond's gun out of my briefcase.

"Look at this photograph, Greg. It's the gun that was found on Clarence Redmond." I raised my voice. "Here, look at it, now."

Greg eyed the photo of the Smith & Wesson Model 19 detective's special, a two-inch blue-steel snub-nosed revolver. "How could you have seen this small gun from two hundred yards away?"

Kimble kept staring at the photo.

"Talk to me."

"It was...The first shot hit Kenny Boyd?" He slouched in his chair.

"Considering the location and credibility of the witness, I believe that's the truth. Did you know inmate Browning, the prisoner killed in the showers of South Block? He was standing right in front of the stage and his last words to me before he died were that you were a dead man. I believe it was because he knew you had shot and killed Kenny, his idol."

"I can't believe that I—"

"That you what Greg? Speak up, boy, don't be afraid."

"He was standing there, right beside me, looking down there with his binoculars. He said, 'Redmond's got a gun. Take him out, Greg.' I was squeezing the trigger, slow and steady, trying to keep Redmond in the sights. He started screaming and yelling at me, 'Shoot him, goddamn it. Shoot the motherfucker now!' I couldn't stop shaking. Just before the gun went off, he slapped my shoulder and yelled, 'Kill the bastard!' When he hit my shoulder the gun jumped, but it looked to me like I had hit Redmond. I just couldn't tell from that far away." His shoulders began to shake as tears streaked his face.

"Who was in the tower with you?"

"I can't tell you that, sir."

"Who was in the tower with you? I need to know!"

"I think I'm gonna be sick." Greg had turned white as a sheet. Beads of perspiration dripped from his forehead and he was openly crying.

"Who was in the tower with you?"

"Everybody's gonna be fired over this, sir."

"It would help a lot if you would tell me the truth."

"I just can't do that."

"It was Captain Walsh, wasn't it?"

"No."

"Greg, you're not a very good liar. Do you want me to bring the warden in here? It was Captain Walsh, wasn't it Greg?"

"No, Sir."

"Then who the hell was it? Damn it, tell me right now!"

"It was Halsey."

"Who?" The name sounded familiar, but I couldn't place it.

"Jack Halsey, sir. He doesn't work here anymore. He was fired."

I stood and paced the small room while I thought about the latest revelation. "Wait a minute..." It dawned on me where I had heard the name. "Wasn't he involved in the incident with Don Barrett? He was one of the people who nearly beat Barrett to death out at the quarry. Am I right, Greg?"

"Yeah, that's him."

"But how the hell did he get into the gun tower if he had already been fired?" I leaned on the wall next to the bewildered rubber plant, flustered and confused.

"Well, he had a pass to get into the facility that day. I saw him get out of a patrol car. He was dropped off below tower three. I figured he was okay."

"You didn't ask him what authority he had to be there with you?"

"Why should I hassle him? He had a pass. He wasn't even driving his pickup truck—he got out of a facility patrol car that day."

"Halsey drives a pickup? Is it black?"

"Yeah, it sure is."

A black pickup truck! I wasn't just being paranoid after all. The idiot was out to get me—he was out for blood. "Who brought him in? Who gave him the pass, Greg?"

"I don't know. I couldn't see who was driving. He's a big buddy with Captain Walsh. Or maybe the warden gave him the pass. I just don't know."

"He's friends with the warden, too?"

"Not exactly...more like with the warden's secretary."

"Leslie Kirby?"

"Yeah, she lives with Jack Halsey."

"You've got to be kidding, Greg!"

"No, everybody knows that."

Everybody except me. Apparently, cock is her preference—at least for now. I was in a state of terrified shock. I started to get jittery. I had opened a can of worms that could easily get me killed. And the Tarantula was just outside the door, pretending to mop.

"Okay, you've got this guy, a visitor, in the tower telling you that he sees a gun in Redmond's hand. Why did you listen to him when he told you to shoot?"

"Because he used to be my sergeant! He was a damn good one, too."

"He was fired for trying to kill a fellow officer. Did you know that?"

"I don't think I want to talk to you anymore. I want an attorney."

He shifted positions in the chair and turned away. Although I couldn't see his face, I knew he was sobbing. I sighed. "Greg, I think you should get a lawyer right away. Don't talk to anyone—not even Captain Walsh. Don't tell anyone what we discussed. Just get a lawyer! Do you understand?"

"Yeah, okay." Greg's eyes were glazed and bloodshot as he stood. He looked weak and walked like his heart was broken as he left the room. I could only hope that he would take my advice.

Discovering that he had probably killed Kenny Boyd in his attempt to shoot Redmond was a shock to both of us. And with a visitor in his tower to boot! I wondered about his mental stability. He was really just a kid who became a correctional officer because he didn't want to work. Now he might go to prison for first-degree murder.

How could an ex-employee get into an armed tower at San Quentin State Prison so easily? I could think of one person who would eagerly help me find out. I decided to call Don Barrett as soon as I arrived home.

Once again, I left the prison with more questions than answers. I decided to take a detour on the Bay to try to clear my mind with a quick beer at one of my favorite spots in San Francisco—Alioto's restaurant, my cousin's place. The ferry ride to San Francisco would supply the sunshine and fresh air needed to recharge my inner soul. Since my cousin Cosmo would be tending bar, I looked forward to a conversation that had absolutely nothing to do with San Quentin.

Fisherman's Wharf was crowded with tourists, as usual. Walking toward Alioto's, the steam from the crab pots and the smell of freshly baked bread made my stomach quiver with hunger. I purchased a small loaf of sourdough filled with steaming hot red clam chowder. It was delightful and took me less than five minutes to finish.

I took the elevator to the second floor of the restaurant and felt more at ease than I had for days. The minute I sat down, my cousin began bombarding me with questions. Leave it to an Italian family to make sure nothing exciting happens to any of its members without the grapevine spreading the news. Cosmo had already heard that I was now, in his words, "a big-shot District Attorney investigator who was going to solve the crime of the century."

"Jesus, Cosmo, give me a break. I'm just interviewing some people and trying to dig up the facts. The governor's office will put it all together."

"Matt, you know I don't believe that for a minute. It's not in your make-up to gather facts for someone else. You'll have to put all the pieces together as you go, or it will drive you nuts!"

"Maybe so, maybe so."

"Let me give you a piece of family advice. The cons have their own rules and laws. They have a system of their own within our system. They also have a code of ethics that would rival the Vatican's. They would sooner take a fall than rat on each other. Hell, it's not just ethics—it's survival in a place like that. If you think that these guys are going to point the finger at each other, you're wrong and crazy. Take my advice—forget the interviews and hang up this assignment. It only takes a minute to pray and a second to die. Listen to me, cousin, some things are better left unsaid. You *capice*?"

Cosmo had a right to his opinion, but I was in no mood to listen to it. I had enough rage and fear inside me without him fueling the fire. I had taken the assignment and I was going to solve the case. Period. Instead of lashing out at him, I quietly drank the rest of my beer and left without saying good-bye. I felt like I had just been just been scolded like a little kid. His words stayed with me on the ferry ride back to Marin County and on the drive home.

As soon as I hit the door to my apartment, my orange, furry friend greeted me. I called the Glass Doctor to fix the window. It was my luck—they couldn't replace the glass until next week. Oh well, I had more important things to worry about. Like Mom and Dad. I wondered again if a thousand bucks a day was worth it as I phoned Don Barrett.

"Hello?"

"Don, it's Matt Belding." The beep of the recording device on my phone punctuated the silence. "Can you hear me okay?"

"Yes. You just surprised me, that's all."

"Don, listen. I'm recording our conversation. I need you to know that before we go any further. I've got a purely hypothetical question for you. Please give me the benefit of the doubt for a minute."

"Okay."

"Let's say that for some reason someone wanted to get inside San Quentin and they didn't work there. Like I said, this is purely hypothetical. If you wanted to get into San Quentin, but you weren't an employee anymore, could you still get inside?"

"Not very likely, Matt."

"But is it possible?"

"Anything's possible, but considering how Captain Walsh feels about me, I doubt if I could. Now...if I was on his good side, I probably could."

"How's that, Don?" I'd been right; it was the captain!

"The captain of the guard out there is like God. He can do just about anything he wants."

"Could a visitor under Walsh's authority go anywhere he wanted in the prison?"

"I doubt it."

"Could a visitor go up into one of the gun towers?"

"Well, that depends on who was assigned to the tower. Personally, I'd fire a warning shot and ask what authority they have to be approaching my post. I'd put the next bullet right between the eyes of anyone trying to get into my gun tower. That's standard procedure at that facility. Nobody is allowed in the gun towers or on the gun walks except the officers assigned to those areas."

"Would it have been possible for a visitor to be in the tower on the day of the bike show?"

"Sure, why not? They had bikers in the lower yard, why not visitors in the gun towers?"

"How could a visitor get into Tower Three?" I went into the kitchen to warm the coffee I had made earlier as I listened to Barrett.

"Well, you could come in off the bay in a boat, but that would be really stupid. By the time you got to the facility, there would be so many gun barrels pointed at you, it'd be like staring down a pipe organ."

"Matt, it would have to be some way that wouldn't be so obvious."

"I guess the easiest way would be to go right through the east gates."

"The east gates? The main gates into San Quentin?"

"Yes, depending on who's working at that time, you could probably get in without any problem. The west gates might work, too."

"I can't believe what I'm hearing, Don."

"Well, look at it this way, San Quentin was designed to be difficult to get out of, not to get into. Besides, the guys on the main gates are usually old-timers. It's a status job assigned by the captain—they get to deal with the public instead of the convicts. If it were somebody I knew or somebody who's got a little bit of a drinking problem, which most of them do, I'd take 'em a bottle of booze. I'd just tell them I'm going into the Administration Building to apply for reinstatement. You don't have to go inside the walls to get to Tower Three. All you have to do is turn left down the main road at the Administration Building, drive about three hundred yards, and you're there. If you walked in with the captain, there wouldn't be any questions asked."

I poured myself a hot cup of mud. "I still can't believe it would be that easy."

"You remember the girl that Wilcox was living with, the one who had been busted for fucking everybody and hooking?"

"Yes, Nikki Buckner."

"Well, the guards kept letting her back inside because she kept giving them blow jobs. The captain finally put a copy of her I.D. photo at the east and west gates after she tried to smuggle a gun inside to one of the inmates, so the guards wouldn't let her in anymore."

"Don, do you know anything about a grudge between Captain Walsh and Clarence Redmond?"

"No, other than the obvious. I mean, there's bound to be friction between a right-wing law-and-order type like Walsh and a big-time loser like Redmond."

"You don't know of any specific incident that would make Walsh hold a grudge?"

"No. Why?"

"Let's go back to the incident when you were beaten up by Walsh and the others at the rock quarry. After they left you, how did you get from the quarry to the emergency room at Marin General?"

"Well, that's a good question...I really don't know. I blacked out before they were finished beating me. The next thing I knew, I was in the emergency room in Marin General. I have no idea who found me or how I got from the quarry to the hospital."

"Who could have found you out there, Don?"

"Nobody I know—the quarry's surrounded by hills. I was told someone left me at the door of the prison hospital. When they saw what a mess I was, they called the ambulance to take me to Marin General Hospital."

"Did anyone witness the assault on you besides Walsh, Kirschner, and Halsey?"

"I don't think so."

"Was there anyone else in the captain's office at the time he ordered you to report to him?"

"No."

"Did you pass anyone while they were dragging you to the patrol car?"

"Just Redmond coming the other way. He was bringing in an armload of files from what I can remember. What are you getting at?"

"Could Redmond have carried you back from the rock quarry?"

"No—but, hell, he could have had one of his underlings from the ranch, even one of the guards under his control would have done it for him."

"You're telling me he had guards under his control?"

"Oh, yeah, you bet he did."

"Don, I'm beginning to believe there are a lot of bizarre things about San Quentin State Prison not too many people know. I can't even begin to imagine an inmate controlling a guard."

"Don't feel bad. I'm having trouble believing that Clarence Redmond may have saved my life!"

"Suppose that Redmond wanted to send a guard after you in the rock quarry. How could he have enough power over a guard to make him go fetch you?"

"It's pretty simple, actually. If you get greedy and bring in some dope just once, that's all it takes and the inmate has got you over a barrel. If you cease to cooperate with that inmate, he rats you out, which means he turns you in to the authorities. But you don't have to be a bad seed to fall in with a guy like Redmond. Some really decent guys end up working for somebody like Redmond. Can you keep a secret, you know, like off the record?"

"I can, but I think it's very important that everything we talk about be on the record. Let me hear it first, Don. If it's something that would hurt an innocent person or something that doesn't pertain to the investigation, I'll make sure it just stays between us."

"You know Sergeant Eudon, right?"

"Of course I do. Don't tell me he was working for Redmond, too!"

"No, not working for him, but Redmond got to him, too."

"Got to him, how?"

"Redmond knew that he was about as straight as they come and went right by the book. He couldn't bribe him, couldn't scare him, he just couldn't do nothin' to him. He really didn't need Eudon for anything, but I guess it was a challenge to Redmond. You see, Eudon's got this six-year-old daughter named Heather. She's that man's only reason for living. Has he shown you the pictures he carries in his wallet?"

"Yes. I've seen them all."

"Well, she came home from school one day with big tears running down her face. She said that a tall African-American man came up to her while she was walking home and stole her lunch pail. Three days later, Eudon's wife received an overnight package in the mail with a Sacramento post-mark. It was his daughter's lunch pail. Inside the lunch pail was a kitten with its throat slit from ear to ear. His wife got absolutely hysterical. He had to go home and calm her down. He didn't tell anyone about the incident. No one knew a thing except Eudon and his wife at the time. The next morning Redmond said, 'Hey, Eudon! I heard your little girl got a new kitty cat.' It took seven guards to pull Eudon off him. Redmond was laughin' his ass off the whole time Eudon was tryin' to clean his clock.

Redmond never asked Eudon to do anything for him that I know of, but he had proven that no one was unreachable or untouchable."

"Why didn't Eudon ask for protection through the system?"

"Protection, are you joking? These guys have contacts everywhere on the outside. The sheriff's department followed one of the guards around for weeks because he was receiving death threats. Finally, they decided that there was nothing they could to. They pulled the undercover officers off the detail. Four hours later, a white sedan pulls up beside this guard's car while he's driven' north on Highway 101 and bang! Someone blew the right side of his face off with a twelve-gauge shotgun."

After last night, I completely identified with his story. "Don, where do you get all this information?"

"Hell, Matt, that one was in the newspaper. You're a reporter. Look it up. You'll find it. Most of the stuff I've been telling you has been in the local newspapers or is common knowledge among the correctional officers."

"I'm not accusing you of making up things, Don."

"Well, if someone was trying to kill reporters, you'd probably take notice, wouldn't you, Matt?"

"Point well taken." Little did he know that in the last twenty-four hours someone had already gotten my utmost attention.

"By the way, how come you keep bringing up Halsey's name? Have you been talking to that idiot, too?" Don asked.

I sighed. "No, but he may have...I really shouldn't discuss anything about Halsey at this point. Please, just forget I mentioned his name."

"Wait a minute. Everything's starting to add up. You ask me about a grudge between Redmond and Walsh. I realize that Redmond probably saved my life, almost ruining Walsh's career in the process. It did ruin Halsey's career or rather—he ruined it himself. Come on man, what the hell's going on?"

"I can't say anything right now, Don. It's very important that you not mention anything to anybody either!"

"It's just about going to kill me not knowing."

"I understand. You've been a big help, and I really appreciate it. I've got to go now. I'll talk to you soon."

"Okay. And thanks for the courtesy."

"What courtesy is that Don?"

"You know, telling me that our conversation was being recorded, using that beeper on the line. I'm not used to that you know."

"What do you mean?"

"They record every phone call in and out of San Quentin, but they don't use a beeper. You don't find out until later that everything you thought was private is on tape."

"That's illegal."

"So is bugging the rooms where the inmates have confidential conversations with their attorneys, but they do that, too."

"You aren't serious, are you?"

"Yes. A whole bunch of people got in trouble over that one. The State Department made the upper administration rip out the whole system, but they still do it."

"How do they do it if the system's been removed?"

"I guess they figured that it took the attorneys fifty years to find the old one, so it will take them another fifty to find the new one."

"Are the phone calls still taped?"

"Yes, all of them. They keep the tapes for about a year, transcribe the important things, then erase and reuse them."

"Thank you, Don. You've been more help than you'll ever know!"

"You take care of yourself, Matt. I mean that."

"I plan to. Thanks, Don."

"See ya."

Tapes! I may have hit the jackpot! Sometime, someone had to have slipped. There had to be hints, if not outright confessions, just waiting to be discovered in those tapes. I couldn't wait to tell Sal.

12

I needed to call my good buddy and give him the great news. I picked up the phone and dialed his office. Sebastian was rubbing my lower leg with his head, so I opened a box of Kibble and poured him a bowl.

"District Attorney's Office, Sheila speaking."

"Sheila, this is Matt Belding. Is Sal in? Please, tell him it's urgent."

"One moment, please."

"Hey, Matt. What's up?"

"Sal, I need your help. I just discovered that every phone conversation in and out of San Quentin is recorded. Do you know anything about that?"

"Yes, Matt. That's pretty common. Police departments do the same damn thing."

"Have you also heard that the rooms where attorneys and inmates have confidential conversations are bugged?"

"That's old news and it's been handled already. All of the equipment has been removed."

"No, the equipment has been replaced with newer technology that's more difficult to detect, that's all."

"Who told you?"

"It doesn't matter who told me."

"Well, it matters to me, Matt."

"I'm not asking you to look into it. I'm just looking for some professional advice."

"For free, I suppose!"

"Of course, for free. If I could pay for it, I would have called a good attorney." I had forgotten how much I enjoyed our banter.

"Fair enough, what's the problem?"

"Sal, is there a legal way to confiscate all the tapes that are on file at San Quentin?"

"All you have to do is request them."

"That's the problem. If I request them, the ones I want are probably going to disappear."

"Are you onto something, Matt, or are you just being paranoid again?"

"Maybe a little of both, I guess. Is there a way we can march in with a subpoena or something to make sure I get every tape that exists in the facility? I don't want to take possession of anything illegally seized that might be thrown out of court."

"I don't know, Matt. A subpoena might be possible. What are you looking for—tapes of conversations between attorneys and inmates?"

"No, not really. I want the telephone conversations from the upper administration offices and officers' telephones, especially anything that originated from Captain Walsh's office. It may be a long shot, but it would be nice to prove that the people who run San Quentin considered themselves to be above the law."

"Matt, do you think Captain Walsh would say something incriminating over the phone, knowing the lines were monitored?"

"I think he would. Are you familiar with Captain Walsh?"

"I'm afraid so. I worked on the case a few years ago when he and two other morons beat up a guard out there."

"Which side were you on, Sal?"

"As always, I was on the morally correct side."

"How would you like to have another shot at Walsh?"

"What do you mean?"

"I am beginning to believe that, in spite of the front he puts up, he has a great deal of contempt for the law. Sal, the man sees himself as completely invulnerable and indestructible."

DR. GREGORY VILNER

"Judging by his past performance, I would say you're right. What could Captain Walsh be charged with?"

"Nothing juicy...just conspiracy to commit murder."

"Are you serious?"

"I think Walsh and some of his cronies from that case were trying to settle an old grudge. I think they put their heads together and plotted a murder. They went to great pains to carry it out in a way that would leave them blameless. Only problem is they killed a famous singer by accident. Now they're scurrying around trying to cover their tracks before they get into trouble."

"Have you talked to Warden Cooper about this?"

"I'm afraid to talk to anyone but you. I don't know who to trust at this point."

"I don't think you have to worry about him. We're going to need a lot of probable cause in order to get a subpoena."

"Sal, do you really think I can trust Cooper?"

"Go talk to him, Matt. Trust your instincts. If you feel like you can confide in him, do it. If not, call me back and I'll see what I can do."

"Thanks, Sal. Thanks so much."

"I've got another piece of advice for you, too."

"What's that?"

"Be careful with Walsh. During the trial with Barrett, I learned things about him that gave me the creeps. The man is cunning, merciless, and very intelligent. Be careful and watch your back from this point on, okay?"

"Funny, you're the third person this week who's told me to be careful."

"Listen, I want you to think about something. If you have any evidence that might incriminate Walsh, I need you to leave it with me as soon as you get your hands on it. I can lock it in the office safe. If you're treading on thin ice, it may serve as a good a insurance policy in case something happens."

"You may be right, Sal."

"Do you really think you're in danger?" Sal seemed genuinely concerned and that worried me. I used a hankie to clean my glasses.

"Well, I found a threatening note on my apartment door yesterday. Do you think you could have it checked for fingerprints?"

"Sure, no problem. What did it say?"

"That I'd better back off or I'd end up dead. Right now, I'm more concerned about one of the guards. He actually pulled the trigger for them and I'm more than a little worried about him."

"Can you meet me at Fisherman's Wharf for dinner about seven? You can fill me in on what's really going on." He paused for a moment and then added, "Off the record, Matt."

"That sounds good." An evening with Sal would be a welcome diversion.

"Great. I'll meet you at Alioto's."

"Thanks again, Sal."

"My pleasure, good buddy."

I kicked back on my bed for a couple of hours and tried to rest, then headed toward Fisherman's Wharf, which is about thirty minutes south of my place. Although I had been to Fisherman's Wharf a thousand of times in my life, I didn't remember it ever looking so vibrant. At night, the garish neon colors designed to distinguish each building were dazzling. The brisk night air smelled of fresh steamed crabs and sourdough French bread. I knew almost instantly why it had such an impact on me. After all the time I'd been spending inside San Quentin, I realized that these were the familiar sights, sounds, and smells of freedom.

I waited for Sal outside Alioto's restaurant, drinking a soda in the surroundings that always revived wonderful memories from my childhood. They seemed to draw me back to this very spot every now and then, this place I called home. Near the docks, sea lions darted to the depths of the bay then returned to the surface, barking at the tourists to feed their already-bloated bodies. The commercial boat lines, drooping and straining to hold the bobbing fishing boats, pulled against the aging railings of the pier, causing them to creak rhythmically like my father's favorite old rocking chair.

Home is a special place for each of us, but when home is San Francisco, it's that much dearer still. The fog was starting to roll in over the Golden Gate Bridge. As I stood there, the damp ocean air began to collect and drip off my hair. I couldn't believe the prison where I had spent the last few days shared this same bay. What a cruel twist of fate that San Quentin had been placed so near the dazzling City by the Bay.

Sal pulled into the parking lot across the street. His car caught my attention—the same yellow Volkswagen convertible he'd been driving for twenty years. We purchased VWs at the same time and we both still had them; his was a convertible and I had a hardtop. Although the car originally made a social statement against the materialism that obsessed many of his colleagues, the VW was now a classic, far more valuable than some of the German luxury cars.

That's the way it was with Sal. No matter how poorly he appeared to be doing at any given moment, he always managed to end up on top. We had been friends for more years than I cared to remember. I was reluctant to admit that middle age was hurtling toward us. As Sal strolled across the parking lot, I began to get a familiar and welcome feeling. Ever since we had been in college together, Sal's presence meant I was going to have a great time, no matter what we were going to do. He had an air of peacefulness, grace, humor, and ease in social situations I had never been able to master. He was, in many respects, my alter ego. Where I was withdrawn, he was gregarious. Where I was concerned about how other people perceived me, he was completely self-assured. Why did we always manage to let so much time go by without seeing each other?

I held out my hand to shake his but he brushed past it, trespassing through my boundaries, breaking my invisible protective barrier. He put both arms around my shoulders and hugged me so tightly I couldn't breathe.

In his booming baritone voice he said, "God, it's great to see you! How the hell have you been, good buddy?" He took a closer look at my face. "I guess the right question is what the hell happened to you? Exciting night in the sack, you little devil?"

"Yeah, in the sack." I'd never admit to Sal that I'd taken a potshot at my cat by mistake. As I tried to wriggle out of his grasp, he squeezed tighter and started bouncing me up and down along the sidewalk like going for a ride on a pogo stick. "Sal, let go of me for God's sake. I can't breathe!"

"Not until you loosen up a little," he replied.

"Okay, I'm loose, I'm loose! As a matter of fact, my teeth are getting loose. Put me down—please!" Relief washed over me as air filled my lungs again.

Sal stepped back to appraise me. With a smile, he said, "Yeah, I guess that's about as loose as you get. When are you going to start enjoying life? Did I ever tell you that you take everything too seriously?"

"Only a couple of thousand times," I laughed, since he had been telling me the same thing since the day we met.

Sal put his arm around my shoulders and together we jostled our way through the never-ending parade of tourists along San Francisco's most popular wharfs.

"God, it's great to see you!" he said.

"You're repeating yourself, Sal."

"Well, it is. I mean it, good buddy."

We climbed two flights of stairs to Alioto's elegant three-tiered dining room with its marvelous view of the Golden Gate Bridge. Every table offered a wonderful view of the bay, but Sal didn't wait to be seated. He led us to a front row table beside the expansive window. The lights on the Golden Gate Bridge were beginning to sparkle as darkness fell. Out of habit, I took out my tape recorder and set it on the windowsill next to our table. Rather than be offended or suspicious, the way many people would be, Sal looked at the old little machine and laughed in my face.

He went on to say, "I bet you still don't know your right hand from your left hand. I see your memory hasn't gotten any better." He laughed so loudly everyone in the restaurant paused to stare at us.

Before I could answer, our waiter arrived and immediately disappeared to fetch menus, which we would have been given had we waited to be properly seated. He was back in a flash. "I can't believe it doesn't offend you that I drag out a tape recorder while we're having dinner." It amazed me how he could be so incredibly secure.

"Do you remember our phone conversation? I said this would be off the record."

"Why should it be, Sal?"

"I know that you'd forget your name if you didn't write several checks each month. Besides all we ever do is lie to each other anyway—so what's the difference? You always tell me what a great time you're having, and I always tell you about all the cases I'm winning. In all the years we've known each other, have we ever said anything that could be even remotely be construed as the truth?"

I laughed at him. Thinking back, I realized that, as usual, Sal was right. I asked his permission anyway, "You don't mind if I record our conversation, then?"

"No, I don't mind, besides, there's a really nice looking lady three tables over, and the tape recorder is making her curious. Even if I did mind, I would be willing to make the sacrifice on her account."

I doubted whether she was interested in the tape recorder or anything else at the table besides Sal. His swarthy good looks, finely tailored clothes, and athletic build had always attracted attention from women. And my thick black glasses and large snout for a nose seemed to send them right into his arms.

Over the years he had developed an unintentionally malevolent code of ethics to handle their advances so that we remained friends. When the girls contacted him, which invariably they did, he would always tell them that he was not interested as long as they were still dating me. The results were swift and predictable. The "Dear John" letters would usually come within a few days. However, none of them had successfully courted Sal for any length of time. He was an unusual and precious commodity in San Francisco—a single, straight District Attorney—and he was as much of a *bon vivant* as anyone from our generation could be. Most of all, he was trying his best not to squander a very large inheritance from his father.

Alberto, a balding Italian in his sixties, returned to take our order. "Where's my cousin?" I asked.

"He left a few hours ago."

"Please tell him I said hello."

"I'll do that."

"I'll have the linguini with crab, prawns, clams, red snapper, and squid in the red sauce." Alberto suggested a Mediterranean salad with balsamic dressing and imported cheese from Italy to go with the meal.

"Sal, what would you like?"

"Pasta shells stuffed with salmon, lobster, and herbs and I agree that the salad would be a perfect complement."

"Well, Matt, are you going to turn that thing on and lend me the air of mystery I need or not?"

I made as much of a production as I could of pushing the red record button. Sal grinned and looked admiringly at the woman three tables away. When he winked at her, she winked right back.

"Sal, I'm really worried about the guard who acted as the trigger man for Captain Walsh and his buddies. He's not exactly what you would call sophisticated. I think they used him and that he's become a liability. I'm concerned they'll decide to make things a lot easier on themselves and get rid of him."

"Lower your voice. Who's this guy?"

"This is just between us for now, right?"

"Right."

"His name is Greg Kimble. He's the one who actually fired the first shot in the crowd of inmates. Well, let me back up a little bit."

"Please do."

"First of all, Warden Cooper made it his personal mission to rid San Quentin of the drugs that flow into the place. He did a pretty good job of it, too. The inmates who needed the drugs and the people on the outside who were supplying the drugs figured that they had to do something to get back into business as soon as possible. Someone, I'm not sure who at this point, came up with the brilliant idea to have a motorcycle show and a rock concert inside the prison walls on the same day. So, Clarence Redmond—he's the ex-inmate who was supplying the drugs to the inmates from the outside—set up a meeting with the warden and sold him on the idea. We're getting into heavy speculation now. I also think that Captain Walsh, who was really in a position to put the brakes on this whole event, saw it as an excellent opportunity. He could get the bikers (including Clarence Redmond) on his turf for a day, settle his grudge with Redmond by having him killed, and make the warden look like an incompetent idiot all at the same time."

"What kind of a grudge did Walsh have that would make him want to kill this so called biker?"

"Remember the case you worked on where Walsh, Halsey, and Kirschner beat up Don Barrett?"

"Yes, I do."

"Redmond was an inmate at San Quentin at the time this all happened. In fact, he was the most powerful inmate there. He ran everything from drugs to their form of prostitution to contract killings. He was also Captain Walsh's clerk. If it hadn't been for Redmond, Barrett would have died in that rock quarry. If he had, they probably would have blamed Barrett's death on one of the inmates or classified it as an accident."

"Why would Captain Walsh want to kill a fellow correctional officer? And better yet, why would an inmate want to save a guard?"

"Sal, I can't answer that question yet, because I don't have all the answers. I think it was just to show Walsh who was really running the prison. Anyway, Walsh and Halsey—that's the sergeant who was fired for the rock quarry debacle—decide to set up Redmond. Walsh puts the dumbest guard he can find in a remote gun tower and drives Halsey into the prison as an official visitor. He puts Halsey in the tower with this guard who's a lousy shot and can't see distances well."

"This is the Jack Halsey I busted for almost killing Officer Don Barrett a few years ago?"

"Yes."

"Right at the beginning of the concert, Halsey starts jumping up and down in the tower yelling to Kimble that Redmond has a gun in his hand and he's holding three guards hostage. Halsey orders Kimble to shoot Redmond."

"Couldn't the guard see it wasn't true?

"Well, the fact of the matter is there wasn't a gun at all in Redmond's hand. Plus, Kimble couldn't have seen the Rose Bowl Parade from that tower if it were right in front of him without a set of powerful binoculars."

"So, this guard Kimble tries to shoot Redmond right then and there?"

"Kimble thinks he has Redmond in his telescopic sights, pulls the trigger, but the bullet hits the famous rock singer in the head instead."

"Do you realize what you're saying, Matt?"

"That was my first thought too, Sal. It looks as if they had a fail-safe system built into their plan since Redmond was killed a split second after Boyd was shot. Someone else had his or her rifle up, sighted, cocked, and ready as soon as the first shot was fired. For all I know, they planned on Kimble missing the target. It's no secret that he's a terrible shot. I think they just needed somebody to fire first in order to justify everything else done to quell the riot. But I don't think they planned on Kimble hitting Boyd and bringing all this scrutiny on their heads. And I'll tell you something else, that I haven't told anybody. I think that the whole damn thing was the brainchild of the warden's secretary."

"What?"

"Sal, the warden has this sweet little Southern belle of a secretary.

Honey just drips from her lips when she's talking and just looking at her is enough to give any guy a hard-on. But let me tell you something—her heart is like an ice cube and she has rubbing alcohol for blood. She sat there, looked me in the eyes and deliberately lied to me the whole time I interviewed her."

"And you probably believed every word, didn't you?" Sal chuckled.

"Well, I did at first, anyway." That was the understatement of the century!

"You never change, Matt, do you?"

"Listen, I found out later that she used to be a guard there. She got in some scrapes and was having an affair with an ex-hooker, who was also a female guard."

"They had a hooker working as a guard?" Even Sal was shocked.

"Can you believe it? Anyway, the warden's secretary was in on this motorcycle show from the beginning. It turns out that she swings both ways and lives with Jack Halsey on his ranch in Sonoma County. Jack Halsey is still buddy-buddy with Captain Walsh. Also, Halsey was the chief beneficiary of Redmond's life insurance policy and he's the main man inheriting Redmond's drug empire. I'm dying to know just how large Leslie's part was in all of this."

"Matt, can you prove that Halsey was up in the tower with Officer Kimble?"

"You bet, as long as I can keep Kimble alive, I can."

"Can you prove that the first shot was fired on Halsey's command?"

"As long as I can keep Kimble alive."

"Can you prove that Halsey was there on Walsh's authority?"

"I believe so, as long—"

"I know, as long as you can keep Kimble alive. What do you want me to do, Matt?"

"Help me get the tapes of the phone conversations. I want all of them, not just the ones they want me to hear."

"When are you going to talk to Warden Cooper?"

"Tomorrow morning, I hope."

"Call me after you talk to him. If you don't feel that you can trust him or if you think he's in on any of this, I'll do what I can to help you get them."

"Thanks, Sal."

"Sure, any time. It sounds to me as if Kimble is your whole case, though."

"I'm not trying to build a case. That's up to you. San Quentin is a living, breathing, stinking unflushed toilet. The whole system is based on revenge, and there's no way anything good can come from it. The guards are the real prisoners and a lot of the inmates are nothing but victims."

"You're starting to sound like a liberal. What's happened to that cold, cynical person I once knew and loved, good buddy?"

"It's easy to be cynical when you don't really know what's going on. Our prison system is like a criminal training academy. If someone gets caught, they obviously weren't doing it right. We send them there to get better informed, better trained, so they can come back out in society and try again!" The anger that had been building over the last week had finally surfaced. I had a surge of emotion and barely caught my water glass before it went flying off the table as I gestured.

"Okay! Okay! Don't get upset. Put that energy into your final report and maybe you can change some people's minds."

"Actually, I think the Department of Corrections is painfully aware of their shortcomings. One of the guards said something that I've been mulling over for the past few days. He said that I should write a book about this whole experience. The people who need to know what it's really like are the voters and the taxpayers. They're the only ones who can change the way things are done within the system."

"Well, I'm glad to see you're not getting emotionally involved."

"Somebody had better get emotionally involved!" I was shouting. Suddenly, I realized that most of the restaurant patrons were staring at me. Awkwardly, I raised my glass to Sal as if in a toast and smiled.

"Hey, I'm sorry. I didn't mean anything personal."

"I know. I'm sorry. This whole thing is making me crazy."

"No, you've always been crazy, Matt. This is just making it evident to the rest of the world. Oh, shit."

"What?"

"You can turn off the tape recorder."

"Why, what's wrong?"

"Well, someone just joined my blonde friend over there. Looks like even my air of mystery isn't going to give me the advantage I need for this one, my friend."

"Don't you ever quit, Sal?"

"Never, the early bird always catches the worm."

Our waiter arrived with our salads. Sal insisted that we change the subject before we took the first bite, but not before he pointed out that I was taking things too seriously. He told me that if I weren't careful, I would be perceived as a zealot or a fanatic. Everything was a political process to him. In many ways, he was right.

Over a lifetime, there is often just one person with whom you click perfectly, a relationship that goes untouched by time and lack of contact. Conversations resume where they were left, in spite of the years that pass from one word to the next. As always, I lost myself in the conversation with him, the challenges, the victories, the defeats, and life's funny little things. We ended up laughing uncontrollably over things that probably weren't funny enough to warrant such behavior. But it always happened that way, and tonight was no exception. Our salads were tasty. The main course arrived with the white wine and more sourdough French bread. The seafood and wine were exceptional as usual. We ate in silence. Sal was only a bit perturbed that he didn't get to hit on the blonde.

Sal picked up the check, as he invariably did. I had learned a long time ago not to argue with him about it. It didn't have anything to do with his wealth; it was part of his personality. Sal needed to be in control of the situation without rhyme or reason. If he were down to his last dime, he would fight over the check.

As we walked toward the parking lot, Sal said, "Matt, leave your evidence with me. It's going to be important down the road in developing a criminal case and I'd sure feel better if you had an ace up your sleeve. If you ever need it, you can rest assured it is secure in my safe at work."

"You're probably right. I don't have the evidence with me but let's get together at the end of the week. I hope to have the case wrapped up by then. I'll get organized and give it all to you when we meet. In the meantime, can you have this paper checked for fingerprints?"

Sal took the baggie with the note in it and tried to read it under the streetlight.

"You can read it later. Suffice it to say, I'm taking it very seriously. Let me know if you find out anything, okay? Oh, by the way, I need a check. Can you have your office drop it in the mail to me?"

"No problem good buddy. By the way, how's your dad feeling?"

"The same. Right now, he's very sick from the chemo treatments. I'll feel so sorry for him."

A tear rolled down his cheek. Sal grabbed me around the shoulders and squeezed me like a bear. Predictably, he said, "God, it was really good seeing you again! I hope your father's health improves soon. Let's do dinner again next month."

"We always promise that we'll get together and we never do!"

"This time it'll be different. I mean it, Matt. You'll see."

"Okay."

Both of us knew that deep down inside for some reason or another it wouldn't happen. If not for my investigation, I probably wouldn't have seen him again for years. Some friendships are just like that—the mutual affection is always overshadowed by an indefinable need for distance.

He turned just before getting into his car. "Matt, watch your back."

Sal pulled out of the parking lot, his VW disappearing into the damp fog. I located my car and fumbled for the keys. Just before putting the key in the lock, I dropped them, something that seemed to be happening more and more all the time. I had tried to blame it on being thirty-five, or the cold, or on the ever-increasing number of keys I carried, even though I had no idea what locks they opened.

As I bent to retrieve them from the shallow puddle they were lying in, a loud blast filled the air. Shattered glass rained all around, hitting my head and shoulders. For once, I was glad that I wore thick glasses; they served as eye protection. People were screaming and running in different directions. I tried to remain calm. Out of instinct and a strong sense of self-preservation, I stayed in a crouched position until the commotion ended.

When it felt safe, I finally stood. All the glass on the driver's side of the car was gone. The passenger's side had five fresh pockmarks in the door. It was painfully obvious that I had been the target. A shotgun filled with buckshot had been fired from very close range at me. Thank God I had dropped my keys.

I walked around for a few minutes in shock, shaking, trying to find out whether anyone had seen who fired or had a description of the vehicle or a license plate. No one shared any useful information. As usual, the wharf was loaded with tourists but most of the people didn't speak English. They were practicing self-preservation. I called the police, more out of a desire to provide a report to my insurance company than to apprehend the offenders. I had a pretty good idea who was responsible.

Eventually I crawled into my damaged car, thinking that I needed to solve this case as soon as possible. I decided I needed additional help. The drive home was nerve-racking and cold. I couldn't stop shaking. I knew in my heart that there was a man in a black pickup waiting for a chance to kill me. Don Barrett's story of the guard killed by a shotgun blast on Highway 101 was repeating in my head. Instead of going straight up the hill when I exited the highway, I took side streets, constantly watching for lights in my rear-view mirror. Only when I was positive I wasn't being followed did I head up the hill to my place. It was the longest twenty-minute ride I had ever had in my neighborhood. I paused once more to look around at the top of my street before slowly working my way toward my driveway, constantly searching the shadows.

My relief at arriving home safely was short-lived. I needed to call a body shop and make an appointment to have my car fixed as soon as possible. As I walked through the front door of my apartment, it was clear that it had been ransacked.

I started shaking and felt sick. The floor was carpeted with paper, some torn, some shredded. The furniture was barely visible through a blanket of documents. My gun! Where's my gun? I had stupidly left it on the floor by my bed. Without paying any attention to what I was treading on, I ran to the bedroom. The gun was still on the floor. Thank God. But Sebastian was nowhere to be found.

"Sebastian! Sebastian!" I yelled. "Where's my furry little friend, baby where are you?" The kitten with its throat slashed in Eudon's daughter's lunch box flashed through my mind. "Sebastian!" I looked all around, especially in his favorite napping spots. "Sebastian! Sebastian!" I yelled again. "Baby, where are you? Come to Daddy!"

I finally found him on the top shelf of the linen closet. God only knew how he got up there.

The last thing I wanted to do was talk to the police tonight, but that's what I had to do. I carefully worked my way back to the phone. Just as I started to dial 911, I hung up. There was no use calling the police because of my cat's frenzy. I realized that while my desk was bare, stripped of every last thing as though a tornado had touched down, nothing else had been disturbed. I began to recognize the distinctive shredding and tearing of the papers on the floor. Sebastian had gone on a search and destroy mission.

When he'd first moved in with me, I amused him while I wrote by tossing crumpled paper balls at him. He would chase them throughout the apartment. When he got bored with one, I'd toss him another, creating a trail of confetti. Unfortunately, I had inadvertently taught him that any paper was fair game. I picked up the cat and carried him to the bedroom with me. He'd have to pay for his mischief by keeping me company all night long.

While sleep probably wasn't a real possibility, I needed to lie down. I'd been bushwhacked too many times in the last twenty-four hours. One more time, and whoever was trying to steer me off the forbidden path wouldn't have to worry—I was on the edge of a nervous breakdown. There was an urgent message on the recorder from my mother. I decided to call her before I got too comfortable, plus I wanted to know how my father was doing.

Mom blurted, "While your sister, brother-in-law, and the grandkids were over for dinner, two fat men with shotguns came to the door looking for you! I told them you didn't live here anymore. We all hit the floor after slamming and locking the front door. Your brother in-law grabbed your father's gun, then we called the police. What the hell did you get yourself into this time? Have you lost your mind?"

No, I am quite lucid. "I really don't know, Mom, but trust me I'll straighten things out."

"I hope so."

"Sorry this happened. How's Dad?"

"He's doing better. He wants to move. He says he wants a sheep ranch."

Sheep ranching suddenly seemed like a nice, safe job. "As soon as I finish this assignment I'll help him find one. I love you, Mom. Give Dad my love and tell him I'll be up to see him this weekend." After I put the receiver down, my head started spinning. I went to the bathroom and took two Valiums. I had to get some sleep. If I didn't solve the case by Friday, I promised myself I'd drop it before somebody in my family was killed—me.

13

There are mornings in the San Francisco Bay Area when absenteeism in the workplace can be directly blamed on sheer, natural beauty. The sun was shining brightly on the deep emerald foliage dotting the golden hills, set off by a crystal-clear, deep blue sky. The bay waters were calm and the temperature was sixty-nine degrees with no humidity. Life couldn't be more perfect.

The thought of returning to San Quentin, to be locked up inside the rotting bowels of that psychological torture chamber, made me feel cheated. Running my hand through my rumpled hair, I found another piece of glass. Last night's events didn't increase my desire to press on with the investigation, but the thousand bucks a day I promised my parents would them help them financially and I'd need cash to fix my car.

I kept worrying and wondering who the two men were and how they found my mom and dad's house. After checking to make sure there wasn't a black pickup parked nearby, I stuck my head out to take another good look around, then grabbed the morning newspaper. I was immediately blown away by the headlines: "San Quentin Guards Arrested in Marin County Drug Bust." I was flabbergasted to discover the guards were Frank Bezel and Greg Kimble. Frank Bezel wasn't familiar to me, but not in my wildest imagination could I picture Greg Kimble masterminding drug deals. The article stated that another unidentified San Quentin correctional officer was under investigation because the gun confiscated during the arrest was registered in his name.

I had to talk to Kimble as soon as possible. I threw on my clothes and ran out the door without a shave, shower, or food. On the way to the

Marin County Jail, which was literally at the bottom of my hill on the west side of Highway 101, I couldn't help wondering if I had completely misjudged Greg. As the wind blew through my open window, I wondered if I could've been wrong about him. Was he more than a simple-minded, childlike pawn in the schemes of his superiors? Were my concerns that he might be further used, possibly endangered by the devious minds that had led him to kill Kenny Boyd, wrong? These new developments seemed strangely out of synch.

Less than twenty minutes after I read the headlines, I was at the security desk of the Marin County Jail. The young woman behind the bulletproof window glanced at me as I announced, "I need to see Greg Kimble."

"Are you his attorney?"

It hadn't occurred to me until this second that I had no real authority to visit Greg since he was incarcerated on drug and weapon charges. For one fleeting moment, I was tempted to tell her I was indeed Greg's attorney, but I had recently experienced too much of the inside of a prison to try something that flagrantly stupid. Instead, I tried to sound very official. "No, I'm a special investigator with the District Attorney's Office."

I presumed that she could only have two responses. The first would be "So glad you could come. Please step this way." The second, and far more likely, would be, "So what?" Her actual response was apparently based on a desire to establish some sort of law enforcement-based kinship with me.

"That was some bust last night. You guys must have been surprised to find out your drug dealers were prison guards, huh?"

She had apparently accepted me as part of the Marin County Drug Task Force, the law enforcement unit responsible for last night's arrests. My unshaven, unkempt appearance, so popular among officers assigned to undercover drug details, ostensibly helped my cause. I wasn't about to clarify my role in the investigation.

"Yeah," I said. "What jerks! Working inside a prison and making drug deals on the outside. That's hard to believe, isn't it?"

She shook her head and clicked her obvious disapproval.

"I need to see your I.D. card."

I searched my pockets for the laminated card, and then realized I had left it behind in my rush to get out the door. The only other identification card I had was my press pass, which would have to do. I cradled it in the palm of my hand, using my fingers to cover everything except the picture and my name, and flashed it briefly at her. She smiled and nodded approval.

The metallic buzzing of the security door alerted me to pull on the big stainless steel handle. Something stopped me, though, before I crossed the threshold. My conscience and my newly acquired fear of prisons insisted I run through a mental checklist before I went beyond this point. I never said I was with the Marin County Drug Task Force. I hadn't misrepresented myself to be a police officer or lawyer. Any crime I had committed was only by omission. None of the charges that might be brought against me had statutory bails that were beyond the financial capacity of my bank account. Those considerations made, I stepped through the door and into the atrium.

My new friend smiled again and held out her hand. I stared at it, then at her face, for a clue to what it was that she wanted.

After a very long silence she said, "You have to check your weapon, remember?" Just then, the entry door slammed locked behind me.

I stammered something unintelligible and desperately wished I hadn't let the door close so fast. After fumbling under my jacket for a moment, I said, "I don't have my gun. I must've left it in the car."

She looked at me incredulously and shook her head. "You task force guys are really a different breed. You're out there chasing dangerous criminals, the ones that kill for the fun of it, and you don't even know where your guns are!" She was clearly enamored by the rumpled, unshaven character that routinely risked his life without giving it a second thought. If she only knew...

The buzzer on the second gate sounded as it opened and an enormous correctional officer on the other side met me. He was at least six-foot-eight and weighed no less than three hundred pounds. He was bald, of Latin descent and had a large white scar across his cheek. I was beginning to wish I had stayed home. Although I had lost the self-esteem and self-confidence to push on, I followed him into an interview room—an eight-by-eight cubicle with acoustic tiles on the walls and ceiling—painted the same color of green as every possession of the county government.

The graffiti on the walls provided a diversion while I nervously awaited his return. Most of it was familiar. There were big hearts with arrows through them, assorted names and initials, someone named Lucas vowed eternal love for Gina, a very artistic pair of entwined silhouettes proclaimed David's love for Ronald. Someone else had tried to connect as many of the dots in the acoustic tile ceiling as possible before being caught. He or she had succeeded in connecting more than I would have thought possible during any one span of stay. Other graffiti reflected the times. "AIDS Casual Contact Test Station Eight" appeared to be the most recent of those with fresh blue ink. In the space between the tiles someone else had written, "Do not write in the space between the tiles." My favorite, however, was the plea written boldly under the one-way observation mirror, "Every man here is innocent? Please let me out before I corrupt one of them."

I had set up my tape recorder and was starting to read the third wall when Goliath returned with Greg Kimble in tow. Before he got a chance to say anything stupid, like, 'What are you doing here?' I grabbed him and sat him in one of the only two chairs in the room. I thanked the officer profusely and closed the wooden door.

"What are you doing here, Matt? I told you before I don't want to talk to you anymore."

"You better talk to me now. You're in a lot of trouble, Greg. I don't think a jury is going to be too sympathetic toward a couple of San Quentin guards who supplement their incomes by dealing drugs."

"There's not going to be any jury. There's not going to be any trial because this is all bullshit, every bit of it!"

"I could be arrested just for being here, but I need to hear your side of the story first. I'm not here to get a confession. I just need to understand what happened. You're the weakest link in the chain of people who were involved in killing Clarence Redmond and Kenny Boyd. Do you know what kind of danger that puts you in?"

"I've been thinking about it a lot."

"Good. You did a big favor for some very dangerous people and I doubt they're going to show their appreciation in the form of expensive gifts."

"What do you think they're going to do with me?" Greg looked genuinely worried.

"I don't know." I wasn't about to share my fears with him.

"Do you think they're going to kill me, Matt?"

"I think it's a possibility. If the riot was actually a contract on Big Red, and Jack Halsey tricked you into pulling the trigger, getting rid of you would make life a lot easier for all of them. Right now, you have no protection. We're the only people who know the truth. If anything happens to you, what I know won't mean a damn thing. None of it would be admissible as evidence without your testimony. You have to help me so that I can help you."

Greg half-nodded, which I took to mean he wanted my help. He started crying, thick tears rolled down his face onto his shirt. I gave him the hankie from my shirt pocket.

"Look, my good friend is the District Attorney. I don't know what he will be willing or able to do, but I know he can help. I can't promise you anything but I can't do anything at all unless you help me, do you understand me? Do you understand what I'm saying?"

"I guess so." Greg stopped crying for a moment.

"All right, what happened last night? Greg, don't leave anything out. Don't hide a single thing from me. I need to know every detail if I'm going to be able to help."

"Okay." He almost looked relieved.

"Was this the first time you have ever been in on a drug deal?"

"No. It all started about three months ago. Frank Bezel—he's the other guard I got busted with—said he had this great idea. He asked me if I'd like to pay back some of the local drug dealers for selling drugs to kids and stuff like that and I said, 'Yes.' He wanted to set up drug deals with these guys, make it look good, talk about how many contacts we had and flash a lot of money. You know, like the real undercover cops. Frank's grandmother had this big white Bentley we could drive to make the deals. We would grab our off-duty guns and go out and take drugs from the pushers and dealers. Frank made it sound like we were modern-day Robin Hoods who would steal from the rich and give to the poor, like we were doing something really good for society. I believed him. We ripped off a lot of drug dealers."

"What did you do with the drugs you stole?"

"I asked Frank a few times how he got rid of the stuff. He was really vague. Said he'd ditched the stuff so that the drug-pushers would never get their hands on it again. I didn't press him, maybe because I didn't really want to know. I figured as long I didn't know, I wouldn't take a rap if he'd screwed up and given any of the drugs to his pals. At least I figured the drugs would be thrown out and that's all I wanted. Frank kept all the stuff and I figured he was dumping the junk in the bay. I didn't find out until last night that he wasn't dumping the drugs."

"What was he doing with them?"

"I didn't know any of this, you gotta believe me, Matt! If I knew, I would have gotten out a long time ago." Greg started crying again. "Last night one of the investigators told me that he was selling the drugs to the inmates at the prison!"

"Tell me exactly what happened last night."

"Well, it was like every other time. We set up the deal and the exchange with these guys at the Holiday Inn in Marin County. They were from out of town. We met them and they had the stuff. Frank checked out the drugs on the spot, like he usually does with his little drug tester. Then, like always, we pulled out our guns. We were starting to handcuff them so we could steal their drugs and money, when all of a sudden the doors to the room fly open and guns are everywhere! There must have been ten gun barrels pointed at my forehead. They screamed, 'Throw down your weapons and put your hands on your head.' They read us the Miranda Rights, then handcuffed us, loaded us into the police cars and brought us to jail. We gave up our rights, they questioned us all night."

"What have you told them, Greg?"

"I tried to cooperate; I mean, as far as I knew, we were on the same side. But every time I told them what I knew, they refused to believe me. They kept talking to me like I was behind the whole damn thing, like I was the mastermind behind it all, but you know I'm not. I just got all caught up in this bullshit."

"But, why Greg? You had to have known how dangerous it was going to be!"

"It was exciting, you know, and it was a rush like a new career. I really felt powerful. For the first time in my life, I was having a great time. I guess I figured I was doing some good in a way." Greg sighed and fresh tears covered his cheeks. "I never thought it would end up like this."

"Do you have any idea how close you came to getting killed last night?"

"Yes, I do now. When all those guns came out and they told us to drop our guns, my mind just froze. I wanted that Smith and Wesson model .38 to fall out of my hand more than anything else in the world, but my hand just wouldn't let go of it. I didn't know if these guys were really cops or just drug dealers. If they weren't cops and I dropped the gun, we were dead for sure. If they were cops and I didn't drop the gun, I was dead anyway, so I finally dropped it. When they put handcuffs on me, I was relieved they were real cops. I never thought handcuffs could feel so good!"

DR. GREGORY VILNER

169

"How do you figure the task force found out about you guys in the first place?"

"I think we were pissing off a lot of drug dealers and word got around."

"Why in the world would you want to do that?" I had underestimated Greg's stupidity. Besides being extremely shortsighted, I was certain he had some serious emotional issues.

"It felt kind of nice to get even with the drug dealers. They come into San Quentin and take over like animals. The only way to hurt them is in their pocketbooks."

We both jumped from our chairs as the door slammed open and bounced off the wall.

"The officer said, "Hey! What the hell are you doin' in here? Put your hands on the wall. I thought the guard was talking to Greg. Get over there right now," he yelled. "Now! Right now!"

Before I could begin to move, I was propelled and slammed against the wall, courtesy of the behemoth guard who had let me in. He roughly frisked me, letting me know he was not happy, then shoved me down the hall to lock me in a holding cell. He did the same to Greg.

The real Marin County Drug Task Force confiscated my trusty tape recorder. They were trying to decide what part of the California Penal Code they could make a permanent part of my virginal record. I hadn't impersonated a police officer. I hadn't quite interfered with an investigation. The only violation I could think of was trespassing on county property.

While they were deciding what to do with me, I tried to establish contact again with Greg. The holding cell I was in had bars on three sides with a concrete back wall. I could see Greg pacing hysterically two cells down. Between us was a man who appeared to be a frequent guest of the county. His clothes were filthy and tattered, and he reeked of urine and half-processed alcohol. Despite the presence of a bunk in his cell, he was curled up asleep on the bare, cold concrete floor next to a malodorous drain.

I called to Greg several times. I knew he could hear me, but he wouldn't answer. I was getting more and more frustrated and worried. I knew he'd been seeing a psychologist for alcohol problems and that he was close to going over the edge.

"Greg, listen to me. I'm going to call some friends to get me out of here. Then I'm going to try to get you out on bail. I don't think you're going to fare too badly when all the evidence is brought into the open."

Greg continued to pace hysterically. He never looked my way, but he did yell, "Go to hell, asshole! You caused all this shit to happen!"

"Look, this isn't as bad as it seems right now."

"Are you fuckin' crazy man? I killed a man. I killed a rock star who had a lot of very powerful friends. People loved him. Do you think that Browning is the only nutcase who would like to break my balls for killing him? Man, I got convicts passing me notes saying exactly the same thing that Browning said— 'You're a dead man fucker face' –and now this. They're going to hang me out to dry."

There was no emphasis in his voice, no inflection of anger or fear, no emotion at all. He just paced in the cell, talking in a frighteningly quiet tone of voice that cried for help.

I believe the most important psychological breakthrough of this century was the discovery of "self image." Whether we realize it or not, each of us carries a mental blueprint or picture of ourselves. It may not be consciously recognizable, but it's there, complete down to the last details. It has been built from our own beliefs about ourselves from our experiences, our successes and failures, our humiliations, our triumphs and the way other people have reacted to us, especially in early childhood. Once an idea or belief about ourselves goes into this picture in our minds, it becomes "true" as far as we are personally concerned. We do not question its validity, but rather proceed to act upon it, just as if it were true. I believe Greg was recalling years of negative self-images of himself.

"Matt, they're going to say that I'm a pathological killer, an alcoholic, and a drug dealer. What if I get put in San Quentin? Do you know how long I will last in there? Do you have any idea what those emotionally unstable convicts would do to me?" Even though the thought of incarceration at San Quentin terrified Greg, there was no hint of his fear in his voice. He continued to pace the cell. His weakened personality was far more frightening than his earlier bursts of emotion.

"Greg, listen. You were used. Maybe you pulled the trigger. Maybe you hit Kenny Boyd by mistake. But quite frankly, it was Jack Halsey and Captain Walsh who had the intent to kill, not you. You're in trouble for trusting the wrong person. You honestly believed that Redmond had a gun and you never intended to shoot anyone else. The rest of what you did was simply your job! That's all. You were just doing your job."

"That's not going to make any difference. I know one thing. I'm not going to San Quentin for murder one. They're not going to lock me up. I'm not going to give them the chance."

I knew exactly what he was saying and I was terrified. Hopelessness causes suicide. And at that moment, Greg Kimble had lost all hope that anything in his life could ever change for the better.

He walked to the back of the cell and pulled the sheet off the bed, then held one end of it up to his chest.

I yelled, "Greg, what the hell are you doing?" even though I already knew.

He pulled on the sheet with all his might. His face reddened, but the sheet refused to tear. I was relieved. Had the county found some type of sheets that couldn't be torn and were suicide proof? He held the end of the sheet up to his chest, his face reddening again, but still the sheet refused to tear.

"Greg, that's not what you really want to do. It's not going to solve the problem!"

"It's the *only* thing that's going to solve the problem!"

Greg looked around the cell, then walked over and slipped the center of the sheet over the sharp metal edge of the bunk. The sound of the tearing cotton softly echoed off the concrete walls. I was overcome by a sense of panic. "Greg, this is crazy! They're not going to let you get away with this. I'm not going to let you get away with this!" My shouts were going unheeded. "They'll pull you down from there and put you in a psychiatric ward at Napa State Hospital, and that's even worse than this place. Just put the sheet back on the bed and talk to me. Greg? Greg? Greg?"

He didn't respond. I helplessly watched as he looped one end of the sheet he had made into a rope through an overhead air vent and tied it in a knot.

"Greg, that's it! Stop it! That's enough, Greg! If you don't stop, I'm going to call the guards. Greg, listen to me! Greg?"

He was sitting on the top bunk fashioning a noose around his neck and then he removed it. I quickly figured out that I was not going to change his mind with my inept negotiations so I started yelling again. "I'm going to call the guards. I mean it!"

Actually, it dawned on me that I had been yelling so long that they guards should have already responded. Where were they? Why hadn't they already come to see what the commotion was about? I yelled some more. He pulled the noose over his head and then removed it again. I could clearly see now he was making his final adjustments. I could only hope that he was having second thoughts about what he was about to do.

I begged, "Greg, please don't do this. I promise you, people will understand that you were used. I'm going to help you prove that, but I can't do a thing if you're not alive to help me. Don't do this! Please, Greg, I'm begging you. Take that thing off your neck. Let's talk."

He continued to ignore me. Just as I was about to try another tactic, he leaned forward and propelled himself off the top bunk. I became hysterical. The sheet tightened and stretched, but stopped him before his feet touched the floor. He was swinging back and forth, spinning in a deadly pirouette.

I screamed at the top of my lungs. "Guards! Guards! Guards! He's hanging himself! Help! Help! Please! Guards!"

My voice echoed through the bare concrete cellblocks of the basement where we were caged like wild animals. "Guards! Guards! Please, God..." I had never been particularly religious, but I inserted truly heartfelt pleas into my screams. God, please forgive me. "Guards! Please, please, God, don't let him die. Guards! God, make that sheet break, make the air vent break. Guajardo! Please guards! Where are you mother fuckin' Guuaaards?"

No one was coming to rescue Greg. The cellblock was quiet.

"Guards! Guards! God damn it! Guards! He's hanging himself! Hanging! Guuaaards! Hanging!" My voice was growing hoarse. Much longer and I wouldn't be able to yell loudly enough for anyone to hear.

"Guards! Fire! There's a fire in here! Fire! Guuaaards!"

I looked at Greg again. The pendulum swing, which seemed like an eternity ago, had stopped. The spinning motion had stopped. From the glazed look in Greg's eyes, it was obvious that his life had stopped, too. I refused to believe that the only living souls in that cellblock were those of a wino who had not stirred through the death of Greg and my yelling. I had to try again.

I pressed my face tightly against the bars and tried to shout one more time. My face flushed; my vision blurred. I was mute with rage, then with guilt. I could taste the salt of tears.

I had failed Greg Kimble. I began punishing myself by banging my head against the iron bars. Why were they so cruel to him? How could we be so indifferent? How could someone so young be allowed to take his life in a jail cell without intervention from anyone? How could screams of "hanging" and "fire" go unheard? Blood ran down my forehead and burned my eyes. I sat on the bunk and sobbed, wiping the blood from my forehead. How much longer would I have to look at Greg's body, a symbol of failure framed in a dead person? When would someone cut him down? I had many questions, but no answers.

I wanted to call Sal, but it was a long time before the door to the cellblock opened again. Two correctional officers came in. The older one yelled back toward the door, "You can forget that third lunch tray today! We won't be needing it!" The guard started singing, "Another one bites the dust..."

I watched silently as they cut Greg down from the ceiling vent. I started to shake and begged them to let me call the District Attorney's Office. They ignored me. After they left, I curled up on the cold damp concrete floor and cried myself to sleep.

14

It took most of the day to secure my freedom. After Greg was found dead, people finally started asking questions. There was a ton of paperwork and millions of questions. I had the answers. Once Sal was finally called, I was allowed to leave the jail.

Driving down Sir Francis Drake Boulevard, I looked at the passing scenery in an entirely new light. I was on my way to San Quentin, true enough, but it was my choice to go there and finish the case, which I had started working on a week ago. More importantly, I could leave when I wanted to and never to set foot there again. I relished every second of freedom.

If I were sentenced to one year at San Francisco's Mark Hopkins Hotel on Knob Hill—that bastion of the good life with all the pampering and privileges the address implies except the ability to come and go at will—it would probably take me less than a week to begin searching for an escape route. I felt more empathy for the prisoners of San Quentin State Prison now than ever. Furthermore, San Quentin was not the Mark Hopkins Hotel. There were no privileges, just ridiculous little concessions earned through intimidation, humiliation and dehumanizing bootlicking labeled as good behavior. The greatest pampering any inmate could hope for was simply to be left alone once in a while.

I thought about the guards. Why had they chosen to be correctional officers? It didn't pay well, and there was certainly no prestige attached to the position. Why did they stay after they discovered what was really going on? Mark Wilcox had entered corrections as a dedicated, industrious, recently discharged Marine Corps veteran. He was the all-American boy from the bottom of his cowboy boots to the top of his tousled curly red hair. Four years later, he was divorced, fighting a constant battle against alcoholism, and living a life that consisted primarily of going to work at San Quentin, drinking himself blind to forget San Quentin, and sleeping it off so that he could return to work the next day.

Don Barrett had been a carefree, happy-go-lucky Southern boy, raised on the banks of the Tennessee River, where he fished, did chores, and inherited that region's love of common sense and good humor. Now, after being humiliated, beaten, and left for dead by the people he worked with, his aspirations were reduced to collecting news clippings and gossip he could share with anyone who would listen. He was suspended between a career that was a part of his past and a present life in search of hope or new direction.

Ed Eudon had somehow survived his tenure at San Quentin. At first, perhaps, because of the music and poetry he wrote and his young daughter. He had miraculously avoided the corruption within the walls and was finally approaching a state pension that would allow him more peace of mind than he had had in the past twenty years.

But most of all, I thought about Greg Kimble, a young man wandering through life with no idea where he wanted to go and accidentally got off at San Quentin. He had the mind and heart of a child. I couldn't erase the vision of him locked in his cell, fearful, hopeless, seeing suicide as the only logical solution. The frustration and anger I felt from being completely powerless, first to reason with him, then to intervene and prevent him from taking his own life, would stay with me until the day I died.

As I pulled up to San Quentin's main gate, I was overcome by disgust and sadness. The yellow and pink colored complex with its red tile roofs that just a week ago had looked like a country club to me, now looked like the cold heap of rock and stone it really was. Driving up the road to the Administration Building, I recalled the story Eudon had told me about the day, many years ago, when workmen, cheered on by inmates and guards alike, had taken chainsaws to the old hanging gallows in the lower yard. They had destroyed a symbol of the cruelty human beings inflict upon each other.

The hangings had often been cited as the most objectionable duty in every warden's job. They were neither swift nor specious. Back in the 1930s, an incident on the gallows became a legend. The condemned man was on the platform, blindfolded, seconds away from death. The three guards assigned to cut the thin cords holding the trap in place did their job, but the trap door refused to open. The gallows had never before failed to operate in all the time they had been in use. Not wanting to prolong the doomed man's agony any longer, the warden and a guard dove for the ropes leading down from the executioner's control booth. The guard reached them first and yanked on them frantically until the trap finally fell from under the condemned man's feet. Within minutes, they received a telephone call from the executed prisoner's attorney. He confronted them with the fact that they had killed a man whose case was on appeal due to new evidence that which proved he was not responsible for the heinous crime.

I hoped that someday I could return to watch crews obliterate this malignant tumor, San Quentin, once and for all from the landscape of the beautiful bay.

Warden Cooper had seemed curious about my request for the phone tapes when I called him just before I left the Marin County Jail, but he hadn't asked many questions. I had been able to secure the tapes without divulging my suspicions. Now that I thought about it, I wondered whether his suspicions were aligned with mine. He had said he had to leave the prison grounds for a meeting, but he'd have all the tapes waiting for me in his office.

Leslie Kirby, long since departed from my dreams, was at her desk when I arrived. She had replaced her gracious greeting and luring smile, which used to trigger my lust, with a cold glare that made me shudder. She must have known I would have found out she had used me like a ten-dollar whore uses a virgin boy for kicks. What a shame such beauty should be wasted on a malicious, conniving charlatan.

The tapes were stacked in the corner of Leslie's office: over one hundred, fifteen-inch reels in eleven relatively equal columns. Without wasting any energy on pleasantries, Leslie informed me that the warden had ordered a compatible tape deck installed in my interview office. From my conversation with Warden Cooper, I was certain that he hadn't told Walsh I was coming to get the tapes—but Leslie must have called Walsh as soon as she found out. She had probably already called Jack Halsey, too. I was sure the Tarantula was under orders to listen carefully and report back to Captain Walsh.

The Tarantula and I carried the tapes to my office. Each of the reels contained twenty-four hours of phone activity, each line recorded on one of twenty-four tracks. At least the tapes were clearly labeled with the proper dates, tracks, and lines. If I were going to listen to every minute of tape, it would take nearly six hundred hours per reel. I decided to start with track five, Captain Walsh's line. Most of what I was looking for should be there, but I needed to be careful the Tarantula didn't realize I was focusing my investigation on Walsh.

I asked the Tarantula to arrange the tapes on the left side of the desk, by date, from the oldest to the most recent. I loaded the first reel that he gave me. After many minutes of silence the first conversation played. It was severely disappointing. All of the calls that I monitored for the next two hours were Captain Walsh at his administrative best. He attended to dozens of little details as I struggled to stay alert. To amuse myself, and to make use of the blank yellow tablet in front of me, I began marking the number of times I heard, "Yes, sir."

The Tarantula appeared as though he couldn't have been less interested in what was being said. Now and then, he would doze off in his chair or stare at the ceiling and watch me doodle. After listening to several hours of conversations that went nowhere, I needed a break. The ashtray in front of me was filled with cigarette butts from the Tarantula. I took my glasses off and cleaned them. I had consumed enough coffee to keep me awake until Christmas and I was beginning to doubt whether I was ever going to find any incriminating evidence against Walsh. Most of all, I was hungry. My last true meal had been at Alioto's with Sal, almost forty-eight hours ago.

As he cracked his knuckles for the hundredth time, I asked the Tarantula if he knew where to find a couple of cheeseburgers. He suggested I lend him my car and he'd be glad to go to Burger King. We both laughed and agreed that the employee snack bar would be much easier. I gave him all my tokens and told him to get whatever he wanted. He was back within twenty minutes with a tray full of burgers and more coffee. Just as I was about to bite into the first burger, I remembered Mark Wilcox telling me that the inmates who ran the snack bar would spit on the food, or worse, if they didn't like the guard who had ordered the food. My mouth was open, poised to take the first bite, as I looked imploringly at the Tarantula.

"Don't worry, I stood right there and watched 'em make it. They didn't honk on it or nothin'." It must have been as common as Wilcox had said! Watching him devour his cheeseburgers, I finally bit mine, but with far less gusto.

As the night wore on, I realized it was possible to monitor three tracks at the same time. I would listen for promising tidbits, then, if I thought I heard something pertinent, I would go back and isolate that track. Anyone standing in the hall would have thought a big argument was underway in my office, but it kept me amused and awake. I continued to take tapes from the left side of the desk, listen to them, and then stack the monitored tapes on the right side of the desk. It went much more quickly than I had first estimated because ninety-five percent of the tapes were recordings of unused phone lines. By the time the stack on the right side was nearly equal to the stack on the left, I had uncovered nothing of any consequence. The Tarantula had long since curled up on the floor and had nodded off. I was fighting to keep awake.

I was ready to admit Walsh may have been smart enough not to use the phone lines from San Quentin. Oddly, something caught my attention through the three conversations playing at the same time. *I didn't know you were so hot. Let's switch phones.*

Although I didn't recognize the voice that asked to switch phones, I knew the other voice –Captain Ted Walsh. I ran the tape back to pick up the beginning of the conversation and played it again after switching off the other two tracks. The conversation was highly suspicious:

Captain Walsh here.

Ted, listen. There's a slight hitch.

Are you nuts? Why did you call me here? Captain Walsh sounded furious. You know these lines are monitored.

Nobody ever listens to those damn tapes, you fool.

The unknown man was unruffled by Walsh's tone of voice. *I don't care. You just stay at the ranch and I'll take care of everything here.*

I didn't know you were so hot. Let's switch phones.

With the mention of the ranch, I was tempted to believe that the caller on the other end of the line was Jack Halsey, but I couldn't be sure. They could've been discussing the ranch at San Quentin, the minimal security work program for inmates about to be paroled. But more importantly, there were obviously lines into San Quentin that were unmonitored private lines.

I searched the tape forward and backward on all twenty-four tracks, but couldn't find the balance of Walsh's conversation. The conversation was suspicious, but a long way from the hard evidence I needed.

The tapes continued to move, one by one, until I was almost back to the present. My watch told me the sun was coming up as I started another tape, but I could only imagine dawn breaking over the bay from my windowless vantage point. My sleeping clerk was motionless as I did a few stretching exercises before sitting down again. My eyelids became heavier and I kept nodding off only to wake sharply as my head fell back. I convinced myself that what I wanted wasn't going to be on the tapes. I was almost asleep when I heard a familiar voice coming from the cacophony on the tape recorder.

He knows exactly how it happened, you idiot. He knows that you spear-headed the whole damn thing. He knows you had the two convicts burned to death in South Block because they were trying to expose you to the FBI. He probably knows about Jack Halsey—

I almost jumped out of my chair. Damn it! Whose voice was that? The quality of the tape was fair to poor. People do not sound the same when they talk on the telephone. But I knew the voice was familiar.

Captain Walsh here.

What are you doing out there?

What do you mean?

I mean, what the Sam Hill are you doing? You left too many loose ends dragging around behind your ass.

Belding doesn't know a damn thing.

The hell he doesn't!

It was at this inopportune moment that the Tarantula started to stir. I knew better than to let him wake up and hear this conversation, so I quickly stopped the tape and replaced it with another. I held my breath and prayed that he would slip back into slumber land. Unfortunately, I wasn't so lucky. He sat up, rubbing his eyes then jumped to his feet with a look of sheer panic on his face.

"Did I fall asleep?"

"Gee, I don't think so. Think I did, though—I'm bored to death. Think you could round us up some coffee?"

"Uh, sure. You about finished?"

"As a matter of fact, I've heard all I can stand for now. Think I'll just turn the tape machine off and call it a night or a morning, to be more exact."

"Well, I'll start carrying the tapes back."

"What about the coffee?"

"Yeah, well, I'll get some, but I might as well take an armload while I'm going."

"No, I'm not done with all the tapes. Just leave them here for now."

I knew then without a doubt that someone was going to make sure I didn't hear anything that might be incriminating without it being reported, but to whom I wondered. The warden? Walsh? Or maybe the familiar voice on the tape? I knew by the Tarantula's panic that he was in big trouble if that person discovered that he had fallen asleep, which meant I had to worry about the tape being taken, but that didn't solve the problem of what to do with it. I couldn't take it with me. I had come straight from the jail, so I didn't have my briefcase to put it in, and the tape was too large to hide under my jacket. It had to be concealed quickly. But where was the question? I frantically searched the room. Damn it, there was no hiding place that I could see! Okay, okay. Where's the last place anyone would ever think of looking. Buried under the plant? No, the dirt might ruin the tape...

My gaze settled on the trashcan. That's it! No one had ever bothered to empty it before. I had no choice but to pray that the poor housekeeping routine would continue. I quickly shoved the tape into the bottom of the trashcan and covered it with the garbage from the previous days. I had no sooner finished than the Tarantula returned with two cups of black coffee. I hoped he couldn't hear my heart pounding. Maybe there was nothing else important on the tape, but I knew I'd never rest until I put a name with the familiar voice. Although I was exhausted as I walked out of the prison, my latest find had left me energized.

By the time I opened the door to my apartment, nearly twenty-four hours after I had raced out to rescue Greg Kimble, Sebastian welcomed me with a beseeching meow, a sure sign that his food bowl was empty.

As anxious as I was to return to San Quentin and hear the rest of the tape, I knew I'd never be able to solve the puzzle of the familiar voice until I had some sleep.

15

Nearly ten hours of sleep had helped soothe my frayed nerves, although I still felt numb and detached from the rest of the world. I had spent nearly all my waking hours over the last week in San Quentin State Prison. Never before had an assignment consumed me, yet left my soul so frustrated and unnaturally empty. I had totally convinced myself the tape would incriminate the conspicuously famous Captain Ted Walsh. Without it and Greg Kimble, I still had nothing significant to solve this case.

After lingering in a long, hot shower for an unspeakable length of time in drought-stricken Marin County, I had recuperated enough to call Warden Cooper to arrange an interview with the second inmate on my list. I had to continue, though I had learned nothing new and had no reason to be chomping at the bit. Since I had to retrieve the tape as soon as possible, I was thrilled to hear that inmate Parker was a trustee and could be interviewed in my office.

I rolled through the main gates at approximately 3:45 in the afternoon. The Tarantula was hovering around the Administrative building with a shit-ass grin on his face. He did not follow me back to my office. It looked like a bomb had gone off after my tape marathon yesterday. I started to sweat; all the reels were gone. I checked the trashcan immediately—sure enough the garbage and tape were untouched. There was a smile from ear to ear on the man's face. I quickly put the tape in my briefcase and closed the zipper, breathing a long-awaited sigh of relief.

I rushed to Leslie's office to ask what had happened to all the tapes. She said that Captain Walsh had taken them back for the District Attorney's use in another court case. I returned to my office thinking that was a bunch of bullshit. After gathering the wrappers from the cheeseburgers, the multitude of used paper cups, and the ashtray's contents, the trashcan was overflowing. I took it to the Tarantula and told him to empty it. My final act of tidying my office was to unplug and remove the tape deck from the desk and put it in a corner of the room on the shelf. I had just returned the second chair to its place beside my desk when inmate Parker knocked on the door.

"Thanks for coming in, Mr. Parker. I'm Matt Belding." I reached to shake hands but he kept his firmly planted in his pockets. "Please sit down." This time I didn't even bother with the tape recorder since I knew the cons weren't going to let me tape their conversations.

Parker was a tall, thin man around fifty. His skin was dark—a shade lighter than a typical African-American yet a different tone from most Hispanics. His glasses, even though they were prison issue, gave him a studious, intelligent look I had not observed in other inmates. Except for his blue denims, I would have easily mistaken him for a guard or other state employee.

"Mr. Parker, I'm with the District Attorney's Office and I'm talking with people who were in the center of the action during the riot. Will you discuss the riot with me?"

He nodded.

"You were in the lower yard on the day of the riot, weren't you?"

"Sure was. Just standing there grooving on the sounds, when all hell broke loose. People were dying all around me. I didn't want any part of that, you know."

"Do you remember where you were when the first shot was fired?"

"Right up by the stage where the music was real loud. I was watching Kenny Boyd, when all of a sudden he just like exploded. There was blood everywhere. I turned to see where the shot came from. I was looking over at Big Red's head and boom, he gets shot next. So I took off running. I wasn't standin' on a particularly choice piece of real estate, if you know what I mean. I headed for the safety of the yellow walls. In other words, I got the hell out of Dodge."

"Did you see a gun in Clarence Redmond's hand?"

"No, not at all."

"Did any of Redmond's men have guns?"

"I don't know. I only saw a couple of the bikers the whole time. I didn't see any guns. I try to mind my own business, you know."

"Did any of the bikers have drugs?"

"You better believe it. It was like Santa Claus had come to town. Things had been kind of dry around here, so everybody was looking to get what they could."

"Were drugs being distributed to the inmates during the concert?"

"Are you kiddin'? When the guards weren't looking, they were flying through the air! I'm not into that shit, so I didn't pay a whole lot of attention to it. It was kind of funny to watch, though."

"Go back to when the first shot was fired. What happened next?"

"Well, like I said, the first bullet hit Kenny Boyd. He was hurt real bad 'cause you could see the blood flowing out of his mouth and onto his clothes. The second shot came right after and hit Big Red, his blood and brains splattered across the motorcycles and the walls."

"How long was it between those two shots?"

"Not even a second. It was like bang-bang, just like that. Then it was like everybody just froze like ice cubes. Nobody made a sound for a few seconds. Then it sounded like firecrackers going off. Shots were coming from every direction. One of them went right by my ear. All I wanted to do was get the hell out of there."

"What did you do?"

"I ran toward the walls of the lower yard, where everybody else was heading. I tripped over one body, didn't even look to see who it was. I just raised my hands up over my head and headed toward the walls. There were people falling all over. The guards didn't know what to do. Some of them were trying to get to the walls, too. They were trying to help the wounded cons. These guys don't know shit about what they're supposed to do."

"What do you mean?"

"It's just that, well, they don't know what to do when somethin' like this breaks out. There was one guard, one of the new guys, he killed this con by trying to help him."

"Killed him?"

"Yeah. He was probably gonna die anyway, but this guard made sure of it."

"How?"

"This con was stabbed and he was layin' on the ground with the knife still sticking out of his chest. This new guard ran over there and started to pull the knife out. After he got about three inches of the knife out of the guy's chest, blood started spurting everywhere. One of the older guards says, 'Are you crazy? He'll bleed to death if you pull that knife out!' So this new guard says, 'I'm sorry. I didn't know!' Then he puts all of his weight over the knife and pushes it back in. The con let out one last groan and died. The guard killed him. I know he didn't mean to, but, Jesus, they ought to be trained to know how to handle these situations."

"What else did you notice?"

"These other two guards had picked up a con that had been shot and put him on a stretcher. They were running toward the hospital with him when another guard came around the corner and said, 'Hey, we've got an injured guard over here.' So they turned the stretcher over like they were flipping pancakes. The poor con hit the pavement face first, and they just left him there. There's no reason to treat injured inmates like pieces of shit."

"What were the inmates doing at the time all this was going on?"

"Most of them were just trying to get out of the way. Some used the opportunity to settle disputes. That's how come so many people were stabbed. The Mexicans, the ones that are part of *La Familia,* were trying to find someone from the A.B. to stick while they could and vice-versa."

"A.B.?"

"Aryan Brotherhood."

"Is there that much racial tension at San Quentin?"

"You gotta be kiddin'! This place is the worst it's ever been, and I been in and out of a lot of joints. It's so bad here the guards are even into it. While the riot was going down, there were three brothers beating up a white guard. He was calling to these two black guards to help him, but they just turned around and walked the other way, like they didn't hear him."

"Does that happen very often?"

"Well, not usually in front of the inmates. But I used to work at the employee snack bar. The guards' parking lot is right down the hill and I used to see a lot of it. They'd get out there, take their uniform shirts off, and beat the shit out of each other. We used to make bets in the restaurant on who'd win."

"What happened to the white guard who was being beaten by the black inmates?"

"Four whites, A.B.s, rescued him. That's the way it is. If I want somethin', I talk to a black guard. If one of the black guards wants somethin' done, they talk to me."

"Can you think of anything else you saw the day of the riot? What else was going on out there?"

"Well, some were still trying to cop."

"Do what?"

"You know, score drugs. Buy whatever junk they could before it was over. People were being knocked down. They got right back up and went back to doin' business as usual. One brother was making a deal and the guy he was dealing with caught a bullet in the chest. He just took the drugs out of the dead guy's hand and stepped over him to start a dope deal with someone else."

"The bikers were still dealing drugs?"

"Yeah, for a little while. When it looked like the riot was cooling off, they was giving the drugs away. They didn't want to get caught with the junk on 'em. Some of them were pouring the drugs out on the ground to get rid of the evidence."

"Mr. Parker, I'd like to explore your suggestions of racial tension between the correctional officers. Would you tell me more about that?"

"I don't get much into it. See, my daddy was black, but my momma was white. When he left us, she took me to the country to live with my grandma. A lotta times I didn't fit in anywhere. I look black, but I think white. Guess that's why I spend so much time in the books."

"What do you mean?"

"Well, my grandma, she made me learn to read, and she'd always be preaching how important book learnin' was. I didn't cotton much to school 'cause I always had to fight the white kids. My brothers and sisters were the only other coloreds in my school, and I kept getting in trouble because I tried to protect them from the white folk. Then one day I ended up in jail for fightin' the wrong kid. Been in and out of the joint ever since."

"What did you mean about spending time in the books?"

"While I was doin' my first time, I started to read. I found out I liked learnin', and I'd read everything I could get my hands on. I got my high school diploma back then. Ever since, I've tried to get assigned to the library whenever I'm back in the joint. Over the years, I learned a lot about the law, so now I help guys get appeals going and stuff like that. That's why they leave me alone."

"Do you mean the gangs leave you alone?"

"Yeah. See the racial thing here is big. The Mexicans and Puerto Ricans have *La Familia* or Mexican Mafia, the whites get into the Aryan Brotherhood, the blacks are into the Crypts, Black Gorilla family or Moslems, well, and they're all brothers. If you don't belong to a gang, you don't get any protection, and doin' your time can be hell."

"What about the guards?"

"Mister, some of the guards get involved in gangs, but I don't know too much about it." Parker paused and stretched in his chair. "And even if I did know somethin', the second-to-last bunch of people I want to be talking about is the guards. The last bunch of people is the gangs. So that kind of settles that, don't it?"

"Why is everyone so afraid to talk about the things that go on here? I can't get any cooperation from anybody, especially about corrupt prison officials." My frustration came through loud and clear. I wanted to listen to the tape.

"That's not so hard to understand, not if you got any sense. Some guys have tried to report it and some guys were stupid enough to go up against Captain Walsh with his goon squad, but they're not around here anymore."

"What do you mean? What happened to them?"

"The lucky ones get booted down to a lesser position than the one they had or maybe shipped over to Folsom to finish their time. There was this one inmate, a guy up in South Block B section, who wrote a note to the FBI. Well, the letter was intercepted in the mailroom. Instead of going to the FBI, it ended up on Captain Walsh's desk. One night when everyone was locked down, you could hear these two inmates swearing at someone or somethin' for spraying shit all over them. Then there was this rude smell of lighter fluid or somethin' like it. Next thing you hear is this big whoosh sound and about three minutes of screaming and yelling. You know, while those inmates were burning to death, Walsh walked up and down the tier, yelling something like, 'Get the fuckin' keys.' But, if you ask me, he wasn't making his subordinates haul ass to bring those keys up to that tier."

"Would you be willing to testify to that in court?"

"Testify against Walsh? Yeah right, with no proof that he was out-of-line? Are you out of your fuckin' mind? Nobody goes up against that man, nobody. Only person I know ever went up against Walsh was Clarence Redmond and you saw all the good it got him."

"If no one will help me bring Walsh down, he's going to just go on doing the same thing to other inmates for as long as he's Captain of the Guard."

I was beginning to agree with the inmates. This interview was exhausting. I was beginning to believe Walsh was practically invincible.

"People like Walsh will go on doin' that anyway. There's people like him in every prison I ever been in. They're always at the top or on their way. The one we got now breeds 'em. The rookies try their best to do the right thing. But before they can do any good, they either end up like Captain Walsh or they get sick of all the bullshit and quit."

After a moment of silence passed, I thanked the inmate for visiting with me and for sharing what information he had. He was gone when I looked up to ask him another question.

16

I had always put a great deal of faith in forensic medicine, in the ability of a good physician or evidence technician to reconstruct an event through the footprints that violent death leaves behind. In this case, though, the number of people involved, the number of weapons used, and the fact that the crime scene had been badly contaminated by guards made the task of establishing what actually happened virtually impossible. Since they were trying to get help for the wounded as well as maintain order, the three volumes of drawings and official reports were highly inconclusive. Although I wanted to believe the answers I was looking for were in these reports, no matter how hard I tried, I couldn't find them.

I needed to reach Sal, but he was out and I didn't know if anyone else in his office could be trusted. The only other person I could think of who could probably make sense out of all the evidence was Sergeant Tom Moss, a rather strange but incredibly gifted evidence technician with the San Francisco Police Department. I decided to stop by his office before going home to listen to the telephone tape of Captain Walsh.

I headed out of San Quentin with the stolen tape hidden in my briefcase. I didn't have to roll down my driver-side window because I didn't have one. I took a deep breath of fresh, clean bay air and enjoyed the wonderful sense of freedom that I'd recently began to appreciate. I headed to San Francisco to find Tom. The traffic was smooth sailing and the weather was perfect.

I parked my car next to the police cars and climbed the wooden stairs to find him. Tom lived in his own world for the most part, a twenty-by-twenty foot room on the second floor of the San Francisco Police Department's central headquarters. The room had been reduced to an aisle, barely wide enough to allow walking from the door to Tom's desk twenty feet away on the opposite wall. On either side of that narrow aisle from the floor to the ceiling were gray metal racks filled to overflowing with brown and white papers, photographs, report files, and samples of everything from expended bullets to splattered blood. There are very few people in the world who could work in such an environment, fewer still who would enjoy it. Tom was one of those rare people who would rather be at work than anywhere else.

After scanning the crowded room, I found him crouched in a corner of the office hooking something to a plant.

His greeting was more friendly than usual when he spotted me. "Get the hell out of here!"

"Tom, I need your help."

"You need *my* help? You should have thought of that before you said that the evidence in the Ryskamp case was handled by an amateur."

"I didn't say that! I didn't have anything to do with that news article."

"You work for that San Francisco newspaper company, don't you? You get a paycheck that has their name on it, don't you?" His face was turning redder with every word.

"Tom, I didn't write that article—"

"Doesn't matter to me. You're one in the same as far as I'm concerned. Get out of my office, Mr. News Reporter!"

I couldn't believe he was still upset about an article that had appeared in the newspaper almost a year ago. It was one of the worst jobs of reporting I had ever seen. The reporter wrote the extremely caustic opinions of the defense attorney into the article as if they had been handed down from God. The comment about the evidence had not been labeled as the expressed opinion of a desperate attorney for the defense, but as the observation of the amateur reporter.

"Tom, I've told you a dozen times before, it was an error. It never should have been printed that way. The *San Francisco Examiner* printed a retraction the next day."

"Oh, yeah." He finally stood, turned to me, and said, "I remember seeing that. It was right there in the women's section, between the recipe of the week and the bra and girdle advertisements. I'm sure everybody read it, Matt."

"Tom, look, that whole thing is history. It wasn't even between you and me. Please just forget about it." Hoping to change the subject, I pointed at the plant and asked, "What're you doing over there?"

"I'm hooking this rubber plant to a polygraph machine."

I should have known better, but I couldn't resist. "Having trouble getting the truth out of him?"

"See! That's exactly what I mean! When you guys don't understand something, you figure that the other person's got to be crazy!"

"I'm sorry, Tom, I didn't mean anything. It just sounds a bit weird, that's all. Okay? No more jokes. Why are you hooking a rubber plant to a polygraph?"

He put his hands into the pockets of his white lab coat and explained, "This isn't something I dreamed up. I'm trying to expand an old experiment a little. Look here—see these wavy lines on the polygraph chart? That's the plant's baseline response. You've got a baseline response, I've got a baseline response, this rubber plant's got a baseline response, every living thing on earth has a baseline response. Are you with me so far, Matt?"

It was everything I could do to keep a straight face. I sincerely hoped that he wasn't going to tell me that he could tell when the plant was lying. I clenched my teeth and nodded, desperately trying to keep my mouth shut.

"Good. Okay, this plant is aware of hot, warm, and cold energies that surround it, which affect its mood. You've heard of people who play classical music for their kids and plants, that kind of thing?"

I clenched my teeth even harder, took a deep breath, and nodded again.

"Well, this is the same principle. It's been proven that plants not only respond to certain pieces of classical music, but they respond to things like danger or like heat and it doesn't even have to be real danger for it to respond. Watch this." I watched as the needles on the polygraph swept slowly up and down on the graph paper.

"Do you have matches?" Tom asked.

"No, I have a lighter," I reached in my shirt pocket and started to hand him the lighter.

"I don't want a lighter. Just listen to me, Matt."

I put the lighter back in my pocket. This was getting strange.

Tom said quietly, as if he thought the plant could hear us, "Do you have something in your pocket that you use to light a cigarette?"

This was so ridiculous I couldn't believe it. It was like spelling I-C-E C-R-E-A-M in front of a two-year-old.

He continued. "That object that you use to light cigarettes can be used to harm this plant. Take it out of your pocket and use it."

I put my hand on the disposable lighter in my pocket. My mind quickly pictured taking it out and setting one of the leaves of the plant on fire. Before I could tell Tom that I didn't want to do that, the needles on the polygraph started jumping wildly.

"Tom, what the hell is it doing?" I asked.

Tom started laughing wildly. "You scared it. You scared the plant!"

"I didn't do anything! I just thought about setting one of the leaves on fire for an instant! Why is the plant acting like that?"

"It doesn't know how else to react. It thought you were going to set it on fire!"

I looked at him, disbelieving. "Bullshit! You've got some kind of switch on there or something. I don't believe the plant did that on its own."

"It doesn't matter whether you believe it or not. It did it. If you want to see something more interesting, watch this!"

Tom squeezed and side-shuffled his way across the room and dragged back another rubber plant similar in size and shape to the one wired to the polygraph. He set them about ten feet apart, and then ran out of the office. He came back a couple of minutes later with three police officers. They obviously weren't excited about helping him. In fact, one kept reminding Tom that it had taken almost six weeks for his hair to grow back after Tom's last impromptu experiment.

Tom dismissed it, saying, "That's why the department issues hats to everyone." The three finally agreed to help after being assured that no personal harm would come to them.

Tom sent the three of them into the hall. He had each one enter the room, pass by the rubber plants, and leave while I watched the slow, easy waves penned by the polygraph machine. Oddly, he whispered something to one of the officers. Each of the officers passed by the plant one at a time repeatedly, with no response from the plant hooked to the polygraph. I was curious, but getting restless. The case I was working on was more important than this far-out experiment. I impatiently watched as Officer Davidson entered the room again. He walked up to the unmonitored plant, ripped the leaves off it, pulled it out of its pot, broke the stalk and threw it on the floor. I was so surprised by his actions that I had forgotten about the polygraph test. When I looked back, the pens were scribbling in wild rapid patterns. The untouched plant was extremely upset over the fate of its neighbor.

"I'm impressed, Tom."

"Tell me when the polygraph returns to a normal, relaxed, sweeping motion, Matt."

It took several minutes, but the relaxed pattern eventually did return.

"It's back to normal."

At that moment, Officer Watson walked in, strolled past the carnage, turned, and walked back out of the room. Officer Hurley did the same.

There was no response reflected on the polygraph either time. But when Officer Davidson walked back in the room, the machine, or should I say the rubber plant, went wild! The polygraph needles scrawled wildly back and forth across the graph paper.

Tom was waving his arms wildly. "Do you see that? Do you? Do you understand the implications? If a man were killed in a room with a plant like this, the plant would know who did it! Like an eyewitness to a murder who doesn't know how to lie!"

Although I had seen it with my own eyes and understood the implications, I still had trouble believing what had just happened. "That's incredible! Did you figure that out yourself?"

"Like I said, it's a very old experiment. The first person who documented it was a man named Cleve Baxter. He was a special interrogator for the CIA. Later, he trained police officers in New York on polygraph techniques. It has been duplicated at every university in the United States, probably the world. The trouble is, his work was just the tip of the iceberg, and people have treated it like a goddamn party game. Nobody experimented or did further research on the rubber plant from that point. No one applied the science. Now that you have a grasp of the basics, let me show you what I'm trying to develop."

Fascinated by his work, I was curious to see what else the mad scientist had up his sleeve.

"Okay, let's say you have a suspect and you know he's lying, but he refuses to submit to a polygraph test. Or maybe you don't want him to know that you doubt his credibility, right? So you put a plant in the room and hook it to the polygraph, then you bring in the suspect and ask him questions!"

"Tom, are you trying to tell me that the plant will tell you when the other person, the suspect, is lying?"

"Yes and no. It depends on the questions you ask. At first, I thought that my theory was a failure. The responses were undependable and erratic, but that's because I was thinking like a human and not a rubber plant.

First of all, you have to understand that plants are completely nonjudgmental. A rubber plant doesn't care if you cheat on your taxes, lead a covert life as a drag queen or if you screw your neighbor's wife."

"Unless you use a condom!"

He grinned at my clever reference to a rubber, and then replied, "You're closer to the truth than you think. They react to any act of violence, any thought or plan of violence, or, this is the important part, Matt, any memory of violence. That's my theory. Plants don't have memories. Some people think they do, but it doesn't make sense to me. People have memories. Do you remember when you simply thought about setting that plant's leaves on fire? The plant reacted to you, right?"

"That's right."

"Okay now, the plant reacted to Officer Davidson, but was it reacting to Officer Davidson because it remembered what he did or was it reacting to Officer Davidson's memory of what he did?"

"What difference does it make?"

"It makes all the difference in the world! If the plant reacts to a person's memory of violence, the plant doesn't even have to be at the crime scene! If I ask you a question about some act of violence that you committed, your mind will automatically start to paint a picture in your head. You can't help it, you can't control it. Any act of violence will stay with you, very vividly, for the rest of your life."

"What if I try to ignore it?"

"That's even better! Here, I'll show you. Look over in that corner."

"Okay, now what?"

"No matter what, don't see a giant pink elephant. And if you do see one, just ignore him. What do you see?"

"A giant pink elephant."

"See, Matt. The harder you try not to see something, the more you see it. If I ask a suspect where he was on the night of a murder and he was in bed with his secretary, he might not want to tell me. But the plant tells me, by not reacting, that it means he wasn't committing an act of violence. That's all I care about. On the other hand, let's say a suspect was committing a murder, and he tells me he was in bed with his secretary. Maybe his secretary is even willing to substantiate his alibi, but the plant says, no way, baby, because the harder this guy tries to block it from his mind, the more the plant reacts. I know it's not responding to the other little transgression, because the plant doesn't give a damn."

"Tom, this is really fascinating. Thanks for showing me your experiment, but I'm short on time. Would you take a look at this report?" I struggled to pull it out of my briefcase. "It's the summary of the crime scene investigation after the riot at San Quentin State Prison. Could you help me understand what really happened that day?"

"Just leave it on the table. I'll try to digest it and get back to you next week."

"Thanks, Tom, but there are a couple of things I need to know right now."

He looked at the three volumes I had brought, then back at me. "I can't tell you anything that fast. You want me to scan a thousand pages and tell you what happened, *right now*? God, you reporters can't wait for anything. You'd rather have a half-truth now than the whole truth in an hour!"

Trying to calm him, I said, "Let me just tell you what I need to know right now, then you tell me how long you may need with the reports to make those few determinations. I'll leave the reports with you and come back to get the whole picture later, okay?"

His disgust was evident. "What do you need to know, *right now?*"

I had him hooked. "Okay, the first two people killed were Clarence Redmond and Kenny Boyd. They were standing very close to each other, one on a stage and the other on the ground in front of the motorcycles. I need to know which one was killed first."

Tom was looking at the ceiling, rubbing his chin with his hand. I could tell he was trying to get a vivid geographical picture of the scene I had just described.

"It may be possible for me to tell you that and it may not. It all depends."

I decided to strike while the iron was hot. "I really need to know where the shots came from that killed them. That's all, just those two little things. Then, I'll give you all the time you need to decipher the rest."

Tom was still looking at the ceiling, rubbing his chin. "Okay, I think I can do that, but it's going to take an hour or so for the report to be done properly. Probably longer because it's my lunch time."

"I can wait an hour. Look, I'll go get us some lunch, anything you want. When I get back, we can go over the report, okay?"

"I want a blood sausage."

"What's that?"

"Blood sausage and muenster cheese on white bread, lots of mayonnaise and pickles. There are only two places in the city you can buy it."

"Where are they?"

"You're a big shot investigator. You find them quick and then go get my lunch."

"Thanks a lot!"

"Matt, don't come back without my food."

It took over twenty-five phone calls to find a delicatessen that stocked the ingredients to satisfy Tom Moss' vulgar appetite. The nearest one was across the city in the Pacific Heights area of San Francisco.

By the time I returned to the police department holding Tom's lunch at arm's length, he was deeply engrossed in the report. He had about ten photographs in his left hand and was flipping back and forth to reference points he had marked in the summary report. Spread across the top of his desk was a close-up aerial photograph of San Quentin's lower yard.

Without looking up he said, "This is the worst piece of shit I've ever seen. I wish they had let me work this case. Five dead bodies, twenty or more injured, every blood type, and every weapon imaginable—some even homemade. Jesus, you spend your whole life waiting to wade into something like this! Then it happens in your own backyard and some-body else does a half-ass job."

I placed the lunch bag on Tom's desk and looked over his shoulder at the summary.

"Does that mean you can't tell me what I need to know?"

"No, it's all here, Matt. The evidence is there. The Federal Bureau of Investigation Crime Lab did the evaluations and nothing is wrong with their findings. It's just that the conclusions drawn by the state investigators completely ignore the facts. There are no logical reasons to support their conclusions. The evidence is right in front of our eyes. Tons of it—can't you see it?"

I sat next to him. "Then let's ignore their conclusions. Please tell me what you think happened."

Tom jumped up. "Evidence doesn't lie or estimate or approximate or guess! It's either there or it isn't. If it's misinterpreted, that's not the evidence's fault, it's because some people value their own opinions more than the truth. It's all there, Matt—even better than if you had a movie of the riot. Your eyes play tricks on you, camera angles distort the truth, but evidence can only tell the story exactly the way it happened."

He certainly was a passionate man. However, at that moment, I needed him to focus on a few very specific questions. "Tom, have you determined who was killed first? Was it Clarence Redmond or Kenny Boyd?"

Tom looked at the photographs, then a sheet with his scribbled notes.

"I don't know these guys by name." Holding up a picture of Kenny Boyd, he said, "This guy here, according to the database, he's victim C-1, okay? This unfortunate fellow is victim C-5," he said, pointing to the picture of a badly damaged Clarence Redmond. "Matching their blood types to the blood splatters on the front of the stage, the location and patterns of the tissue that were transferred from the point of exit of C-5's and the order in which those elements layered themselves on the front of the stage, the only possible order of contact is C-1, then C-5."

"In English, please?"

Tom reached into the bag, removed the foul smelling sandwich, and took a bite. "When this C-5 guy—who is this?"

"That's Clarence Redmond."

"Okay, when Clarence Redmond's brains came flying out of the place that used to be the right side of his face, they landed *on top* of the motorcycles and blood that were already on the stage. That blood was typed as AB positive. According to the FBI analysis, only C-1 had that rare blood type."

"That's Kenny Boyd."

"If you say so."

"Okay, so Kenny Boyd, C-1, was shot first."

Tom took another bite of the sandwich and nodded in agreement. The smell of his sandwich and the graphic photographs in front of me were making my stomach very queasy. It was all I could do to concentrate on what we were doing. Tom walked across the room to a small refrigerator. Reaching through a collection of recently dismembered body parts and fresh blood samples, he pulled out an open pint of buttermilk. He brought it back and set it on the desk next to the sandwich.

"You're not going to drink that, are you?" I asked.

He looked at me in disbelief. "You come in here, you interrupt my work, I drop everything to help you, and you're going to tell me what to eat for lunch?"

I turned away and started toward the window for a breath of fresh air.

"Get away from there, Matt! You open that window, the wind blows a couple of papers around, and ten murderers walk free because I can't find the evidence the D.A. needs to convict them!"

I turned back to the desk and tried to keep my mind on the questions I still had to ask. "Can you tell what kind of guns the bullets were fired from?"

Tom picked up a list of weapons supplied by San Quentin officials.

"Yes and no. The gun that killed C-5 was a twenty-two caliber and the bullet that killed him matched the ballistics test from this weapon, a mini-fourteen, serial number 768NG294. On the day of the riot, that weapon was issued to one Officer Gregory Kimble."

"Kimble killed Clarence Redmond? That's impossible!"

"No, it's not impossible. It's a fact." Tom pulled the map of San Quentin closer and drew an "X" in front of the drawing of the stage. "Now, looking at the place where the bullet entered and exited the body, the shot came from some point along this line."

He drew a line from the "X" directly to Tower Three, Kimble's post on the day of the riot.

"He didn't shoot Kenny Boyd? Oh, my God."

"What's the matter, Matt?"

"This kid, Kimble, committed suicide because he thought he killed Kenny Boyd, and it's partially my fault. I'm the one who convinced him he shot the wrong person. Who shot Kenny Boyd, then?"

Tom wrinkled his brow and scratched his head. "That's a lot tougher. Because no one found the projectile, it's more difficult to be exact. Judging by the similar size of the entry wound, the exit wound, and the fact that no one found the projectile indicates that it was a bullet of approximately the same caliber, probably fully jacketed, armor-piercing. It went through old C-1 here like an ice pick through a parachute, put a hole in the stage here, another hole in the back of the stage skirt here, and is probably ten feet underground in the lower yard somewhere."

My mouth was hanging open in astonishment. "Jesus Christ, Tom! What kind of gun was that? What did they use to kill him with, a guided missile?"

"No, it was probably another mini-14, but I can't say for sure without the bullet, and those bastards were too lazy to dig it up."

"Can one rifle be that much more powerful than another?"

"No, it's not the rifle. It's the projectile and the gunpowder. It's jacketed, in other words, covered by a thick hard brass shell so that it won't deform when it hits objects."

"Why would they use something like that at San Quentin?"

"Well, they don't, Matt."

I was completely confused. "They don't? Then I don't understand..."

"Somebody must have brought it in from the outside. The ammunition they use at San Quentin has a tunneling effect when it hits with a lot of impact. The bullets deform very quickly, tumble through the body tearing up everything in their paths, then exit another part of the body. The only reason someone would use a jacketed projectile would be to shoot through a car door, or engine block, or—"

"Or what, Tom?"

"Or if someone wanted the bullet to go through the victim and keep on going so that it couldn't be found later—no bullet, no ballistics comparison. No one could say for sure which gun the bullet came from. If you were shooting from a position higher than the stage, you could almost count on the bullet either burying itself or ricocheting off the ground and never being found."

"Where did that shot come from?"

Using a ruler, he drew a line that went from the center of the stage to Tower Two. "It was somewhere along this path."

I was astonished. "Whoever killed Kenny Boyd was in Tower Two! That makes it easy enough. Thanks a lot, Tom."

From the way Tom looked at me, it was obvious that I had said something wrong. He jumped up, waving his arms, shouting, "I didn't say the killer was in Tower Two, I said the shot was fired somewhere along the path to Tower Two!"

"But that line leads directly to Tower Two, doesn't it? What are you trying to tell me, Tom?"

"Look, Matt, this is a two-dimensional drawing of a three-dimensional world. I need more time to determine what elevation the bullet came from—then I can tell you exactly *where* it was fired."

I was too excited to listen. The line led directly to Tower Two. All I had to do was find out who was in that tower and I had Kenny Boyd's killer. I had all the information I needed. I gathered my materials and headed for the door. "Thanks a lot, Tom! I really appreciate everything. You've been a big help."

He followed me, saying, "Don't go off half-cocked. Let me do some more studying on that second shot before you do something rash."

I walked quickly toward the elevator. "Sure, Tom, whatever you say. Give me a call at San Quentin if you come up with something new."

"You've got an office there now?"

"Yeah, sort of."

"Well, well. Don't get too comfortable in some big fancy prison office."

I laughed at his comment as I waited for the elevator to arrive. "It's not fancy, Tom. I just have an old desk, a couple of chairs, and a big ugly pot with this tired looking old…"

"Tired looking old what, Matt?"

I ran back down the hall to Tom. "Why didn't I think of it before? That's the answer! You're a genius!" I kissed him solidly on both cheeks while a group of police officers in the hallway gawked at us.

Tom stepped back, wiping his face repeatedly on his sleeves. "Are you crazy? What the hell are you talking about?"

"Tom, I've got to borrow your polygraph tester. Please!" I was not above begging.

"Sorry. Not a chance."

"Tom, please. There's a rubber plant in my office at San Quentin. What better place to test your theory? Can you think of any place in the world that has more people with more memories of violence than San Quentin? Can you? It would be perfect!"

"But you don't know what you're doing, Matt. Besides, I can't let you run off with a thousand dollar machine. It doesn't even belong to me, it belongs to the police department."

Tom had made a grave mistake. I could tell by the tone of his voice that the idea of using the polygraph at San Quentin excited him. I knew if I persisted long enough, curiosity would overcome caution. "I won't let anything happen to it, I promise. I'll protect it with my life."

He was looking at the ceiling, rubbing his chin again. I knew from experience that was his body language for *I'm thinking about it, just give me a second.* He looked me right in the eye, and then turned and walked away, "No, I can't do it. You don't know how to hook it up or adjust it for baseline response or anything. You don't know how to interpret the plant's responses. No, I can't do it. It would be like turning a five-year-old loose with a machine gun. Forget it, Matt."

I ran up behind him, grabbed his shoulders, and turned him to face me. "You can teach me. Please. I learn very quickly. I'll do everything exactly the way you tell me! Tom, come on, please. This is the opportunity of a lifetime. Just think, Kenny Boyd was a rock star for Christ's sake! If your theory helps crack this case, just think of all the good publicity you'll get. Everybody will be talking about you and your rubber plants."

"Whatever, Matt."

"I'm telling you, this is the opportunity of a lifetime! You can't pass this one up!"

He started rubbing his chin again, started to say something, then stopped.

"What is it? Tell me. If there's a problem, we can work it out, please trust me."

He rubbed his chin harder, and then buried his hands deep in the pockets of his white lab coat. "I'm not going to let you use the polygraph. I just can't. But I can do something else that will work just as well for what you want to do."

"Sure! Whatever you think will work is fine. Please show me and I'll do it."

"I want you to understand that this is simply in the interest of science. I'm not concerned with publicity or anything else."

I was itching to know what he was going to do or show me. "Sure, Tom whatever you want. I can keep your name out of it—you can remain completely anonymous."

"Well, I don't want to be anonymous. I'm already anonymous. I mean, if you're going to give somebody the credit for this, I want it to be me. However, I just want you to understand that's not why I'm helping you."

Tom walked over to a big metal cabinet and pulled out a small black box with two wires attached to it. It had only one recording pen and a roll of graph paper attached to the topside.

"Matt, this is a psycho galvanic reflex meter, a PGR meter for short. It measures the electrical resistance of a person's skin. Its mechanisms are very similar in function to the part of the polygraph that I showed you when the rubber plant reacted to threat. Do you understand so far?"

I nodded enthusiastically. I would have agreed with anything at that moment—even eating the rest of the blood sausage and Muenster cheese sandwich and washing it down with buttermilk—to get my hands on that little black box.

Tom continued, "The only bad thing about this particular unit is that the tracing pen is a little noisy. Here, I'll show you." Tom attached the sensors to the rubber plant. "You need to adjust the sensitivity like this until you get a baseline reading on the paper. Give me your lighter, Matt."

As he threatened the plant with my lighter, the pen began scrawling all over the graph-paper making a light noise similar to the grinding sound of an old computer searching for information on a floppy disk. It was audible, but certainly not objectionable.

"It's perfect! I'll take it."

He disconnected the PGR meter, packed it into a box, surrounded it with plastic foam, and handed it to me. "Thanks, Tom. I owe you one," I said before racing down the hall to the elevators. I was too anxious to get back to San Quentin and test Tom's theory to worry about listening to the tape I stolen first. Tom was still calling instructions and warnings as the elevator doors closed.

17

Although less than an hour passed, it seemed like it took forever to drive back to San Quentin. Dread made my stomach sour, but I was more anxious to get there than I was the first day. At every red light along the way, I frantically searched my car for the July fourth duty roster, which I knew were somewhere in the boxes of documentation.

I parked my car and ran up the stairs to the Administration Building as I reviewed the roster. When I flung open Leslie Kirby's office door, she looked like she had just awoke, her hair was a mess and her clothes were wrinkled. She appeared like the tramp that she really was.

"Please, get Roy McCoy down here, now!" I was shocked at the authoritative tone of my voice. Without giving her a chance to reply, I went to my office. The small room was still littered and the rubber plant was drooping badly in the corner. Would this rubber plant be forgiving enough to serve me after all the indignities I had heaped upon it? I had repeatedly knocked it over, poured cold coffee over its roots because it was faster than going to the water fountain and ignored it when it was obviously calling for deliverance. I noticed the Tarantula at the other end of the hallway when I left to fetch a cup of water for the plant. I hoped he would keep his distance.

I bent to hook the PGR meter to the rubber plant exactly the way Tom had shown me. "Okay, Sherlock, you help me and I promise you I'll find a way to get you out of here. I have a great apartment in mind with a big picture window, a view of the San Francisco Bay and the Golden Gate Bridge, plus lots of sunshine and plant food. Do this right and I promise to spring you from this joint."

I wanted to get at the truth so desperately I was talking to a plant. What's worse, I was trying to bribe it with a window spot in my apartment. If, as Tom believed, this plant could read my mind, it would know that I was full of shit. But still, it was worth a try.

I scooted the plant close to the credenza, ran the wires from the sensors to the black box, adjusted the sensitivity control exactly the way Tom had shown me, and checked to make sure there was plenty of graph paper on the spool. I placed the heavy mechanism inside the credenza and closed the door.

Wringing my hands and sneering in a self-satisfied manner, I sat at the desk to await the arrival of my first suspect. He was one of the two guards who had been assigned to Tower Two on the day of the riot. Perhaps Officer Roy McCoy thought he would never have to answer for his crime, but he had no idea that within a matter of minutes, Sherlock Houseplant was going to do him in.

I was certain that Officer McCoy was either guilty of or had first-hand knowledge of the criminal activity that ended Kenny Boyd's life. I had virtually ignored the Miranda card since the day it was given to me, but I pulled it out of my briefcase and placed it on the desk.

Officer Roy McCoy walked in and seemed to be a pleasant enough fellow, but my experiences with the likes of Captain Walsh had taught me not to rely on impressions. "Good afternoon, Officer McCoy, I'm Matt Belding. I'm investigating the riot, and would like to ask you some questions. Your cooperation in this matter is entirely voluntary, but anything discovered during this investigation will be included in the report to the Governor's office. All evidence discovered could be used by the District Attorney's Office to file criminal charges against you if found guilty. You have the right to have counsel present during questioning, and if you can't afford an attorney, one will be provided for you. Do you understand those rights?"

"Yes." Roy McCoy looked confused to say the least. His eyes continuously shifted from left to right.

"Are you willing to answer a few questions concerning the events of July fourth, the day of the riot?"

"Sure, why not."

"What was your assignment that day?"

"Gun Tower Two."

"What did you see or hear that day?"

"Well, we didn't see anything, really."

"What do you mean? You were in the tower watching, weren't you?" No more fooling around. I was on my way to the bottom of this vile mess. "You must have seen something!"

"Well, John and I were—"

"John. Is that Officer Johnson?"

"Yeah, Officer John Johnson. He was assigned to the same tower that day."

"Go on."

Officer McCoy started scratching his head.

"Well, it took a while before John and I realized what was going on. We were—well, Jesus, I don't know what to tell you. If I tell you everything that happened that day, I'm probably going to lose my job."

"Officer McCoy, all this is going to come out eventually. You might as well tell me now. Sometimes it's better to get things out in the open and pay for the consequences up front rather than let something haunt you for the rest of your life."

"Damn, it wasn't that bad! Certainly not something that's going to haunt me for the rest of my life. It's over and done. There's not a whole lot I can do to change what we did, but I don't want to lose my job over it. This is the best job I ever had, you know? I don't think what we did is enough to give up our jobs."

What a cold bastard! I couldn't believe this idiot. He kills somebody and thinks he can still keep his job!

"Listen, McCoy. We're talking about a man's life here, and you're worried about a fuckin' job?"

"What the hell are you talking about?" McCoy jumped up and slammed his fist on the desk.

I shouted, "McCoy, I'm talking about snuffing a rock star!"

"You're fuckin' nuts, Mr. Investigator! You must be out of your mind! I'm talking about the naked girl on the boat."

"What...what do you mean?" It was my turn to be shocked.

"We were up in the tower, and this girl came by on a sailboat—one of the boats from the yacht club. I guess she heard the music and got curious. She brought her boat almost in to the sandy beach of San Quentin. We got on the bullhorn and told her she was too close to San Quentin property, and she had to move on. She shook her head no, so we told her again. Instead of starting the motor and backing the boat up, she dropped anchor and took the top of her bikini off. She had a great set of lungs. We were standing up in the tower, taking turns watching her through the binoculars and listening to the music. That's why we didn't even look at what was going on in the lower yard until we heard the first shot fired. We didn't snuff out a singer, that's for sure. The riot was over so quick I didn't even have time to grab my gun."

"That's a real good story, Roy. Is your friend John going to have the same exact story?" His feeble attempt at lying made me furious.

"He will, if he decides to tell you the truth, but I don't think he's going to even bother talking to you."

"Why do you say that, Roy?"

"Because he doesn't put up with crazy people like you. If you accuse John of shooting somebody, you better have someone a lot bigger than you in this office."

"Why is that?"

"'Cause he'll jump over that desk and kick your fuckin' ass, that's why!"

"The forensic reports show that the shot that killed Kenny Boyd came from Tower Two."

"Then your forensics report is wrong!" McCoy shouted. "Get off my fuckin' back, Mr. Investigator!" He rose, started pacing, and then opened the office door.

"Where you going?"

"I'm leaving before I decide to kick your fuckin' ass myself. I probably would get fired, but it just might be worth it."

"Officer McCoy, I'm not finished here." I followed him into the hall.

"Fuck you, asshole Investigator!"

"Warden Cooper has pledged the cooperation of the guards in my investigation and—"

"Fuck the warden, too!" he shouted as he headed out the wooden doors.

I knew I had the goods on this guy and his partner. Talk about political corruption, what a grafter. His warning about his partner didn't scare me, by God! I had the forensics report. I had concrete evidence that the gunshot that killed Kenny Boyd came from Tower Two. And I had my rubber plant. My God, the rubber plant!

I spun in my chair and opened the credenza door. The PGR meter had recorded five minutes of baseline response. There wasn't any sign of reaction or violence until the very end. Either Tom's theory was garbage or I had hooked the machine up wrong. The little peak at the end of the graph paper, though, made me wonder if he had been serious about kicking my ass.

So the plant did react somewhat to the present thought of violence, but sensing memories still remained the unproven theory of a man whose brilliance and imagination walked a very fine line between genius and insanity. At the moment, I was somewhat confused and thoroughly disappointed in Sherlock Houseplant's performance. On the other hand, it could be this particular rubber plant. It looked half-dead. Perhaps in its present state of health, it was unable to respond or maybe it was its environment. Possibly, the plant had grown immune to the constant stream of violent memories.

I tore the used sheet of graph paper from the PGR meter, wrote "Roy McCoy" on the back, and placed it in a file folder. I planned to give it to

Tom Moss as soon as possible. Perhaps, he could see something on the sheet that wasn't apparent to my untrained eyes. Maybe this was much more delicate of a science than it seemed at first glance.

I put the file folder in the credenza, closed the door, and swiveled around in the chair. Immediately, I wished I hadn't. There were two hands on the opposite side of the desk, one on each corner. With the fingers curled, each of them was about the size of a desk telephone. Not the modern, low profile desk telephones either, but the old multilane, three hundred pound Western Electric monsters that used to come from the telephone company. I looked from the hands up two massive arms to double door-width shoulders, culminating in a scowling face. Even for the record, and in the interest of accuracy, I couldn't describe the man's neck. He didn't have one!

Before I could say a word, he bellowed, "What did you say to Roy to get him so upset?"

There hadn't been a time in my life that I chose my words more carefully. Very calmly, I said, "I was very abrupt with Officer McCoy. I wanted to apologize to him, but he left before I had a chance to do so. I feel really bad about the conversation."

His hands squeezed the corners of the desk as he roared back at me. "Roy wouldn't tell me what you said and he always tells me everything! I don't know what you said, but it couldn't have been very nice."

I was sweating profusely. "You and Roy are pretty good friends then?"

Officer Johnson took his furniture clamps off the front of the desk and stood fully erect. There were only a few inches between his head and the suspended ceiling.

"Roy and me, we're tight." He smiled broadly, and then the smile disappeared. "I don't mean we're funny or nothin'! You don't think that's what I mean, do you?"

"Oh, no! I didn't think that for a minute! Listen, Officer Johnson, why don't you have a seat and relax." I pointed to the chair. This guy was making me sweat armor-piercing bullets. What was he going to do when I questioned him?

"Officer Johnson, there are some questions I would like to ask you. However, before I do, you need to understand that your cooperation in this matter is entirely voluntary and that anything discovered during this investigation will be included in the report to the Governor's office. Any evidence discovered could be used by the District Attorney's Office to file criminal charges against you. You have the right to remain silent, you have the right to have counsel present prior to questioning, and if you can't afford an attorney, one will be provided for you. Do you understand those rights?"

"Not really." It wasn't that he hadn't been listening, because he had. In fact, he was intently paying attention to my every word.

"Which part didn't you understand?"

"Just the part after entirely voluntary."

"Which part?"

"Most of it."

"It just means that if, while we're talking, you tell me that you did something illegal, then it will be included in the report and it will be read by the Governor of this state. If he decides to have the District Attorney press charges, the evidence in this report could be used against you."

"I didn't do nothin' illegal!" He jumped to his feet and started shouting.

My worst fears were coming to pass.

"Who said I did something illegal?"

"Nobody did, Officer Johnson, nobody did. It's just a warning that I have to read to you before I can ask you any questions. It's there for your protection. Please sit down, please relax."

"You don't think I'm stupid, do you?"

That was an understatement if I had ever heard one. "No. Why would I think something like that?"

"Because I didn't understand it the first time you said it."

"No, I think that shows that you're pretty smart, actually. It's all legal double-talk. I don't think anybody really understands it the first time they hear it. But rather than ask what it means the way you did, they just act like they understand it. I think it's foolish to act like you understand something when you don't. Asking what it really means, I think that's pretty smart."

"Did Roy understand it the first time?"

"I don't know but I think so. I think Roy is very smart, don't you?"

"Oh, yeah, real smart."

More like a smart ass, I thought.

"He's real smart! He knows about all kinds of stuff. He's going to night school. He built his own color TV. It's got a remote control and everything. He built the remote control, too. He's real smart."

"Yeah, I thought so, too."

"You sure got him mad, though, Mr. Investigator."

"I promise you, I didn't mean to." My eyes were pleading with him to believe me.

"He'll get over it. Sometimes he gets real mad at me, too, but he always gets over it."

"Was he real mad the day of the riot?"

"Boy, was he mad ever!"

"What about? Did it have something to do with the girl on the sailboat?"

"How do you know about that?"

I had caught Officer Johnson off guard. "Roy told me all about it."

"He did?" He was dumbfounded and looked confused.

"Yes, he did. You guys aren't going to get into trouble over something like that. It's no big deal. Why did Roy get mad at you that day?"

"Because I wouldn't give him the binoculars, and he couldn't take 'em away from me. He gets to see women like that all the time. I've never seen a naked woman up that close before. Then, when they fired a shot down in the yard, he got even madder 'cause we were watching that girl instead of doing our job. Like I said though, he gets over it."

"Did you miss the whole thing?"

"Pretty much. By the time we turned around and picked up our rifles, it was all over."

"Do you remember hearing the first shot, Officer Johnson?"

"Yeah, actually it was like the first two shoots. They were right together. There wasn't even a second between them. I thought that was really strange."

"Why?"

"If everybody had their guns down, how could someone fire that second shot so close to that first shot? I've been wondering about that a lot."

"Me, too, Officer Johnson."

"The only thing I can think of is that they might have been shooting at the same thing, do you know what I mean?"

"Officer Johnson, I want to ask you a question, straight out, because I believe that you wouldn't tell me anything but the truth."

"I wouldn't lie to you, Mr. Investigator, even if it meant I was going to get in trouble because of it. I don't like liars."

"Did you fire a shot on the day of the riot?" The way he snapped to attention in his chair made me think he was honored that I would be so direct with him.

"No, sir."

"Did Roy fire a shot on the day of the riot?"

"No, sir."

"Do you have or have you ever had armor-piercing or fully-jacketed ammunition?"

"No, we don't use that kind around here, sir."

"Have you ever seen Roy with that type of ammunition?"

"No, sir." Officer Johnson was starting to sweat.

"Was there anyone else in the tower with you on the day of the riot, other than Officer Roy McCoy?"

"No, sir."

"Officer Johnson, thank you for being so helpful. I really appreciate all your cooperation." As he stood to leave, I added, "Please tell Roy I didn't mean to upset him."

There was no need to look at the graph paper on the PGR meter. I doubted whether John Johnson knew how to tell a lie. There was something about him, a gentle-giant air that led me to believe every word he said. While social graces weren't his forte, he wasn't a murderer. If he ever were to harm anyone, it would only be a result of not realizing his own strength. He had a natural grace and a great deal of consideration for others. I opened the door to the credenza and found exactly what I had expected to find. In fact, if I was reading the tracings correctly, Officer Johnson had a calming effect on the rubber plant. He had the same effect on me, once I was relatively certain that he was not going to rip my head off with his bare hands.

I had obviously placed too much faith in Tom's crazy rubber plant theory. I had been so sure that it would help me solve Kenny Boyd's murder. I was wondering if this was Tom's idea of a joke. There probably wasn't anybody named Cleve Baxter in the CIA or anywhere other than in the fertile imagination of Sergeant Tom Moss, whom I thought was a good friend. I pictured him back at police headquarters, telling any officer who would listen that I was trying to use a half-dead rubber plant as a lie detector in my investigation of the San Quentin riot. I could see him laughing his ass off. The more I thought about it, the angrier I became. "Damn him! Shit! Shit! Shit!"

I slammed the aerial map on the desk in front of me. The line Tom had drawn went from the point where Kenny Boyd was killed to Tower Two. Maybe he had lied about that, too. Maybe that was part of the big joke. I had reached a dead end again. I knew as much as I did the first day the investigation started. What I really wanted to do more than anything, was punch Tom Moss in his big fat nose. "That son-of-a-bitch! He fucked me good this time!"

I peeped out of the office and saw groups of officers coming in the front door of the Administration Building. I didn't wave or say anything, even though I knew a few of them. I was so deflated that I just wanted to crawl under my desk and cry. I turned and sat down. At the height of my self-pity, the only person I would have wanted to see, if I had wanted to see anyone that day, stuck his head in the door.

"Hey there, Matt! How's it going, my good friend?"

I looked up at Eudon and told him the truth.

"It's not goin' for shit! I'm just sick and tired of this whole shitty mess. I thought I was onto something there for a while, but it didn't quite turn out the way I thought it would, not at all. I'm actually pretty disgusted with what I've discovered about this place, and I just wish the investigation were over. Maybe—maybe I got in over my head. I should pack my bag and just say I did the best I could do."

Eudon sat in the chair across the desk. "Back home, we'd say that you've 'got a real big dose of it'. That doesn't sound like you at all, Matt. You just stay with it. Most of the guys around here think a lot of you. If anybody can get the state to pay attention to what needs to be done and change this place, we know deep down in our hearts it's you. You're the only person they will listen to."

A smile crept onto my face. There was something about this man's sincerity and gentleness that was infectious. I was grateful to him for taking a few minutes to cheer me. I looked at him warmly and stood to shake his hand. "Eudon, I'm just going to say thank you. I don't know what else to say...Thank you."

He grabbed my hand firmly.

"That's the most anyone can ever say. Maybe after all this is over, we can get together and have another beer and talk about the good old days."

"I'd like that very much."

Eudon started toward the door, but stopped and cocked his head, then turned back to me with a frown on his face. It was the first time I had ever seen him with anything other than a smile since we talked at Melody's.

"What's the matter?"

"I don't know. Do you hear something strange? Like a computer or something?" He was listening intently.

I did indeed hear it. It sounded exactly like a computer, a computer searching a floppy disk for a program.

"Oh, that. Ignore it. It's some crazy person's idea of a practical joke."

"I didn't think there were any computers around here, but that would be just like the State of California. Feed the inmates food with fried cockroaches, then buy a computer nobody around here can use."

He shook his head as he walked off.

"See ya 'round, okay?"

"Yeah, thanks again, Eudon."

"My pleasure, Matt."

Once Eudon was out the door, I turned around and yanked open the door to the credenza. The pen on the PGR meter was jumping up and down all over the graph paper. I ripped the sensors off the rubber plant, threw them in the credenza, and slammed the cabinet door. I stood in front of the plant and raged, "You stupid fuckin' plant! What the hell's the matter with you? That's the nicest man around here. I'm going to donate you to science. My gift to posterity—the the world's dumbest rubber plant! Shit, nothing's going right today."

I sat back down at the desk. The aerial map was at my fingertips. Tom Moss had based his drawing on the evidence I presented to him. Even in his worst mood, he would never misinterpret evidence. To him, evidence was sacred. I could expect Billy Graham to produce pornographic movies before I could expect Tom Moss to misrepresent what was being explained by a trail of blood spatters and body parts.

I retraced the line backward from the stage, across the lower yard, across the ball field, past Gun Post Five, across the access road, right up to Tower Two. Wait a minute...past Gun Post Five? I had looked at this map a dozen times and never noticed that Gun Post Five was only a few feet off the fatal bullet's path. Mark Wilcox and Eudon had been assigned to Gun

Post Five. Maybe I hadn't wanted to see it. Tom Moss had tried to warn me not to jump to conclusions...

I looked at the rubber plant, and then opened the door to the credenza. Before I turned the PGR meter off, it had traced wild, erratic patterns across yards of graph paper. By my best time estimate, the pattern coincided with Ed Eudon's brief visit.

I walked outside and sat on the front steps. The fresh air and the warm sunshine seemed like trespassers about me. I really didn't belong there. My title was Investigator for the District Attorney, but I wasn't really an investigator. I didn't have the experience or skill needed for the assignment. I had conducted a terrible interview once today, because I thought I knew who killed Kenny Boyd. And I was at that crossroads again. This time the suspect was someone I knew, someone I liked. By all accounts, he was a devoted and loving father to his young daughter, Heather.

Did I have the right to pursue this option? Did I even want to? It could go undetected, probably forever if I didn't utter a word. But could I live with myself if I didn't acknowledge my suspicion or findings? Then again, could I live with myself if I did?

18

I sat on the concrete steps in front of the Administration Building until I couldn't sit still any longer. Finally, I went to Leslie's office. I could barely get the words across my lips. "Could you ask Captain Walsh to send Sergeant Ed Eudon down as soon as possible please?"

She nodded and picked up the phone.

I sadly walked down the hall to the interview room. The Tarantula was conveniently missing. I sat at the desk and looked at the aerial map of the grounds again. I couldn't believe that I had looked at this map repeatedly and not noticed the proximity of Gun Post Five with the trajectory line Tom had drawn. I had held Ed Eudon and Mark Wilcox above suspicion until that moment. So much of my investigation had been based on what they had told me. If Eudon did fire that first shot, it was very possible that Mark Wilcox would be charged as an accessory in the crime. More than anything else, I wished I could to home and forget about this can of worms.

I looked up to see Eudon standing in the doorway. The expression on his face was exactly as it had been when he stopped in to cheer me less than an hour ago. I stood and motioned him to sit in the chair. This time I wanted privacy. I closed the door behind him and we sat down.

"I know that you don't like to have discussions here, but I hope you'll make an exception for me this once."

"Sure. No problem, Matt."

"Eudon, I think I've got to tape our conversation, okay?"

"Okay."

I turned on the tape recorder and began.

"Sergeant Ed Eudon, there are some questions I would like to ask you, but before I do, you need to understand that your cooperation in this matter is entirely voluntary and that anything discovered during this investigation will be included in the report to the Governor's office. Any evidence discovered could be used by the District Attorney's Office to file criminal charges against you. You have the right to remain silent, you have the right to counsel to be present prior to questioning, and if you can't afford an attorney, one will be provided for you. Do you understand these rights?"

"Whoa, this sounds serious. What's up?"

"Did you understand the warning I read concerning your Miranda rights?" I watched the full-of-life expression on Eudon's face fade to that of a condemned man.

"Yes, I did."

"When we talked earlier this afternoon, I was frustrated with the investigation. I was upset that I had done all this work and wasn't any closer to the truth than when I first set foot in San Quentin." Looking him square in the eye, I continued, "But now, I think I know who killed Kenny Boyd."

"You do?" Eudon looked more resigned than surprised. He didn't flinch. Although he maintained an ambiguous expression, he started to sweat.

"I'll tell you something, Sergeant Eudon, the knowledge I have is very upsetting because it is inconsistent with my previous findings. The person who shot Kenny Boyd is someone that I've come to admire and respect over the course of this investigation. He's someone who I felt a certain kinship with, someone who I thought was above all the hatred and violence in the world. As a matter of fact, the reason it took me so long to figure out was because I simply refused to believe the truth when it was staring me right in the face."

"Those are very kind words, Matt. I appreciate you saying them."

"You know who I'm talking about, then?"

"Yes, I know Matt. I had my fingers crossed. I knew it wouldn't stay a secret for very long. In a way, I'm relieved that it's over."

"Eudon, as an investigator, I'd like to listen to every word you have to say about this. But, as your friend, I think you better stop right here. You need a good attorney before you say anything more, okay?"

"Thanks for your concern, but I want to finish. I need to finish. I'd rather talk to you about this than anyone else."

As much as I wanted to hear everything that he had to say, I really didn't want to hear any of it. I wanted desperately for this to be another bad dream from which I would wake up at any minute. "Eudon, please don't say anything else until we can get an attorney in here."

"No. There's only one thing I hate more than lawyers and that's car salesmen." Eudon laughed.

"Jesus Christ! Don't be stupid."

"I just want you to understand, that's all."

"I want to understand, I really do. Out of all the people out here you're the last person I would think might do something stupid like this. Why you? Why?" I would never understand why a kind, loving man could have done something do wrong. "You need a lawyer now."

He ignored me. "It mostly concerns my daughter, Matt. The day she was born, that was the greatest day of my life. The first time I held her in my arms, right there in that delivery room, I decided things were going to change. I didn't want her to think that her father went through life as a loafer or Mr. Nobody. I wanted her life, that is, our lives, to be something special. I wanted her to know that her daddy left his mark in this world."

His eyes filled with tears. The tears flowed down his face onto the table, but his composure stayed strong. "That's when I started writing. I worked every night from the time I got home until I couldn't keep my eyes open any longer. I wrote poems, short stories and submitted them to magazines. I just kept writing, but they just weren't good enough. No one wanted to publish them."

"You chose a very hard path. Most people never get their writing published, let alone make a decent living from it. Take it from me, I know first hand."

He didn't seem to hear what I was saying—he just kept talking. "But every time I looked into Heather's eyes, every time she put her arms around my neck, in my heart I knew I had to keep on writing. Matt, one day Heather came home and said that some big tall black man had taken her lunch box from her while she was walking home from school."

Tears were following like a running stream. "I heard about that."

For the first time, Eudon looked surprised. "Did you hear how we got it back?"

I nodded.

"I almost lost my mind. That kitten in the lunch box could have been Heather. They could have tortured her and killed her. She was so vulnerable. It made me more determined than ever. I started to write songs again, one was an incredible piece of music. It was the best song I had ever written. In fact, it was probably the best song I'd ever heard. I felt that way about it when I played it for some of the fellows at the prison. I had a nervous breakdown the first day I heard it on the radio."

"What do you mean you heard your song on the radio? You recorded it?"

"Unless you were livin' in Tibet last year, you've heard it. It's 'Going Through Them Changes.'"

"God, Eudon, I love that song! You wrote it?"

"Yes, Matt, but nobody knew it."

"How could nobody know it? That song was a number one hit for weeks. It stayed in the top ten for months! It was the song that made Kenny Boyd a star, for Christ's sake!"

"That's right. It made him a star. And it made me a nothing. Kenny Boyd copyrighted that song days after he heard me play it. He mailed the application to the copyright office at the Library of Congress in Washington D.C. right from his cell. After he got out, he recorded it and told everybody he wrote it."

"What are you saying, Eudon? You killed Kenny Boyd for stealing your song?"

"It was a hell of a lot more than a song! It was my ticket to freedom from this shit hole. Boyd made more than a million dollars in royalties off that song alone! It would have taken my family away from this depressing life. It would have taken me away from the cons, the drugs, the filth, and all the threats I had been receiving in the mail the last eleven years. This was my once-in-a-lifetime gift from God or the universe or whatever you believe in. Kenny Boyd stole a whole new way of life from me and from my baby, Heather. I paid him back the best way I knew how and I'm proud of it. He got what he deserved. I didn't think I would get caught. I worked on the plan for months."

"My God! Why didn't you just sue his ass? That's what the laws are for!"

"He had the laws on his side. I went to one attorney after another until I had gone to quite a few, but no one would take the case. He had secured the copyrights of the songs before I put them down on paper."

"Eudon, what about Mark Wilcox? He stands a really good chance of being charged as an accomplice."

"Everything Mark told you was the truth. He was exactly where he told you. I told him I was going to sneak over to the other tower to get a better view and for him to keep an eye on Clarence Redmond. I gave him a direct order to keep his eyes on him, not to let him out of his sight for an instant. That's one thing about Wilcox; he follows orders to the letter. He never knew that I fired that first shot."

"What about the second shot, the one that killed Clarence Redmond?"

"I can't tell you anything about that, except it was fired immediately after I fired my shot. I'm sure that it was coincidence. I wish I would have known what the future held at that time. I should have waited to see if somebody else killed Boyd during the riot. And now, it looks like it is time for me to pay the piper, as they say."

I would have been in a panic after a confession like this, but Eudon was calm and resigned to what the future probably held for him. "I wish there were some other way," I said quietly as I turned off the tape recorder.

"Me, too, Matt. Are you going to arrest me now?" Eudon was starting to become distraught.

"No. I don't have the authority to arrest anyone. Don't think I would arrest you even if I could. Kenny Boyd is dead. It's not like you're a threat to society or anything." There was no way I would take Eudon to jail. Someone else would have to do that.

"How much time do you think I have, Matt?"

"I really don't know. The report won't be put together for weeks, but since the charge will be first degree murder—I don't think it will be long."

"I just want to get things straight with my family, that's all."

"Promise me one thing."

"What's that?"

"Promise me you won't do anything stupid."

"What do you mean?"

"You know, like Greg Kimble. Promise me you won't do anything stupid like what that kid did."

"I won't. I promise you as a friend."

"I'll do everything I can to get your story out, Eudon. I'll do anything to help you."

He hugged me before he left the room. His shirt was soaking wet with sweat.

19

I sat alone, sitting on the hard wooden chair in my office thinking about Eudon. About to be crucified, he would soon be living with the animals in this house of the devil or one just like it. I wondered *who's keeping whom* at the facility—a San Quentin prison guard had killed a rehabilitated convict for stealing his song. Boyd's friends and supporters would make sure Eudon would have a reserved seat in San Quentin's gas chamber. I had no doubt that Jack Halsey's part in this would be thoroughly investigated and appropriately prosecuted. But there was someone else who might slip through the investigation completely unscathed. Before I left this rock pile, I wanted Captain Ted Walsh's head on a silver platter.

I decided that listening to the tape again couldn't wait any longer. After sending the Tarantula on a variety of errands that would take at least thirty minutes, I locked the door and lifted the heavy tape deck from the floor onto the desk. I put the reel on the tape player and rewound it to the beginning. The slowly spinning reels had a calming, almost hypnotic effect as the quiet hiss filled the room. Suddenly, the silence was broken. I turned the volume down low and listened to the conversation

Walsh: *Captain Ted Walsh here.*

Unknown: *What are you doing out there?*

Walsh: *What do you mean?*

Unknown: *I mean, what the hell are you doing out there? You left too many loose ends dragging around behind you. You're a real fuckin' idiot, Ted.*

Walsh: *Belding doesn't know a goddamn thing.*

Unknown: *The hell he doesn't!*

I had heard this conversation and the voices before. I knew the first voice was Captain Walsh. This time I also knew the second voice. There was no question at all. It was my old buddy, Sal.

Sal: *I just got a call from the fuckin' lunatic.*

Walsh: *I thought you said he couldn't get a date with an old hag if he put a bag over his face and couldn't find his ass with one hand and a map. You told me he didn't know his right hand from his left hand. You also said the guy was a first class lunatic and wouldn't be able to solve this case. You guaranteed me this case would go unsolved with him working on it. I'm worried, Sal.*

Sal: *Look, Ted, he got further into this damn thing than I thought he would. Anyway, he's got some pretty interesting theories about the riot.*

Walsh: *Sal, he won't get too far with his theories. He's a first class moron.*

Sal: *What do you mean? He knows exactly what happened, you idiot! He knows that you spearheaded the whole damn thing. He knows you had the two convicts burned to death in South Block, because they were trying to expose you to the FBI. He probably knows about Jack Halsey. I'm going to meet him tonight at Fisherman's Wharf at seven and find out exactly what he knows. I'll see whether I can get him off our backs and onto something else. Don't worry, I'll take care of this dumb shit once and for all.*

Walsh: *What about the information that he already has, Sal? What's going to prevent him from doing something with it?*

Sal: *Look, I know the way he works, Ted. He doesn't share anything with anybody until he's done with it. He'll want enough evidence to convince a damn good jury. I'll get everything from him. I'll make him promise to bring me all the evidence to hold for safekeeping and then I'll destroy it after he hands it over to me.*

Walsh: *What can you do about Officer Kimble?*

Sal: *Don't worry about Kimble. I'll take care of that little punk. The Marin County Drug Task Force has been following him and his friend Bezel around for weeks. I'll just see whether I can get them to speed things up a little. Once we get him locked up in the Marin County Jail, he'll be pretty easy to deal with.*

Walsh: *Can you do that?*

Sal: *Just leave it up to me. And one other thing, Ted...*

Walsh: *What's that?*

Sal: *Lose the monitoring tapes. Matt is coming in to get all of them.*

Sal, what a fucking bastard! He had set me up at Fisherman's Wharf to be killed. He had pushed the Marin County Drug Task Force into moving in on Greg Kimble! There's always somebody around to foul up a perfect fantasy. Even in the Garden of Eden, the serpent was polite. Thus, the deception was painful. My ideal friendship was nothing more than the obvious—one man using another for personal gain.

I stopped the tape where the conversation ended, pulled it off the tape deck, and then slipped it back into my briefcase. I was treading on thin ice and had to proceed very carefully. Whatever Sal was, he wasn't stupid. Neither was Walsh. I put the tape deck back on the floor and decided that I had better get out while I was still in one piece and before the Tarantula, or anyone else for that matter, returned.

I grabbed my briefcase and headed to my car. My VW was covered with fresh white bird shit—which meant I'd be very luck if I believed Italian folklore. Thousands of seagulls were raising hell since it was herring season and the bay was full of small silvery fish. It was too late to do anything that night. I needed to devise a top-notch plan to see Sal without opening myself to another attack like the one at Fisherman's Wharf.

I headed for home with the wind blowing in my face. I was filled with the excitement of finishing the investigation, but sadness over the lives destroyed by malfeasance. Although I hadn't spotted any black trucks, my knees were still shaking when I went through my front door. As soon as I fed Sebastian, I called my father.

"Hi, Dad how are you feeling?"

"So, so."

"I solved the case. I'll tell you all about it tomorrow. I'll be dropping my car off at the body shop. We'll go to Bodega Bay for dinner in the rental car around 6:00 p.m. if that's okay."

"That would be great. I can't wait to see you."

"I love you, Dad. Give my love to Mom."

"Take care, Matt."

I hung up the phone. I decided to call Tom tomorrow and meet Sal in Golden Gate Park. Since I wasn't hungry and my nerves shot, I hit the sack and was out like a light.

I rose a dawn and waited until 8:30 a.m. to call Sal. While the phone was ringing, I fed Sebastian some Kibble and milk. I still wasn't hungry.

"Hi, Sal. I need to talk to you in person. Guess what I found out?"

"Whoa, good morning to you, too, good buddy. What's the hot news, Matthew?"

"I know who killed Kenny Boyd, but I'm not sure what I should do. Can we meet in Golden Gate Park right outside the Japanese Tea Garden?"

Sal paused, then cleared his throat. In his best-buddy voice, he replied, "Okay, sure. That would be fine. When do you care to meet?"

"Let's say in two hours. Ten-thirty. Okay?"

"I'll be there with bells on, Matt."

I had one more call to make. I dialed the number for the San Francisco Police Department and asked for Tom Moss.

"Tom, here."

"Tom, I need your help. Thanks to you, I've gotten to the bottom of the San Quentin State Prison investigation. I have evidence linking Sal Tarantino to the murder plot and I've got to meet him at 10:30 this morning. I need you to back me up. It could easily turn out to be more than I've bargained for—last time I saw him, somebody shot at me with a shotgun and blew out the windows of my car."

There was a short pause before Tom replied, "Listen to me, Matt. It's been a very long time since I've done any traditional police work. I'm not sure I even know where my gun is, much less how to use. I could be doing both of us in danger. Let me see whether I can get someone else around here."

I wasn't going to let him out of this. I pleaded, "Look, Tom, I need you. This man is a *District Attorney*. Unless this situation is handled with kit gloves, he's going to smell something fishy. There's too much at stake. This requires great care and you're the only person I trust."

I could practically see him scratching his chin and staring at the ceiling. I could tell that his brilliant, skeptical mind was already working on a plan of action. Before his intellect had an opportunity to overrule his adventurous spirit, I added, "I'm meeting him at the Japanese Tea Garden at 10:30 this morning. I'll see you then. Oh, by the way, bring a wire and tape recorder or something." I promptly hung up without waiting for his answer.

On my way across the Golden Gate Bridge, I started to think about the good times Sal and I had shared at the Japanese Tea Garden over the years. I couldn't imagine how he had become a willing participant in all of this, especially in an attempted murder of his old friend from college—me! I arrived early to prepare for what I had to say. I parked my car and walked aimlessly around the park. I kept asking myself, how could Sal be involved in murder? How had he been coerced into such activities? Why would he risk his life, his career, everything he had by joining in a plot to kill Clarence Redmond? And Me? He had to have known that eventually he would be identified. I crossed the street to the Japanese Tea Garden and immediately realized that I had should have chosen a less popular spot to meet Sal. The Garden was packed with both residents and tourists, plus the narrow paths and bridges would mean trouble if he decided to run or if I had to run for my life.

I went back outside to the entrance and found a better spot—one with only two benches. I was shaking and the butterflies in my stomach were burning. One of the local homeless had already taken up residence on the bench across from me. He was lying on his back, occupying its entire length. I doubted that he had seen a shower or clean clothes for months. His beard looked more like a bird's nest, matted with particles of food and dirt. He smelled downright awful. A newspaper was folded over his lap like a tent; his right hand was underneath the paper doing God only knew! It looked like he was slapping the monkey. I sat on the opposite bench trying to ignore what he was doing as I nervously waited for Sal.

I looked around and noticed the peacefulness of the giant ferns rustling in the breeze. The brightly colored flowers lining the walks and the restful grassy expanses of the park were in sharp contrast to my state of agitation. The sun felt good on my face, even though the wait for Sal seemed interminable. To make matters worse, every time I glanced at the man on the opposite bench, I caught him staring at me. I wasn't sure what his interest was, but I didn't find it at all flattering. I also began to wonder worry about Tom Moss—he should have arrived already. I felt doomed without Tom or anyone else that looked like a police officer in sight. If he didn't show up soon, there wouldn't be enough time to connect the tape deck and microphone wires and conceal it before Sal arrived.

I grew increasingly nervous with every minute. My stomach felt like it was going to twist out of my gut. Tom Moss, a global-type person, was notoriously late for everything he did. On the other hand, Sal Tarantino was an analytical type and had never been late for anything in his life. I was beginning to realize that I was going to be left to deal with Sal on my own. I was doomed. Depending on how deeply involved he was in this vile thing, the situation was probably not going to be a healthy one. I was tempted to get in my car and head to the nearest police station.

Every time I heard the unmistakable engine noise of a Volkswagen, my heartbeat quickened. I had never realized how many Volkswagens there were in the San Francisco area—it seemed like every third car was a Bug. I took my glasses off to clean them. My nerves were on overload and I was starting to sweat like a fat man in a sauna.

I felt a heavy hand on my shoulder. I turned and saw Sal smiling down at me. I was really in a bad spot. Just as I was about to leave, Sal arrived almost twenty minutes early. On the other hand, Tom Moss and his colleagues were nowhere in sight.

"Mind if I sit down?" Sal asked.

"No, have a seat. Thanks for coming."

He sat beside me, too close for comfort as always, and put his arm around my shoulder.

"This brings back some great memories, doesn't it, Matt?"

"Yes, I was just thinking the same thing."

Sal laughed.

"Do you remember the time that we were dating those twins? What were their names? Carol and Cindy! Do you remember the day we brought them here and—"

"Sal," I interrupted. "I remember a lot of things that happened here, but I've got to talk to you about the San Quentin State Prison investigation. This is really killing me."

He nodded. "Sorry. I'll be serious. Go ahead. Tell me what you know."

I slid over a few inches to a more comfortable distance from Sal. "I told you that I found out who killed Kenny Boyd and that's the part I want to discuss with you."

"Okay. You figured out who killed Kenny Boyd. What's the big deal?"

"The person who killed Boyd is not a correctional officer."

"Yeah, Kimble, right? You told me this already, so what? Just give me the report and evidence for safekeeping. You did bring it with you, didn't you?"

"I was wrong. It wasn't Kimble. Well, it's like this. There is a sergeant named Ed Eudon, who was really trying hard to make a better life for himself and his family, especially his daughter. I've gotten to know him well, Sal. He's a good man. He wrote a song and inmate Boyd stole that song from him while incarcerated at San Quentin. He copyrighted it from his cell and, according to Eudon, made about a million dollars off the royalties after he was released from prison. Since Boyd launched his singing career with Eudon's song, he felt Boyd stole the one chance he had to give his daughter a decent life away from San Quentin. It made him crazy.

When Boyd was up on that stage singing, Eudon lost it and put a bullet through his head.

Sal was listening intently. "Well, Eudon can count on seeing San Quentin from a whole new vantage point, Matt. No jury is going to think the theft of a song is grounds for murder, especially not from a prison guard. Besides, all of Buddy Miles and Hendrix's influential friends in Los Angeles want someone hung out to dry. I could be wrong, but Eudon doesn't have a snowball's chance in hell. He's going down for the count, Matt."

Sal was calmly advising me on Eudon's chances as though he had no part in any of it. If I hadn't heard the tape of him and Walsh, I would still be thinking what a good friend he was. He made me so sick I wanted to throw-up.

"Sal," I went on, "I found something else, too."

"What's that?" his curiosity was genuine.

"A tape of phone calls into Captain Walsh's office."

"Is there anything incriminating on the tape?"

I dreaded answering him. Eudon's chances seemed better than mine at the moment. Who was I really talking to? My old friend, a District Attorney? I had listened to a co-conspirator in the murder of Clarence Redmond? I took a deep breath.

"Yes, Sal. The conversation was between Captain Walsh and another man. They were concerned that I was getting too close to the truth. This person told Walsh not to worry because I couldn't find my ass with both hands and a map. This person also told Walsh where I'd be the night you and I had dinner, the night someone tried to blow my head off with a shotgun at Fisherman's Wharf. Just stop me if any of this sounds vaguely familiar!"

Sal stared at the ground as sweat began beading on his forehead. He didn't speak at all. Finally, he replied, "I didn't know they were going to try to kill you, Matt. I had no idea that's what they were going to do. You've got to believe me!" He continued looking at his feet, then took another deep breath, as if he wanted to say something. Tears began to roll down his face. "They had me over a barrel. I didn't have any choice, Matt."

I was furious.

"Everybody has choices, you fuckin' asshole. You have more than almost anyone in this world. What do you mean, you didn't have a choice? You're full of shit, Sal. Who the fuck do you think you're trying to fool? Do I have stupid written across my forehead or something? I have a college degree just like you."

"Look, Matt, it all started with the case against Walsh, Halsey, and Kirschner, the one where they beat and almost killed that guard. I found out that they were responsible for most of the drugs coming into San Quentin. That's why Clarence Redmond turned them in. He didn't care anything about saving that guard; he was tired of trying to compete with the brass. He wanted the San Quentin drug trade all for himself."

"My God, what's that got to do with you?"

Sal stood and looked up through the trees. "About three years ago, I hit a real low spot in my life. My career wasn't going anywhere. I felt like I was never going to find someone to share my life with again. I seemed to chase away all my friends. So I found new friends. I was just chipping at first, a couple times a week to lift my spirits. Then it got to be an every day ordeal, twice a day, three times a day. It wasn't too long before—well, I was just stayed high all the time. Then, after a while, I got to the point where I began freebasing, just to get back to normal."

"Cocaine?"

"Yeah. Before I knew it, I was broke."

"Sal, your father left you a fucking fortune!"

"It's all gone, Matt."

"There was a time when I didn't think I would ever spend the interest it was earning, but it's all gone. It's been gone for about a year."

I didn't know what to say. I couldn't picture Sal dependent on anything, certainly not drugs. Nor could I imagine him penniless. If anyone other than Sal had been telling me this, I never would have believed it. "What does this have to do with the ex-inmate Redmond?"

"It wasn't too long before I was really hurting. I needed it bad and I didn't have any money left. I didn't have any credit with my drug suppliers, but I had my job, and that meant a great influence. I called Redmond and struck a deal. I got my junk. In exchange, all I had to do was lose the cases against his people. Shit, I've been losing cases for as long as I can remember."

I couldn't believe it. Sal was throwing cases to keep his drug supplier. "If you had such a good thing going with Redmond, how did you get involved with Walsh?"

"Walsh figured it out. He told me that I had one of two choices. If I stayed with Redmond, he was going to blow the whistle on both of us. Then I'd lose my job, my influence and my supplier. He said Redmond would leave me out in the cold to dry. I knew he was right."

"What was your other option?"

"Work with him to get rid of Redmond. He said if I made sure their plan went off without a hitch, he would keep me supplied with drugs and never ask me for another favor again. I'd still be a junkie, but at least I'd have my job."

I got up off the bench and began pacing. "Sal, I don't know what to do. Are you saying that you helped them plan Clarence Redmond's murder?"

Sal nodded.

"Did you help plan the bike show?"

"No. I just helped them plan what they were going to do once it got started."

The Sal I knew was strong, determined, and vital. Whoever this man was behind Sal's face was nobody I wanted to know. My contempt for the man I once called my friend overflowed. "Jesus, Sal. Look at you. There's nothing left! They've got you planning murders and helping to cover them up! You're running scared! How long do you think it will be before Walsh starts asking you to do him favors? It's just going to be more of the same bullshit, if not for Walsh then for someone else."

He shook his head. "This arrangement's different, Matt. I've got some control with Walsh."

"Control? Are you crazy? Look at yourself! You haven't got control over anything! You can't even control yourself. Look at your hands! You're shaking like a leaf. Come with me. We'll get you some help."

"I have to get through this somehow. Things will be different, I promise. You'll see. Work with me on this, Matt. I'm done with the junk, I want to go straight."

I had been in this situation before with other people. I had learned the hard way that for some people there is a point of no return.

"No, Sal. I'm not going to watch you do this to yourself. I don't even know you anymore. I'm turning in my report and letting the chips fall where they may. You fucked me, Sal, and I was almost killed because of you."

He grabbed my arm. "I can't let you do this, Matt." Tears streamed down his face as he pulled a snub-nose 38 revolver from under his jacket. "You've got to come with me, Matt. They're waiting for you at the ranch in Sonoma." I looked toward the road and saw a gray Mercury sedan. Ted Walsh was standing by the open rear door.

"Put that thing away, Sal! You're not going to kill me and you know it."

Sal jammed the gun into my ribs and almost broke them as he said, "I will kill you if you don't get in the fuckin' car now."

Before I could open my mouth, somebody yelled, "Hey, there, you!"

I turned to see the vagrant who had been on the bench across from us. He grabbed Sal's jacket and said, "Has one a' you gentlemen gotta—urn— gotta light? Do ya?"

Sal reached in his pocket and handed him a book of matches.

The vagrant looked at the matchbook cover and said, "Holy shit. You eat addax . . . adda . . . Fairmont Hotel? Holy shit. I nibbler med anybody who eat adda Fairmont Hotel before. Hey! Hey! You! You!"

Sal turned and yelled, "What the hell do you want, you fuckin' idiot?"

"I bed anybodies eats adda Fairmont Hotel gotta habba dollar or two on him. I bed you do, do-ya?"

My mind was telling me to make use of the distraction the panhandler was unwittingly providing. I wanted to run but my body wouldn't move—my legs were frozen, my knees were shaking.

"Hey! Hey! What you god dare. Holy fuckin' shit. Haze gotta god dam gun. Hey! Hey! Are yoo a cop? Hey! Ahm asgin yoo a quezjun, buddy? Are yoo a cop? Izat why you gotta gun?"

Sal turned and shouted, "No, I'm not a cop. Get the fuck out of here, asshole, before I fuck you up!"

The vagrant persisted, "Iv your nodda cop, how gum you godda gun?" This vagrant was going to get us both killed! He tried desperately to focus his eyes on me and then pointed at me, "Is eea cop?" I started shaking and almost fell over; I felt pains in my chest. I thought I was having a heart attack.

Sal shouted, "Get out of here!" again and knocked him to the ground.

"Well! Zumbuddy's godda be a cop around here."

I heard a hammer cock and I figured somebody was going to be dead soon. The vagrant stood and grabbed Sal's sleeve. He pulled on it repeatedly. "Hey, buddy! Lemme see that thing. Whadiz that, a Sniff and Wesson?" In an incredibly deft move, the wino reached out and took the gun from Sal's hand. He pointed it in the air, and fired one shot. "Holy shit, dis thing's—urp—loaded! You shouldn't play wit a loaded gun. Somebody made get killed!"

Just then, five black and whites bearing the San Francisco Police Department's seven-pointed star rounded the corner, squealing to a stop in front of and behind the Mercury sedan. Officers poured from the cars and drew down on Captain Walsh and the driver, Nikki Buckner.

The vagrant, still pointing the snub nose .38 at Sal, looked him in the eye and said, "Hey, pretty boy? You did put more than one bullet in here, didn't you?" His voice was familiar.

Sal nodded, but he didn't take his eyes off the ground.

"Well, then, you better put your hands over your head now." Underneath the filth, bad odor, and the shoe-polish facial stubble was my buddy Tom Moss.

"Tom, did you hear what he said about Captain Walsh?"

"I sure did—every word!" Tom was beaming. His first venture out of the office in years had proven that he still had what it took for undercover police work.

"It's too bad we didn't get him on tape."

Tom grinned.

"We did, Matt."

"We did?"

"What do you think I was doing over there; what do you think I had under the newspaper?"

I couldn't help but laugh.

"Well, when I thought you were a vagrant, I thought—well, I won't tell you what I thought!"

"You have a filthy mind! That was a video camera. Got it all, sights, sound, confessions, everything."

The patrol car drove away with the culprits.

I couldn't stop the tears from running down my face. It was finally over. I could hardly believe that Sal had betrayed me for his new best friend—cocaine.

EPILOGUE

San Quentin had been in lockdown nearly twenty-four hours, which is standard procedure prior to an execution. I carefully picked my way through the people outside the East Gate. The first execution in years, the hiatus had attracted approximately fifteen hundred boisterous protesters; the ones who were gathered tonight were quiet, almost respectful. Their signs spoke loudly: "Are we safer now? Don't kill in my name."

My two-week assignment to uncover the truth about San Quentin had ended eleven years ago. My father just succumbed to cancer last week. For the last nine years I've been a full time reporter for the *San Francisco Chronicle.*

The arrests of Sal Tarantino, Ed Eudon, Ted Walsh, Nikki Buckner and Jack Halsey shocked the people of California. The press in and around northern California cried out in moral outrage for over a year, as the myriad of criminal trials and State Assembly hearings progressed. Conspicuously absent from their tirades, however, were mentions of the numerous correctional officers, who, over the years, had tried in vain to focus the investigative spotlights of the media on San Quentin.

In the end, the facility underwent intense scrutiny. Warden Cooper and other upper echelon officials left for higher-ranking positions in prisons across the nation. Many others were demoted, disciplined, or transferred to various California facilities and a few were fired. The racial gangs were broken up by the transfer of their leaders to other facilities like Folsom and Sing Sing; inmates who were determined to be out of control or extremely dangerous were moved to Pelican Bay. As soon as the new warden was appointed, she and the Governor adamantly assured residents of Marin County and San Francisco that the San Quentin State Prison was under control and posed no risk to their personal lives or property.

I have returned to San Quentin once a month for the past ten years to visit Eudon and Sal, and in spite of all the official claims, I haven't witnessed any so-called major improvements. San Quentin is still a hellhole. It still feels the same; it still smells the same. The correctional officers have been left to "tough it out" since their work-related problems have been virtually ignored by the Department of Corrections. Their wives and children still, in effect, become widows and orphans as the psychological damage from so much time behind bars takes its toll. Requests for help have gone unanswered and discovery that a correctional officer is seeking outside professional help still results in "unfit for duty" status and termination of their jobs.

The never-ending debate rages on: are prisons a deterrent to crime, rehabilitation centers, or human warehouses? As far as I'm concerned, prisons are simply an illusion of protection. Dangerous convicts are released every day to make room for those more recently sentenced. The reality is clear: sentences mean nothing.

In spite of convictions for conspiracy to commit murder, along with various weapons and drug charges, Sal, Leslie, and Ted are due to be released this year. All have survived incarceration without incident. Jack Halsey, even though he was initially charged with first-degree murder, plea-bargained to a lesser charge and will be back at his ranch in Sonoma County in another two years.

Eudon will be freed tonight. His state appeals exhausted, he has chosen to forego federal appeals that could buy him another three years of life on Death Row. Heather is now eighteen, and Eudon still believes his greatest gift to her would be to set her free of this armpit of a society in which he now resides.

Eudon stood up straight and tall as he approached the gas chamber.

Tears ran down his cheeks as he turned. In a very low voice, he said, "Now you can tell the people of the world my whole story."

I couldn't seem to find the words that would be an appropriate reply. All I could say was "Goodbye."

In a very low voice he replied, "It's never goodbye, Matt. It's always I'll see you later." Eudon stopped looking at me as they strapped him in the chair, arms first, then his legs.

The door was sealed at 12:08 a.m., and within seconds, the two one-pound bags of cyanide crystals were lowered into wells of sulfuric acid and distilled water. Plumes of dark gas rose above his head. He tried to breathe deeply as he coughed and choked. He gasped for air. His head jerked back and forth like the snapping of a bullwhip approximately thirteen times before his body finally slumped.

ACKNOWLEDGMENTS

All the materials in this book are based on true stories and actual events. Names, dates, and places have been changed to protect the guilty and the innocent. I thank the following people for their special contributions; however hold none of them responsible for mistakes that have been made.

For interviews and assistance with research and guidance: Ross Perot, Buddy Miles, Jimi Hendrix, Band of Gypsies, Harry Connick, Jr., Mickey Hart—Grateful Dead, Dr. Mark and Melissa Weiss, Dr. Mel and Pat Whittington, Dr. Rebecca Wackowski, Dr. Wayne Burkhead, Dr. Walter Peters, Dr. Larry Williams, Dr. James Mayoza, Dr. Jorge J. and Dru Madamba, Dr. John Phillips Jr., Dr. Cathy LaFortune, Dr. R.C. Romero, Dr. Lee Hayes, Dr. Susanne Caruso, Commissioner John Self, Warden Charles Crandall, Warden John Marin, Warden Vasquez, Warden George Sumner, Warden Snider, Assistant Warden Tony Bennett, Chief of Security Red Wakefield, Major Larry Merchant, Captain Jim Hall, Sergeant Don Carter, Sergeant Judy Wood, Officer Rachel Vincent, Officer D. I. Roberts, Officer Edward Pewit, Officer Vicki Tarbuck, Attorney Herbert E. Elias, Jr., Attorney Travis Barnett, Attorney Sean R. Hood, Attorney Jay B. White, John Swain, Marriette Buck, Bernie Jarvis, Kees Twinging, James Mohlman, Ed Schaefer, James Beckman, Roger Gibbs, Mike Dayton, Atti Hughes, John W. Hughes, Boris Vilner, Isaac, Diana, Noah and Megan Triscell, Rebecca, Pat, Patrick and Geno Quecke, T.J. and Susan Sozanski, Ken Howard, Jason Benskin, Linda Weber, Alberto and Pina Salomone, Patrizia and Roberto Balmas, Michael, Kimbelee, Nathan and Christopher Hairston, Joey Yang, Michael S. Tolliver, David Broadhurst, Scott Hopkins, Scott Paulson, Scott Veitch, Rodger and Kristine Walker, Girl Freiburger, Tom and Susan Sullivan, Shayne, Tabitha and Canaan Tipton, Richard Quecke, Christina Holliday, Douglas and Jonne Tartala, the Aliotos family, Marvin and Brenda Jeter, Dan and Holly Cobrinik, Hal and Barbara Hughes, Alberto, Anjela, Tony, Patty and Albert Sollini, Brian and Beky Mooneyham, Cosmo and Rosa Violante, Mike and Mary Violante, Tim and Bonnie Twiss, Peggy Wood, Randy Piper, Steven Mayfield, Michael Lloyd, Donna Willis, Emma Wells, Jonathan Laboube, Noorani and Simon Williamson, Dennis Duvall, Robert L. Bly, Roger Pavlo, Geoff Parkerson, Steve Stockley, Mike and Tanya Patterson, Susan Barrett, Heather Adams, Jim Vaughan, Donna Willis, Ronnie and Thelma Martin, Tommy and Lisa Boullt, Lindsey Boullt, Doug and Susanne Oakley, Sam Wiseman, Nolan Fry, John Floyd Fry, Joe and Angela Garcia, Cheryl Waldeck, Gary, Denise, Laura, Claire and Rachel Newton, Jennifer Hasley, Bernie and Jennifer Coulter, Kristi Adams, Gene, Jo, Joanne and Mark Bertolucci, Stefania Fiorucci, Ernest and Millie Gober, A.J. and Mike Hatfield, Mary, Susan and Laurie Littlepage, George Beatriz Rosas, Marsha Hughes and Cliff Haby, Gregory Bates, Wayne Adams, Shell Cox, Bud Abbott, Michelle and Sharon Dumont, Woody Walker, Joseph Hawk, Bliss, John, Richard, Tess, Jim and Sandy Kok, Albert Perfetti, Cynthia Ann Lloyd, Steve Cook, Cindi and John Pate, Glen Thornson, The Cotton Brothers, Dion Hughes, Timmy Himstrom, Elise Ann Coleman, Bob and Joyce Bolton, Dennis Delay, Kim Avery, Alice Hewett, Shane Garrow, Jeremy Paschall, Carl D. Robison, Marjorie Bohannan, Dana Ivy, Mike McNamara, John Katz, Jane Manson, Amber Stevens, Howard Vines, Patrick Broom, Floyd E. Roberts, Randy Ball, David Garrett, Debra Arms, Bob and Sue Delmark, Skeet Freelove, Pete Chin, Lou Mansfield, Jerry Maddox, and convicted felons Charles Manson, Stanley "Tookie" Williams, Jeffery Dahmer, and Zebra Killer J.C.X. Simon.

I would like to extend my profound gratitude to HAWK Publishing Group's President William Bernhardt. I am also abidingly grateful to his assistant, Jodie Nida, for lighting the way.

I would also like to give special thanks to Professor and Author Jan Price, Author Peggy Fielding, Author Robyn Weaver, Screenwriter Beverly Baroff—Wild Tony Productions, Film Producer Jerry Olson and Margarita Browning, Film Producer Edward James Olmos, Editor Nancy Owens, English Professor David Vilner, Professor, Warden, and Author Sam McCoy, Photograher Ken Ames, The Night Writers, Oklahoma Writer's Federation Inc., Editorial Consultants, Inc., and Charley Spears.

DR. GREGORY VILNER